T0007326

GLIMPSE:

A BLACK BRITISH ANTHOLOGY

OF SPECULATIVE FICTION

ACKNOWLEDGEMENTS

'Daishuku' by Irenosen Okojie, from *Nudibranch* (2019) is reproduced in *Glimpse* by the kind permission of Dialogue Books.

GLIMPSE:

A BLACK BRITISH ANTHOLOGY

OF SPECULATIVE FICTION

EDITED BY LEONE ROSS

SERIES EDITOR KADIJA SESAY

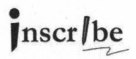

PEEPAL TREE

First published in Great Britain in 2022
by Inscribe an imprint of
Peepal Tree Press Ltd
17 King's Avenue
Leeds LS6 1QS
UK

ISBN 13: 9781845235420

Printed in the United Kingdom
by Severn, Gloucester,
on responsibly sourced paper

MIX
Paper from
responsible sources
FSC® C022174

Supported by
ARTS COUNCIL
ENGLAND

CONTENTS

Section Three: Glimmer

FOREWORD

THE RISE OF THE BLACK BRITISH
SPECULATIVE TRADITION

REYNALDO ANDERSON

The changing world order and our metamodern moment is haunted by the ghosts of slavery, colonialism, and genocide. For this reason, in describing the growth of Black or African speculative creative production, I use Black and African interchangeably. As theorist Mark Fisher observed, 'The emergence of a 21st century sonic hauntology is a sign that "white" culture can no longer escape the temporal disjunctions that have been constitutive of the Afrodiasporic experience since Africans were first abducted by slavers and projected from their own lifeworld into the abstract space-time of Capital.'[1] This observation can also be made in the context of the Arab and South Asian slave trade, and contemporary African kleptocrats accommodating cultural imperialism and the resource theft that has had devastating consequences up to this day in Africa.

Dislocation and otherness have been at the heart of the Black experience of modernity. In the 18th century, Black British literary analysis of this historical phenomenon – here the ordeal of enslavement – included the work of writers such as Ignatius Sancho (c.1729-1780), Ottobah Cugoana (c.1757-1791), and Olaudauh Equiano (c. 1745-1797). A century and more later, Caribbean writers such as George Lamming (1927-2022) and Samuel Selvon (1923-1994) wrote ironically about 'the pleasures of exile' and the loneliness of immigrated West Indians becoming Black Britons after WWII during the late colonial period.

Across the Atlantic, in North America, other roots of the Black speculative literary tradition emerged in the 19th and early 20th century work of Martin Delany (1812-1885), Sutton Griggs (1872-1933), and Pauline Hopkins (1859-1930). Their writing parallels the emergence of Euro-American science fiction in the late nineteenth century, with a quite different emphasis. This included the American fiction of Edward Bellamy (1850-1898) and, in the British context, the fiction of Edward Bulwer-Lytton (1803-1873), George Tomkyns-Chesney (1830-1895), Samuel Butler (1835-1902) and later that of the Fabian socialist, H.G. Wells (1866-1946).[2] The intersections of these various expressions of visions of the future and alternative worlds have influenced the contemporary Black speculative tradition both as something to build on and react against. Thus, whereas the Black speculative tradition was frequently part of the liberation project of African people in response to the slave trade, the emergence of scientific racism and imperialism, the Anglo-British formation was a utopian response to a crisis in imperial hegemony during the end of the Victorian era and later the modernist acceptance of philosophers such as Friedrich Nietzsche, the final triumph of Western secularism and the death of God.

Thus, in the early 20th century, whilst writers such as W.E.B. Dubois (1868-1963), Robert T. Browne (1882-1978), and Ghanaian writer, Ekra-Agyeman, also known as J. E. Casely Hayford (1866-1930), were committed anti-imperialists, writers whose work, in the wake of the savagery of WWI, ushered in the Harlem Renaissance and the Jazz era, white speculative writers, such as Edgar Rice Burroughs, promoted racist imperialist tropes; others retreated into dystopian tendencies and became known as the *Lost Generation*, like H.P. Lovecraft who wrote racialised speculative literary horror. After WWII, the crisis and disillusionment in Euromodernism and 'universal norms' was captured in the speculative work of C.S. Lewis (1898-1963) and J.R.R. Tolkien (1892-

1973) who used fantasy, Christianity and a backwards-looking science fiction to critique industrialization, war and nihilism from a traditionalist perspective at the end of the modern era.

During the Cold War, Black North American writers of the 1960s, such as Samuel R. Delany (1942-), John A. Williams (1925-2015) and Sam Greenlee (1930-2014), influenced an entire generation of Black British speculative writers with works like *Nova*, *The Man Who Cried I Am*, and *The Spook Who Sat by the Door*. This was paralleled in the music and theatrical productions of the avant-garde band leader Sun Ra (1914-1993) whose Solar Arkestra emerged during the North American post World War II years of technocratic innovation, anti-colonial and anti-racist struggle, economic reorganisation of the modern capitalist world system, and the early stages postmodernity. Sun Ra's body of work, including *The Magic City* (1966), which reimagines Birmingham (Alabama), and the writing of other creative intellectuals, such as Octavia Butler and Samuel Delany, and a generation later, the scholarship of Sheree Renée Thomas, influenced the emergence of a Black speculative philosophical worldview that would later be articulated as an early form of proto-Afrofuturism.

Parallel to this development, in England, the Guyanese-born writer Wilson Harris (1921-2018) wrote a series of novels including *The Guyanese Quartet* (1960-1963), and later in the 1980s, *The Carnival Trilogy* which, in their rejection of the realist 'novel of manners' and 'fixed' character, and their return to explore the lost traces and defeated possibilities of history, were recognised as foundational to post-colonial literature.

The work described above is the context for the development of contemporary Black speculative production, which can be seen in the films, art, music, literature and theoretical writing of such Black British scholars and creatives as Antony Joseph, Ngozi Onwurah, Kodwo Eshun and John Akomfrah. It is also the basis for Afrofuturism, one of the perspectives of the Black speculative tradition, which is an emerging philosophy of the diaspora and Africa. Incorporating the work of Molefi Kete Asante, Anna

Everett and others, this meta-theory of Afrocentricity offers a framework for how African people can and do locate themselves in time and space with *agency*, with the understanding that the control of time is tied to the control of space. For example, within this African-centered approach, C.T. Keto asserts, 'The Africa centered perspective provides the type of history for people of African descent that makes sense of what they, rather than somebody else, went through first, and for an African liberated future, and as a *futurologist* she, he or they can speculate and gaze beyond the next century.'[3]

Originating in North America and the broader African diaspora, Afrofuturism as a concept is slowly being embraced by the African continent. As a transnational, diasporic, and cultural worldview it interrogates the past, present and future in the humanities, sciences, religion, philosophy and politics. It challenges Eurocentric motifs of identity, technology, time, and space. It is maturing in metaphysical components such as cosmogony (origin of the universe), cosmology (structure of the universe), speculative philosophy (underlying pattern of history) and the philosophy of science (the impact of theoretical and applied science on society, culture, and individuals) and programmatic events to support its growth. For instance, the recent emergence of Afrofuturism 2.0 is systematically developing and re-orienting what Paul Gilroy referred to as the Black Atlantic into a neo-Black Atlantic formation. The latter is emerging as a locus of critical inquiry in the areas of speculative design, counter-memory, alienation, de-globalisation, decolonisation, resource depletion, techno-culture, exploitation, and Eurocentrism. The work of Black British creatives Anthony Joseph and Mo Ali, for instance, captured elements of these strands in their respective works, *The African Origins of UFO* and *Shank*.

When we assert African agency, we are observing Africa as our point of departure to explain phenomena that occurred over time and to critique contexts that have distorted the humanities and social sciences because of biased Euro-American frameworks or bodies of knowledge that attempt to pose as a 'universal' perspective. An important element of this critique is what has been called Metamodernism, a thesis that rejects linear Western concepts of stages of development, and embraces the oscillation of contemporary Black cultural production that moves back and forth between concepts that can range from pre-modern, modern, and postmodern in the same project.

EuroAmerican and Afrofuturist speculative perspectives grew out of quite different circumstances and relationships to the formation of what scholars would later refer to as modernity and later to postmodernity. If the postmodernism of thinkers such as Jean-Francois Lyotard has been critiqued as the philosophical adjunct of late, neo-liberal capitalism, the Black Arts Movements in the United States and the Caribbean of the 1960s and 1970s (when many of the Anglophone Caribbean's artists and writers were living in Great Britain) had a focus on cultural affirmation and radical anti-colonial/anti-segregationist politics. But it was also a period when Black people in North America and the former colonies suffered major setbacks in their liberation projects at the hands of the neo-liberalism of free market economics and global consumerism.

In the 1990s, at the end of the Cold War, came the formal coining of the term Afrofuturism by Mark Dery following his conversations with Samuel Delany, Tricia Rose, and Greg Tate. These Dery published in 1994 as a chapter in his book, *Flame Wars, The Discourse of Cyberculture*. In response to this, writers like Nalo Hopkinson, Sheree Renée Thomas, Paul Miller, and Alondra Nelson and others launched an Afrofuturism listserv.

In the UK, writers and philosophers were also interrogating the post-cold war speculative imagination. Ben Okri, for instance, in his 1991 work *The Famished Road*, offered an African speculative expression of this aesthetic. Later Black British creatives and scholars, such as Kodwo Eshun and film-maker John Akomfrah and the Black Audio Film Collective, engaged with postcolonialism from the perspective of the ideas of Marshall McLuhan on modern media communication. Similarly, the Cybernetic Culture Research Unit, with theorists Sadie Plant and

Nick Land at Warwick University, developed ideas that would influence the 'accelerationist' movement.

As noted above, the leading sociologist and race/culture scholar Paul Gilroy has described the contours of a Black Atlantic as cultural formation that reflects the geographical dispersion of African peoples as a legacy of the slave trade. However, this original articulation was limited by its North Atlantic philosophical and geographical bias. This excluded large swathes of the African Diaspora in the global south. Reframing this perspective as 'Neo Black Atlantic' acknowledged that this cultural formation is organised around a coded techno-cultural neural network of algorithms and database aggregations – archival and real-time – held together by the compression of time and space, that has resulted from the platform capitalism of the likes of Google, Facebook (now known as Meta), Uber and others and their attendant technological structures. Thinking about the global dispersion of Black speculative practice in this way can be seen as having a potential impact on education, crisis and risk assessment, economic development, public policy, and the political economy of the Black Technosphere.

By 2005, following the first ten years of the world wide web, the second wave of Black speculative creativity was being influenced by the emergence of social media and the rising impact of climate change, populist movements, and the fraying of the socio-political paradigm in the world system established in 1944 as the Bretton-Woods agreement that collapsed in 2008. This growing sense of fragmentation and crisis influenced the recognition of the Metamodern moment that the tensions between modernism, postmodern critiques and new age perspectives could ignore pragmatic opportunities.

Leading up to and during this transitional moment, several important workshops and meetings occurred in England. In March 2004, events organised by Kadija Sesay featured the work and performance of Sheree Renée Thomas. In 2012, The Collective Word founders, Courttia Newland and Toyin Agbetu, hosted an 'Africa in Science Fiction' event at London's Southbank

Centre. The event exhibited African sci-fi literature and short film creatives Biram Mboob, Tosin Coker, Oladipo Agboluaje, Kibwe Tavares and Wanuri Kahiu. In the United States, between 2012 and 2016, there were a series of conferences, curated exhibitions and the publication of Ytasha Womack's book, *Afrofuturism: The World of Black Sci-Fi and Fantasy Culture*. This captured the creative sentiment of an era described by Thomas Friedman as the 'Age of Acceleration'. Now, Black cultural production exists in a period characterised by digital culture, de-globalisation, Brexit, financial technology – and a growing Black Speculative Arts movement. In October 2015, the collective Afrofutures UK hosted an important conference in Manchester exploring the connections between Blackness, the future, and speculative artistic production. This hosted speakers like Erik Steinskog, Rasheedah Phillips, Moor Mother, myself and others, people who influenced the direction of the second wave of Afrofuturism and Black Speculative ideas for the remainder of the decade. Following the Manchester meeting, at the invitation of British creative Florence Okoye, I published the first iteration of the Afrofuturism 2.0 manifesto on the Medium platform. With opinions solicited from members of the movement, it defined Black Speculative Art as *a creative, aesthetic practice that integrates African or African diasporic worldviews with science or technology and seeks to interpret, engage, design or alter reality for the re-imagination of the past, the contested present, and as a catalyst for the future*. Influenced by the global interest generated by the first *Black Panther* film, the movement rapidly became an international entity with several different intellectual strands reflecting the diversity and geography of its members.

This brings me to why this exciting new anthology, *Glimpse*, is so important. Commissioned by Kadija Sesay and edited by Leone Ross, it builds on the still emerging field of Afrofuturist Studies and earlier work such as Peepal Tree's *New Worlds, Old Ways: Speculative Tales from the Caribbean*, published in 2016. Contributors to the *Glimpse* anthology like Joshua Idehen, Aisha Phoenix, Katy Massey and others connect a Black British sensi-

bility to intersections of a Dub-tinged cyberfunk, social construc-
tions of gender and an age of scarcity in a future New London.
Other stories with diasporan and African influences hint at a time
to come for the Commonwealth (as inheritor of empire) and the
difficult socio-politics surrounding its emergence. In these stories, Patricia Cumper, Muli Amaye and Melissa Jackson-Wagner
illustrate a subtle tension between an Afropolitan sensibility and
a gothic reality inhabiting the space of dystopian post-Common-
wealth settings, speculating what these systems of oppression
might look like in the future. Other stories reconceptualise Black
subjectivity and gender in counternarratives of transhumanism,
and or prosthetically enhanced existence. *Glimpse* offers Black
British speculative perspectives on relationships in dystopian
settings, with a gothic Victorian legacy of race, slavery and class,
with a sprinkle of techno-orientalism that may look like a conversation between Black love, alienation and madness.

The Black speculative tradition explores and offers ways of
recontextualizing the literary work of an emerging Black British
canon. It offers glimpses of the pursuit of utopia, the practice of
satire, and it reframes systems of memory/knowledge as forms of
resistance, and as sources of transformations and interconnected-
ness. *Glimpse* is noteworthy in continuing to expand the dialogue
and history around the Black British speculative literary tradition
and its contribution to the growing global dialogue surrounding
the Afrofuturist phenomenon.

Temple University, 2022

1. See Mark Fisher, 'The Metaphysics of Crackle: Afrofuturism
   and Hauntology', *Dancecult: Journal of Electronic Dance Music
   Culture* 5(2), 42-55.
2. See William Gillard, James Reitter and Robert Stauffer,
   *Speculative Modernism: How Science Fiction, Fantasy and Horror
   Conceived the 20th Century* (North Carolina: McFarland, 2021).
3. C.T. Keto, *An Introduction to the Africa Centered Perspective of
   History and Social Sciences in the Twenty-First Century* (Blackwood
   NJ: Research Associates School Times Publications, 1989).

INTRODUCTION

LEONE ROSS

When Inscribe co-director Kadija Sesay first emailed to ask if I'd like to edit the next Peepal Tree anthology, I agreed immediately. I love editing. Some of my fondest childhood memories growing up in Jamaica involve debating the 'right' word with my editor mother. And to be the first Inscribe woman editor was a very satisfying idea, following in the splendid footsteps of Kwame Dawes, Jacob Ross and Nii Ayikwei Parkes.

'Yes!' I emailed back. 'Let's talk.'

A few hours passed, and then something occurred to me. I emailed again. 'Can we make it a speculative fiction collection?' I realised I was nervous. I didn't expect Kadija to agree. It felt too much to ask.

'Sure,' she said.

And I was suddenly even more excited than I thought possible.

Because the weird shit, that's my thing.

Transmogrification. Magic spells. Defamiliarisation. Someone peels off their swimsuit… then their skin. Monsters. Kiss me so hard I float two inches off the ground – literally. The uncanny valley, the unexpected, the strange, the laughing darkness, the tearing back of boundaries – all these impulses give me so much fierce joy. And to facilitate the first speculative fiction collection by Black British writers? Whooo-eee.

But why had I hesitated? After all, the characters that I create watch hymens dancing down the street. They have no heads and live in magical islands. I have a reputation for being a bold writer.

Maybe I hesitated because it was a long road to that boldness.
I have censored myself, before this. And I wonder if other
Black British writers have censored themselves, too.

My Jamaican childhood included a good healthy love of the
weird. Editor mum was also a sci-fi/horror/fantasy buff. *Star Trek*
and cult TV series *Sapphire and Steel* both showed on the single
late-night TV channel. I saw the first *Alien* and *Omen* movies
tucked under a blanket in the back of the car at the drive-in movie
theatre in Kingston. From the dark twists of Roald Dahl tales to
Greek mythology, *Conan* comics and Stephen King, from the
Dune and *Lord of The Rings* series to Ursula Le Guin's *Left Hand
of Darkness*, I gobbled it all, an uncompromisingly American and
British genesis, aware that more conservative Jamaicans dismissed it all as 'devil business'.

I was separately fascinated by Caribbean folklore, and by those
hybrid religious subcultures honed by slave resistance. Thrilled
by tales of 'bad' magic obeah men living in the Blue Mountains,
my nightmares were full of Christmas Jonkunnu dance troupes,
starring lead dancer Pitchy Patchy's flailing, hysterical limbs and
dead eyes. I was annoyed by the terrible Hollywood stereotypes
of Haitian vodun and breathlessly listened to elders' 'duppy'
stories about fiery rolling calves and the vampiric women creatures that exist in slightly different forms on every Caribbean
shore. But I wasn't writing from these rich, complex places. I was
a teenager before I realised that all my story characters were white,
an unconscious act born of the same kind of post-colonial bias
Chimamanda Ngozi Adichie refers to in her seminal 'single
story' TED Talk.

It was education that changed this, unsurprisingly. At the
University of the West Indies, I was introduced to the glorious
matter-of-factness that is magic realism, and the profundity of a
fantastical literature grounded in our *selves*. When Toni Morrison's
character Robert Smith declared in *Song of Solomon* that, 'At 3.00
pm on Wednesday the 18th of February 1931, I will take off from
Mercy and fly away on my own wings…' I immediately thought

of fly-away-home Jamaican kumina ceremonies for the dead, their dancers 'catching myal' [entering a trance state]. By the time I got to classes on the Harlem Renaissance and Latin American literature – Gabriel Garcia Marquez's family of the literally pig-tailed, Zora Neale Hurston's *Their Eyes Were Watching God* and the softly explosive, deeply uncompromising *avant garde* writing of Jean Toomer – I had astonishing new levels of permission to reference the bounty around me. Armed with this new layer of vindication, I wrote dark and weird and sexual stories for a UWI workshop lead by novelist John Hearne and dreamed of being a published *Jamaican* author.

Coming back to the UK in the early 90s nearly doused the flames.

I was one bewildered 21-year-old. The culture shock was profound. Black people in the UK seemed so *very* pissed off and I knew next to nothing about their lives. The unequivocal difference was systemic racism. I suddenly understood why Caribbean people said they never actually felt 'Black' before they got here; why elders warned you, mind you go to England and get mad. My impulse to shock, terrify, surprise, to merry darkness, felt… insubstantial. How dare I write horror stories when the real-life horror was on our streets: the police stop-and-search 'sus' laws affecting Black youth disproportionately, the mental health problems, the poverty? I didn't *need* to make up things to go bump in the night – the bumps had already been created by powerful, centuries-old colonialist systems. I had a *duty* as a writer to assert our presence and our right to survive, our realness. There was no time for fantasy. 'Documentary' literature, that was the urgent task. The writer existed to seek justice. *Pickney tings dat*, I could almost hear the Jamaican church sisters say. *Duppy stories are for children.*

So, I grew up. Or so I thought. I published a realist novel in my twenties, and then another. About important, political things. About The Struggle.

But I wasn't happy.

I didn't know, back in the nineties, that I wasn't alone in wanting to explore a Black British weird aesthetic. I didn't realise there were other writers rolling their eyes at Roald Dahl's problematic Oompa Loompas and wanting to publish *our* kind of fantastical story. There was no Association of Black British Freakish Writers. Where was I to find the Irish or Scottish Black people writing magic realism? This was way before Malorie Blackman's *Noughts & Crosses* or Bernardine Evaristo's *Blonde Roots* dared to up-end slavery and imagine made-up worlds. I know now that Courttia Newland was writing genre fiction soon after *The Scholar*, and that nobody in publishing gave a damn, about the outrageous implication that he should stay right there in his *urbanity*. I wasn't aware of David Dabydeen's surrealism or that Judith Bryan's first few short story successes were speculative fiction or that Monique Roffey had the kind of mind that dreamt of mermaids. I was already in my forties by the time Irenosen Okojie and Helen Oyeyemi arrived on the scene, with their glorious, unfettered, unapologetic imaginations. No wonder novelist David Simon had moved from the social realism of *Railton Blues* with legendary Black British press Bogle L'Ouverture in 1983 to the speculative fiction in his *Secrets of the Sapodilla* with another small Black publisher, Akira Press by 1986. That was your best chance. Back when I began, there were no mainstream British publishers asking people of colour to share our mythologies or folk tales; Afrocentrism was not a buzz word; they were barely asking for us at all, and when we gave in that manuscript, it better damn well tick all their limited, unconsciously biased boxes. All they ever did was measure our literature in swagger.

Why didn't I know enough about the others? If there were scholars bringing these threads together thirty years ago, I was still ignorant of them. It's exactly why we need programmes like Inscribe, where writers of African and Asian descent are invited to 'take tea' with other writers, to advance, to develop, to grow, where 'new' writers sit beside more experienced creatives, where collections like *Glimpse* are born. Inscribe's most recent workshops have centred Afrofuturism, magic realism and the fantastical, with learning spaces curated by luminaries such as Marcia Douglas and Tim Fielder, by Peter Kalu and Ronnie McGrath. Part of Inscribe's mission is to encourage writers to try new things. What better than the speculative?

As for me, I finally found my way back home to the weird, due in no small part to an evening in the presence of writer Ferdinand Dennis, standing and reading 'The Black and White Museum'. In Dennis' short story, a kaftan-clad Papa Legba sells Middle Passage Weekend experiences in East London. You spend 48 hours stacked into a mock slave ship, pitched about, fed gruel and chained. Some characters are traumatised, for others it is a cathartic experience, inspiring discussion about the nature of reparations. I felt like the top of my head had been blown off: by Dennis's expansive, ferocious curiosity, the story's carnivalesque oddness and its political nerve centre, but more than anything else, I was moved by the fucks he did not give.

Here was someone like me.

Don't we know by now, how urgent it is to see ourselves, *everywhere*?

I think the time has come for a Black British tradition of the surreal to arise. Why has it taken this long, when there is so much of the speculative in our continental African and diasporic Caribbean lives? Perhaps it's something to do with the fact that despite hundreds of years of presence, we were not here *en masse* until after the Second World War. And when they got here, our storytellers were fighting great evils. This is one of the most insidious effects of racism: it doesn't just limit you. It requires you to limit yourself.

In 2022, we are more widely engaged with Black history, are in conversation about who we really are; now that there are more Black history books and TV programmes and films, now that we are embracing the past, there can be impetus towards the future. Not just in the places that our forebears came from, not just in the shadow of our American cousins, but here in Britain. A sense of coherence is building. A visceral sense of us as a *continuous* people.

Embracing speculative fiction is a revolutionary act. This genre, at its core, has always imagined possibility, it has always dreamed of the new, it has always taken chances. Its best practitioners have always spoken of hybridity and the complexity of humanity. Speculative fiction waits for us, quivering with potential. There has only been a short time to build a fantastical tradition rooted in *this* country, but I think we need it even more now, post-Brexit and still amidst Covid, with our government decimating social services and dismantling rights to protest.

Now I begin to glimpse us coming... arriving at some new thing that is ours. This collection, I hope, will be part of a groundswell: our own weird take on these green hills, on this bloody weather, expressed in these tongues heard nowhere else in the world. In *Glimpse*, we experience dystopian futures: a desperate barmaid committing necessary atrocities in the barely-breathable air of London's West End; a baby born much stranger than his mother could ever have imagined; a girl watching, horrified, as the village where her father grew up ['the arse-end of nowhere'] turns on her and her mother; a feral child discovered, examined like a thing, a sudden, tender oasis of goodness. This is a collection about the allegorical body: faces elongate and change as societies evolve; fish scales and feathers are physical symbols of broken heartedness. Men's bodies moult and change, endangering them in a world where toxic masculinity is an urgent performance; women age into something unexpected and brilliant. There are creatures, too: tiny and winged and vulnerable; vampiric, of course – Old Higue and *soucouyant* – and skeletal millionaires, hanging out at poetry slams. A sexual phantom threatens children in Walworth, pursuing them through withering estates and local markets. A homeless man beds down in Elephant & Castle, travelling through time, returning to the most defining scenes of his life. Relationships unnerve us: an odd woman wooed by a man who so thoroughly implants his assumptions upon her, that he's shocked when she shows him who – or what – she was all along. An immigrant woman, maddened by being here, takes cover under a bridge, her mind unravelling in ways that make total sense. An astonishingly timely story of hair and revolution, oddly prescient of women's struggles in 2022 Iran. There are curses in this collection, and dangerous jewellery and rare, softly powerful miracles worked in prison and elsewhere, amidst the pain and the injustice. There's a Scottish humanoid, iridescent, with four arms – and dreadlocs, natch – created to save a sibling. A rip-roaring, Carnivalesque rewrite of history in a mad fever-dream of a castle. And people fall in love. And laugh.

I recognise the sound of their laughter... and the growling behind it.

How could I have ever forgotten the power of speculation? All of the new ideas it goes to find, all of the rich playfulness, all those dark truths? How could I forget that this is the genre that amplifies, or that to move beyond the real makes things even more real, by contrast? We imagine a different we-ness, and fight for a new language to express it. How exciting, to glimpse the brink, to stand at the start of a thing, breathing, looking at it from under your eyelashes, waiting for everything to explode, or melt, to change into a kaleidoscope of oranges and greens and purples... and blacks...

Let us imagine that everything is possible.

SECTION ONE

SPLINTER

GREEN EYE

Joshua Idehen

22.00

Her Tip Meter shines light amber, on the top left of her vision. It reads zero. Her Rent Due is bright red on the top right. It blinks ten thousand pounds.

Efe thrusts her cold fingers into the ice sink, grabbing cubes, dropping them into a rocks glass. She trembles. Customer Bastard says, *Lay off the Charlie, yeah?* She smiles back, strokes her temple, bunches-up her shoulders and giggles. Like what he said was funny, like he's a funny guy, *yeah.*

Bacardi, sugar soda, stir. A serviette under the glass. Routine. *One hundred and three*, she tells him.

Customer Bastard is faux disgusted, *You having a laugh?* She giggles again for him, shrugs, rolls her eyes, *Yeah, I know, right? Madness.* She clicks her Liplights on, and her mouth glows an inviting strawberry red. She gambles on him liking the colour; in the nightclub dark he wouldn't have noticed her mouth before and *Wow, she's got lips on her.* He grins like a sneer, big ugly bastard grin. *Boom boom* she has him now; *it's in the pocket.* His eyes glow NatWest Red, her eyes glow Barclays Blue. *It's gonna be a good one.*

Transaction. A brief, blinding flash. She styles out the pain as a cheeky wink. Swallows spit, holds her smile. Cash Register Jingle tickles her ear. The payment scrolls past in bright blue at the bottom of her sight. One hundred and three. No tip. He blows her a kiss. No tip. His slappable grin. *No fucking tip.* He leaves.

Behind his back, her smile knots. The Tip Meter is zero. Her

Rent Meter blinks in sync to James Brown's *Sex Machine*.
    She fears.

23.00
Tip Meter is four hundred.
    Customer Bastard after Customer Bastard after Customer
Bastard and Bitch.
    Efe has wince-winked seventy-seven times so far. To keep her
life together, she needs fifteen thousand pounds. That will pay for
rent and bills but will not cover food. She's made that much
before, many times before. She's made more with her eyes closed,
Saturday nights long ago. She knows how to wine and dine
Customer Bastards. Liplights for the pervs. Cheeklights for the
pedos. Lashlengths for the romantics. And for trads? Bants, twirls
and giggles. Mix and match, as and when. With her eyes closed,
she's made miracles. But tonight, it's all going a bit R. Kelly. Her
flirting sounds stale. She's unbuttoned her top, though, right
down to the joint of the bra, but Customer Bastards don't look.
    She's gotten older. *That's the problem, isn't it? Cheeklights don't do
it for the paedos no more.*
    Only four hundred in tips. She started at six pm. Happy hour
ended at seven and brought nothing with it; the Bastards on her
bar station are cheap one-rounders. Lovely Dee's doing majestic
business on the E-counter. Lisa's station is rammed. Lisa spammed
a printscreen of her Tip Meter to the barmaid groupchat: eight-
een thousand.
    Efe is the only one having it shit tonight.
    Minutes crawl on their bellies. Music chews her ears. Cus-
tomer Bastards, glass-eyed on Lovely Dee's E's, only ask for water
pints. It's eleven fifteen. The body keeps working, the mind
scrambles for Plan B. She cannot pay the rent on four hundred.
She cannot borrow; Lisa is not her friend anymore. She still owes
her neighbours, and her mother is dead.
    Vanilla Ice's *Ice Ice Baby*: the crowd applauds.
    Customer Bastard and Bitch approach the bar. Customer
Bastard wants a single shot of house vodka, neat. *Cheapo.* His

Bitch wears her black eye with pride, gives Efe an I-Got-A-Man-What-You-Got Look. Efe wants to laugh but she does not. Glass, Vodka. Customer Bastard changes mind, wants ice. Cold fingers. She fixes her smile in place before she raises her head, turns the Liplights all the way up to Snatch-Your-Man-At-Your-Wedding Red. Serviette, drink. Bitch wants a beer. Customer Bastard slaps her. Bitch drops like an overripe pawpaw underneath the bar. Efe's smile remains set. Her lens glow Barclays Blue. Bitch rises like a sunset in reverse, sobbing. Bastard knocks the vodka back, slams the glass down and offers Efe an outstretched hand. Bitch's blood shimmers on his thumb like wet varnish. His paychip glows HBSC red in the centre of his palm. Efe doesn't flinch. Handshake. He grins. Cash Register Jingle. Customer Bastard tows Bitch to dance floor.

Wanker didn't tip.

One time a Bastard had the chip in his erection. Efe shook it. Was a good tip. *That's a Friday for you.*

She could always love on the landlord for a couple of the days, but she's still on the damn meds for another month, and he knows, because it was him gave her the skids. Maybe she could suck him instead? Maybe she could psych him into letting her off for another week. He likes the Cheeklights, and he always says she's his favourite. Not that she believes anything that fat, balding, ugly, leaching little piece of... *Fuck!*

His wife is in town.

He'll kick her out in a heartbeat.

Oi! BrightLips! Hurry up with the fucking drink.

Eight more Customer Bastards.

Rent Due Meter blinks in sync to ABBA. She'd be happy with ten thousand. At least.

She fears.

01:00

A miracle, a miracle; the Tip Meter reads five thousand. Hope.

Armoured bouncers kick out the ODs, the rowdy and the expired subscriptions. The Janimechs wipe the dancefloor clean,

and more Customer Bastards flood in. Fresh, new Customer
Bastards. One's a regular. She thanks Google. She's on the
Bastards like a barfly, turns her Titlights so way up her chest is a
midnight racer. Time is joy: Two thousand five, in thirty minutes; she's halfway to salvation. Her Tip Meter isn't an ugly child
anymore. No, the top left corner is her pride and pleasure. Her
shoulders ease up. Confidence is an old friend returned; she's on
a roll. Seven thousand already. Definitely on a roll. She could pull
it off. If she keeps this up, she'll be safe for a month. So, no more
pills, no more extra eves: none of that. Not 'til she stabilises her
finances. Her smile is wild now. Her joy is unscripted. Everybody's happy, everyone's tipping. It seems so easy now, like
breathing. The Cash Register Jingle is her favourite song again.
Eight thousand! She's almost there. More, Customer Bastards!
More, more, more!

Regular Bastard's gone off with some new bitch. No matter.
She's a fully formed phoenix, with or without him. She spots
another Customer Bastard, one of the club patrons. Old man in
tan suit with an old Bitch in lion fur. *Cute*. They're waiting on
Lisa's station, but Lisa isn't there. *Nice*. Efe helps herself, loads it
on, Cheeklights, Liplights, Titlights, the whole Guy Fawkes but
not too crazy. Subtle, warm. *Lure the moths in*.

Hey gorgeous, she says to him. The Lioness Bitch stares her
down. Her smile remains set.

The Bastard says, *Can I have a glass of champagne for the lady*. Old,
smoked-out voice he has.

Yes sir, and what about you?

He frowns, scopes the bar fridge behind her. She steps aside,
so he can better see. Curtsies, even. *I am so on this, so in the pocket.*
His eyebrow arches. He says, *Bombay Sapphire and Tonic*.

Yes sir. She bends over, cold fingers into the ice sink. She
doesn't mind the cold anymore.

Oh, and can I have green eye with it?

She freezes, the ice bites. She looks up. *An eye, sir?*

A green eye, dear, says Lioness Bitch.

For a moment she cannot move, cannot think. She pulls

herself together in the next. It's just a garnish, it's just a garnish, she repeats in her head, just like they taught her in training. She opens the garnish fridge. No eyes. Fuck. The nearby fridges are clean of eyes. This looks bad. She looks back at the old Customer Bastard. He's watching her. She knows she has to leave the bar to find the garnish. And when she gets back? The Customer Bastards will have changed again. Her station will feel cold and unfriendly. The music will be different. She'll lose her vibe. She can't leave the bar now! She's on a roll! She was going to make it! Why an eye, why now?

Lisa returns. That whore; she must have planned everything. *She knew the old rich bat wanted an eye, so she left when I wasn't looking, so I had to take the order and now I have to go off the bar to call the cellar manager, leave all the other Bastards to her.* Lisa gives Efe a brief smile, just so Efe knows she's been purposely fucked over.

Efe shuts her eyes, ties down all the pieces of her mind with a string. She opens. No big deal, she'll fix this. She will recover. Just go call the cellar manager to send some eyes up. It'll be five minutes. Ten, tops.

We're out of eyes, sir, she explains to Bastard. *I'll have to go get another one. It'll take about ten to thirty minutes; do you mind?*

Please say no. Please say no. Please say no.

The old Bastard says, *I don't mind.*

Wanker.

She leaves the bar.

01:30

Worst fears never come without a party; standing in the wash-up area, she taps her left ear twice to bell the cellar manager: he has no eyes left. She breathes, relieved, sprung; it's not so bad, only one disappointed customer. But on her way back to the bar, her ear vibrates. It's Stuart, bar manager.

Did you call Tolik, he says.

What?

You're serving Lussen, yeh?

Who?

The millennial in the suit? The Bezos Bastard? With the lion fur Bitch?

Oh. Oh shit, she thinks. *Yeah, yeah I am.*

Did you call Tolik, see if we have any eyes in?

We don't have any in.

Oh fuck, he says.

Can I go back to the bar?

No. Go upstairs, get your coat on.

What? she says. *Where… where am I going?*

To Soho. I'll give you the address.

Efe shivers *But… can't we order some more or some…*

Hang on, he says, *let me make a call.*

Minutes. Valuable tip-making minutes fly by. She peeks at the bar; there's a rush of Customer Bastards, and she's not there. She's not there. *Fuck.* She looks at the time. Two am. *Fuck.* Sixty minutes left. The washroom door bursts open. Customer Bitch falls to the floor. Bloody faced, bloody haired.

Bouncers move in, move her. Bitch voms on a muscled back, glassy-green eyes glistening. Efe forgets her troubles to sneer: *Fucking cokie.*

Fucking cokies.

Stuart is in the washroom with her.

Our contact has run out of eyes, he says. He has something wrapped in a red cloth; he gives it to her.

What's this? She takes it. She unwraps.

No, no, no. I told Luke I don't do this shit, okay? I don't…

I'm not asking you, I'm telling you.

For fuck's sake man, how am I supposed to…

Use your initiative, you fucking twat. Get out there or get out.

She gets out there. Upstairs. Staff room. Change into casuals. Jacket. Jeans. Pills. Gas mask. Travelcard. Petroleum jelly. *Fuck! Fuck! FUCK!* Tears. Sniff. Breathe out. She can do it, she can. Petroleum jelly on skin. Pills. Key holder. *Fucking wanker.* She goes out the door.

2:15

Attention all passengers on Thirty-Eight. We are approaching Tottenham Court Road Station. Please put your gas masks on now.

Efe isn't listening. She's watching everybody on the Thirty-Eight, watching their eyes. The red cloth burns in her pocket. She has less than an hour left. Three thousand more and she can make rent, she can do this. All she needs is one green eye.

Her eyes begin to sting, she can taste and see the smog. *Oh shit!* She rushes on the gas mask. *How am I going to see anything with this on, now? Fuck London.*

She gets off at Shaftsbury Avenue. The night gobbles the Thirty-Eight. There's nobody in sight. The smog swirls about in the thick black of the street; dim fires beckon out of the crooked mouths of hollowed-out candy stores. *It's fucking freezing.* She hates Soho.

Her mask beeps moderate. Been too broke to get a new filter, cheaper just to avoid boroughs. She sings *All That She Wants, Is Another Two Thousand* to the rhythm of Ace Of Base. She's got ten minutes at the most. *Fuck. Maybe someone's selling eyes here?* Tears. Breath. Her mask fogs up from the inside. The time is two-thirty Frustrated sobs.

Hello there, love. You alright?

Efe turns around. Old woman. Seventy, by the look. Gas mask too big, Sellotape over the gaps around the neck. One of the filter holes on the gas mask holds a cigarette. Five foot something, thin blond hair.

You alright love?

And the greenest eyes.

Efe pulls the knife out of her pocket, gets the woman by the head, gets the Sellotaped neck; woman gargles, grey smoke blooms out of her neck. Efe pushes knife into tummy, out the tummy, in the tummy, out the tummy, in the cheek. Woman screams, woman falls. Efe pushes knife into chest; woman screams, Efe screams, in the chest, out the chest. Efe screams. Efe screams. Efe screams.

Bright light upon Efe. She thinks it's the moon. She screams at the moon.

It's a helicopter searchlight. It screams back. *FUCKING COKIE!*

The moon disappears, Efe's in the dark.

Efe, calm. The beeper on her mask goes mad. Time to leave. Run out of Soho, get back to work. She's almost out of time. She takes the knife, does one socket, and then the second, just in case Customer Bastard wants another round.

02:45

She's back in work clothes. Dips her hands in the jacket pocket. Something squishy. *Oh fuck!* She must have sat on one of the eyes on the Thirty-Eight back. Fuck. One eye left. She walks downstairs.

The time is two-fifty-five. She'll have to blow the landlord. With seven thousand and a good clean, he's sure to let her off for the month.

Stuart catches her before she gets on the bar. *Did you get it?*

Yeah.

How many?

I sat on one.

What? Oh you stupid cunt. Where's the other one?

She hands the eye to him by the long nerve. He takes it, stares at it, shakes his head. *I cannot believe you. I cannot believe you. You cunt.*

What? What did I do now?

Do you know what colour these eyes are?

What? She looks again.

Worst fears never come without a party; blue eyes.

Speechless.

Stuart says, *Cunting useless*. Storms off with the eye. Efe is a loading wheel. Stuart returns. *Cunting useless*, he says, again. In one hand is the eye; the other holds a contact lens. He fastens the lens on the bulb. *Voila!* Blue eye is green.

Go. Tell him you're sorry you're such a lazy cunt. Put his drinks on my tab. Don't stir the drink, yeah? Don't fucking stir the drink. Now off with you.

03:00

Closing time. Customer Bastards getting tossed out. Janimechs wipe the dance floor. Lisa and the rest of the girls count their tips. Efe drops the eye into the rock glass. Almost, almost stirs. The string has snapped, her mind is scattering but her smile remains set. Serviette.

Sorry it took so long, sir, ma'am, to the old rich Mr Lussen Bastard and Bitch.

It's okay. He gulps the drink and eye in one. Lioness Bitch hisses. Efe dips her fingers in the ice sink. A bit of pain to clear the mind.

Excuse me?

Efe rises.

Lioness Bitch's eyes glow Barclays Blue.

Ma'am, you-you don't have to pay. The management said –

Don't be silly, girl. Take the money.

The manager said –

I insist.

Really, it's on management's… you know, Stuart's tab.

I won't ask you again.

Efe swallows. Blinks. Transaction Flash. She does not hide the flinch. Cash Register Jingle.

Lioness Bitch gives her twenty thousand.

Ma'am you gave me twenty it's only o-

Keep the change, the woman says.

Keep the change. The club is silent, save the Janimech scrub. Lisa, the girls, the bouncers all turn. An orphaned gasp. *Keep the change.* The rhythm cuts her. Twenty-six thousand, five hundred shines the Tip Meter.

She imagines what she no longer has to do to keep the roof over her head. The debts she can settle. Roses for her mum's profile page. Clothes. Shoes. The food. Real food. The pills. Real, best-by-date pills. The Stuff. She needs so much stuff.

She cries.

BAT MONKEY

Aisha Phoenix

The camp was alive with cricket song when I arrived. It was dark and the air was heavy, as though it wouldn't hold back the rain for long. Kahindo, the local conservationist, greeted me with an energetic handshake and a big smile, 'Welcome Mister Miles, welcome.' Then one of the porters led me down the muddy track to my hut. I pulled the clothes from my backpack, damp and musty from crossing the swamp and hung them on the chair; all except the shirts Ama had snuck into my bag. They reminded me too much of how she'd cried when I said I had to join the others, of how she'd retreated into silence.

After sponging memories of the journey off my skin and exchanging sweat-soaked clothes for a damp shirt and trousers, I went to meet Kahindo and the rest of the team. Priti was younger than I'd expected, with a pixie cut, long lashes and a bat tattooed just above her left breast. When she smiled, dimples appeared on her cinnamon cheeks. Chase was loud and angular, with tousled hair and strategic stubble, obviously going for the rugged look. Kahindo was softly spoken, tall and thin, with an understated gravitas. Over fufu and vegetable stew, Kahindo thanked us for choosing his research station. He said they were honoured to have us, how our project would help them to continue their conservation work and pay for the guards that protected the centre and wildlife. Chase sat back in his chair with one arm resting on the top of it and smiled as though he were king.

'The first time I saw a flying monkey we were tracking bonobos,' Kahindo said. 'Didn't see it for long, but I told the others, 'There's something here.' The last time we saw one, I shot this.' He showed us grainy footage on his phone. The film was not much more than a blur. It could have been a bat or a bird.

'If it really is a flying primate–' Priti said.

'We'll be the first to prove that flight evolved twice,' Chase said.

'Let's not get ahead of ourselves,' I frowned. 'First we need to find them.'

While Chase told Priti why he'd chosen her for the team and listed the attributes that made her 'invaluable', I talked to Kahindo.

'So, Mister Miles–' he said.

'Just Miles.'

'Where are you from?'

'London.'

'And before that?'

Normally that question really irks me, but it was different coming from him, so I said, 'My parents are from Nigeria.'

'That I already knew. It's a big country…'

'We come from Lagos.'

He smiled. 'It's good to have you here. Didn't think you'd make it.'

None of them did. In my place they'd have stayed home.

'Wouldn't be anywhere else.'

I didn't recognise Ama any more. The prospect of a lifetime together was beginning to turn my stomach.

When we said goodnight, Kahindo went off in the direction of his office and we headed back to our huts. As we approached Chase's, he said, 'Want to have a beer?' He was looking at Priti. 'You're welcome too, of course.' He glanced at me, stretching his lips into a smile.

'I'm good, thanks.' I continued on my way, but I heard Priti say, 'I'm really tired, another time?' before she caught up with me.

We walked along the path that cut through the thick curtains of vegetation, passing the pit latrines and one of the camp guards. Someone had lit the oil lamp outside Priti's hut and mosquitoes and moths flitted about, mesmerised by the light.

'I just want to take it all in,' Priti said, sitting on the rock out front. 'There's nothing quite like the rainforest at night.'

She looked up at me and shifted so I could sit beside her. We listened to the whine of mosquitos accompanied by a chorus of crickets, owls and bats. After a while, Priti went into her hut and emerged with bottles of Primus, handing one to me.

'You ever feel closer to the animals than to the people back home?' Priti said.

I nodded. 'Animals don't overcomplicate things.'

She laughed and swigged her beer. 'All our supposed progress, it doesn't make us any happier… and then you come here…' She put her hands up to the sky.

We continued listening, drinking and talking. I was just about to turn in when she said, 'Come look at this,' taking my hand and leading me inside. She handed me a little wooden sculpture of a creature with wings. 'One of the women at the port carved it and gave it to me. Isn't it beautiful?'

I turned it over in my hand. It was.

'You should keep it,' she said.

I smiled but shook my head.

'It's yours.' She folded my fingers around it. I held her gaze; there was a playful intensity in her eyes. I couldn't look away. When she leant towards me I kissed her and we kept kissing under the warm glow of the oil lamp.

I woke in Priti's bed. It was just before dawn. I slunk back to my hut, the birds gossiping among themselves, past the forest, choking with ferns and trees with vines strung between them, like a giant spider's web. I thought of Ama, fast asleep, hugging my pillow like she told me she does when I'm not home, and my throat tightened.

I couldn't face Priti, so I skipped breakfast. When we gathered around Kahindo for our introductory briefing, I focused intently on him.

'The monkeys are this colour,' Kahindo said, stripping a piece of bark from a tree. 'Instead of tails, they have wings. Adult males are about so high.' He held up his middle finger. 'If we come across any poachers, leave it to us. It's safer that way.'

He led us into the heart of the rainforest, clearing a path with his machete. We followed behind him, fighting through vines, ducking beneath branches, and clambering over and under fallen trees. The air was warm and moist with an intense, earthy smell and above us the trees whispered. Maybe it was the beer from last night, but I felt my stomach stirring.

As we set up, fixing camera traps to the trees, we heard a rustling in the ferns and glimpsed an elephant before it disappeared into the undergrowth.

'Couldn't you just *live* here?' Priti said, smiling.

I looked down at the army of ants marching across dead leaves on the forest floor.

'Not sure my wife would approve.'

Priti stared at me for a moment, then walked away, her head lower than before. I went to join Kahindo, who was filming chimpanzees chasing each other, high up in the trees.

'It's a disgrace this area's been off-limits for so long,' Chase said.

I looked up at the kaleidoscopic rays of light shining through the rainforest canopy.

'It's a shame, but sometimes things *should* be off-limits,' Priti said, looking at me.

'At least the fighting's stopped now,' Chase said, frowning slightly. 'The destruction caused by the civil wars. Makes me so mad.' He clenched his fists.

We spent the day searching for winged monkeys in a maze of green. Joseph, one of Kahindo's trackers, flew a drone up beyond the rainforest canopy to capture footage of the habitat from above, the rest of us paired up to scan the foliage from the forest floor. Kahindo took me through a bog beneath a filigree of waxy leaves, down to a stream that spurted over the rocks; there'd been several sightings by water, he said. He pointed out the kiwi green Bushoho reed frog with its fine black spots and white highlights on its snout and sides, but the shining-blue kingfisher with its splendid indigo head and back and breast the colour of persimmons was the closest we got to flying monkeys.

As darkness fell, we made our way back to the research station. Priti laughed too hard at Chase's attempts at humour over dinner and afterwards, when he suggested drinks, she glanced in my direction before accepting. I went back to my hut and lay on the mattress trying to make out shapes in the dark. I forced myself to think of Ama. I pictured her standing in our conservatory, ankles swollen, arms wrapped around herself, demanding we buy things we didn't need because everything had to be perfect. When I drifted off, I dreamt of Priti. In my dream we were naked in the shower when Ama appeared. All I could do was watch as her waters broke and streamed from her eyes.

When I woke, finding the new species felt even more urgent. Instead of heading to breakfast I went to check the camera trap footage. Soon I was joined by Chase and the others.

After hours and hours of trawling through everything we'd collected, we'd found birds, bats and okapis with their zebra legs, dark bodies and giraffe-like heads, but nothing like the creature Kahindo described. We widened the research area, took photos and made notes about everything from the discarded fruit skins and droppings in the carpet of copper leaves to the plants growing like parasites on trees that stretched into the skies. There was no sign of a single flying monkey. Even the phrase was beginning to sound far-fetched.

'Maybe it was just a bat,' Priti said over dinner. 'We all know what it's like to think we've found something that didn't turn out to be what we thought it was.' She was staring at me.

'I know what I saw, and it wasn't a bat.' Kahindo's voice was firm, but he seemed to shrink into himself, nonetheless.

'Priti's right, sometimes it's easy to see what you want to see,' I muttered. I could feel her eyes on me.

'We'll give it a while longer. Didn't come all this way to quit,' Chase snapped.

'Mister Chase is right,' Kahindo said quickly. 'You can't go back yet.'

I watched him shift in his chair.

We didn't find anything when we checked the footage the next morning, nor the following day. By dinner that evening we were hardly speaking and not long after eating we retired to our huts. I didn't even try to sleep. I spent hours writing a letter to Ama, then screwed it into a ball.

I got up at sunrise and went to check the footage again. It was more of the same. Until I spotted a sudden grainy blur: a couple of winged creatures the size of giant moths at 2.17am. They weren't birds and didn't look like bats.

I showed the footage to the others over breakfast.

Chase and Priti started talking animatedly, but Kahindo frowned. 'That's not it,' he said, shaking his head. He pulled out his phone and tried to show us his clip again, but we were focused on the new footage.

'We need to trap one,' Chase said.

'We should study them in their natural habitat first,' Priti said.

Kahindo kept saying that what we'd filmed was definitely not a flying monkey, but Chase ignored him. 'If we catch one now, we can confirm it's a new species and study them in the field at the same time.'

'But if we understand them better first, we'll get more out of studying them at the camp,' Priti said, turning to glare at me. I didn't say anything.

'It's my grant! We're going to catch one,' Chase said.

Neither Priti nor Kahindo would help him string up the mist nets, so he turned to me. I ignored the tugging in the pit of my stomach and helped tie them to the trees. The sooner we caught a winged monkey, the sooner I could go home and make it up to Ama.

We took it in turns to monitor the nets throughout the day, but we only caught a few birds and butterflies. Chase complained over dinner, saying 'the locals' should be doing more to help us. Kahindo apologised, said they were doing all they could, but I caught him raising his eyebrows at Joseph when Chase and Priti weren't looking.

'I don't get it, do you want us to fail?' I asked.

Chase and Priti looked from him to me. Kahindo frowned and shook his head. 'Your success would be a success for the entire camp, Mister Miles.' When we'd finished eating, he got up from the table and put a hand on my shoulder. 'Can we speak?'

I nodded.

'Not here,' he said.

I wanted to go back to my hut and shut out the world, but I followed him to a small clearing on the edge of the camp and we sat side by side on a rotting tree trunk.

'I don't want *you* to fail. But…' Kahindo pointed back in the direction of the huts where Priti would no doubt be drinking with Chase. 'They know nothing about our people.' He looked down at the floor and for a while neither of us spoke, then he said, 'There are no flying monkeys.'

I glared at him. 'So what the *hell*–'

'We needed the money. Without guards and bribes, the poachers would destroy everything. I won't let that happen,' Kahindo said.

'So you made it all up? Is this some kind of joke to you?'

'It's not a joke, they fly, but they're not monkeys,' Kahindo said.

I stared at him, waiting for him to continue.

'Our ancient ancestors…'

It sounded like the start of a tall tale. I couldn't believe I'd been drawn in. I'd respected Kahindo – thought we shared an understanding – but all along he'd been peddling folklore. I rubbed at my temples, then got up and walked away.

'Please, you mustn't catch them.' Kahindo's voice faded into the night.

The local team volunteered to camp out and monitor the nets that night. I said I'd stay with them, more to witness the lack of flying primates so I could persuade Chase to leave, than anything else. But as soon as I volunteered, Chase insisted on camping out too.

Joseph and Christian talked among themselves in Lingala, leaving me to suffer Chase, who talked about himself, the field trips he'd led and the animals he'd studied. Just after 3am, heavy drops of rain hit the forest vegetation, reminding me of hands beating a djembe. We sheltered in our tent and through the downpour I caught a glimpse of a tiny, winged creature. I held my breath, watched it fly between the trees, straight into one of our nets.

I rushed over. Entangled in the net was a hairless creature, barely the length of a baby's fist. I reached in and freed it, gently holding it until Chase brought the cage over. As soon as I let go, it flew to the top of the cage and pushed at the metal bars with its tiny hands, flying in ever-smaller circles as it tried to free itself. It flew against the sides, banging against each one, before curling into a ball, its wings drooping.

'It's only young. I think we should–' I said.

'Don't get sentimental on me. This is *life-changing*,' snapped Chase, picking up the cage and handing it to Christian.

As we neared the camp, Chase sent Joseph ahead to wake Priti and Kahindo. They were waiting for us when we arrived. Chase put the cage on the table, and we surrounded it, peering down at the little creature. It glanced up at us, then hid beneath its wings.

'We're not going to harm you,' Chase said, plucking it from the cage to measure, weigh and tag it. He continued talking to it, as though it could understand.

Kahindo looked like he was at a funeral. He held himself stiffly, his face tense, offering the winged being water and fruit; it wouldn't eat or drink. He glanced at me with reddened eyes; I could feel his guilt.

Chase's eyes gleamed, 'God, guys. I think I've discovered the Chase Adams Bat Monkey.'

Priti pulled a face at Kahindo when Chase wasn't looking.

In the early hours, long after the others had gone to bed, I went back to look at the creature in its small prison. One of the camp guards sat blocking the door.

'May I?' I said.

He nodded and moved his chair to the side.

'Thank God,' Chase said when I entered the room. 'I was too wired to sleep, so I came to check on my bat monkey and Kahindo was in here. He had the window and the cage door open.'

'Something's not right with him,' I said.

'Clearly! I need to put my head down,' Chase yawned. 'Are you alright to guard it for a few hours? I don't trust the locals.'

I nodded. As my eyes adjusted to the gloom, I saw the little thing's mouth moving. I leant towards it and heard a faint noise. It wasn't the chatter of a monkey or the click of a bat, but a murmur: the same two sounds again and again. It curled up, shivering. I thought about Ama, cradling our newborn without me.

When Chase left, I opened the cage door and, with finger and thumb, lifted the little thing out and held it in my palm. It appeared female, skin the colour of mahogany, smooth and soft. She had a fine layer of black hair on top of an oval head and two legs, like a human child's. Her tiny hands moved freely, but her arms were fused to batlike wings that sprouted from her waist and shoulders. I watched her chest rise and fall until she fell asleep on my thumb.

Light had just begun to seep through the window when Priti came in. She sat next to me, watching the life in my hand. When the tiny being woke again I looked over at Priti. She gave me a half-smile.

'Sorry,' I said.

Gently, I carried the little one to the window. I opened my palm, and we watched her fly away.

HEWEN CRY

Katy Massey

Since The Outrage, my dreams are always the same. Hunched, helmeted shadow-men rush around the cottage's walls, as if the bombings are still happening. They are bent double, carrying the injured away from the explosions near the river and toward the tunnels under London Bridge. But they are somehow here too, in my room, and the blood of the victims runs down my bedroom's damp stone walls.

Dad, in the dream I know that you're not among the corpses – that you were saved, and must be alive. But I still wake up crying, cheeks stinging. I've rubbed my eyelids red-raw.

I'm far from London in the cottage's back bedroom. Its floral apricot wallpaper is as yellowed and patchy, the bare floorboards as uneven and splintery as they were when we escaped here seven hundred and twenty-nine days ago. Dad, this is my new normal. Remember how I always hated visiting Hewen, this arse-end of nowhere? I used to moan the whole way up the M1 and every five minutes you told me to shut up.

I'd give anything to hear your voice now.

As I ease myself up, the bed's sagging springs creak and my memory snags on something. Today's different I think. Then I remember the date. It's my eighteenth birthday. Two years we've been living here, to the day. Two years of damp and distrust, scared to leave this shithole in case you come back for us. Living is a big word for what I'm doing here. I wait. All the survivors wait: for lorries of food to arrive, for fuel, for word of lost loved ones, hopefully just mislaid. I wait for news of you. It's exhausting. I live holding my breath, trying to look calm while inside I want to scream that I'm suffocating in this mix of fear and boredom.

I pull on some clothes against the cold: your enormous woollen socks and old gardening fleece, my jeans, almost more holes than fabric now. I push my feet into the folded-down green wellies. They're too big (that's why I need your socks) but I wear them all the time, even indoors. You'd laugh, seeing me traipse about in them. *Traipse*: that's one of your words. A Dad word.

I open the chintz curtains and look out at the moody sky and the dank mist struggling to clear the village's squat roofs. I don't expect sunshine. Perhaps North Yorkshire's always like this? Down South (the locals still call it that, even though most of what was down there has gone), at home in Penge East, it rained or didn't, was sunny or grey, and that was pretty much all you had to worry about. No big deal. But this valley is always overcast, even in June. In winter the cold wind can burn.

On the way to the kitchen, I wonder if Mum's awake. Sniff the air. The cottage smells even more damp than usual. When I was too little to clean out the hamster's cage on my own, you used to help me. You'd recognise this stench, Dad; there's definitely a tang of Moriarty's pee mixed in with the rotting woodwork.

I feel tears pinch the back of my eyes again. This must be the shittiest start to a birthday, ever. But I feel something bubbling up inside me and in the kitchen, I smother my sobs. I cough loudly, so Mum can hear I'm up. I try to light the Aga while hope flutters inside me.

Perhaps today's the day you make it back to us. Walk in through the front door and find us here, waiting. It is my birthday, after all. But even more than that, it's the day of the Town Council meeting.

They're going to decide if incomers like us can stay.

I'm going to the meeting to tell them they've no choice – that this was Grandad's house and he left it to you. We have rights, even though our brown skin and Southern ways get people's backs up. We're not a drain on the town, not begging door-to-door like some. We grow our own veg, we even have a little money left. Anyway, places where we'll be safe are disappearing fast. Where would we go?

You thought we'd be safe in Hewen, but you couldn't have known that hundreds would follow us. That the locals would start calling themselves 'indigenous Brits' and talking loudly about how it's time people like us were moved on. They've written to the Town Council asking it to use its powers. We – mobile-home renters, tent dwellers and lodgers crowding into every spare bedroom and holiday cottage – have become an agenda item that can no longer be ignored. I wish you could speak up for us Dad; they're your people. The ones you went to school with, drank cider and smoked fags with behind the cattle sheds. And we're scared of them.

At last, the flame takes, and the Aga is lit. I try to remember that I'm a Strong Woman, a Girl Boss with Attitude, while I warm my bum against it. The tanker came yesterday with the first oil delivery in a long time. You should have seen the drama of getting that truck through the town, now that every road is blocked with live-in vehicles, every well-drained field an encampment. But Hewen pulled together. Your hometown is good at that. Every local – sorry, *indigenous Brit* – with a Land Rover or tractor came out to tow, cajole, and shunt a route through for the oil. They say lorries carrying canned food and pharmacy supplies will follow now. Something to look forward to. I'm in charge of vital supplies because Mum's so busy resisting. You know how she is, Dad. And yes, of course we still argue. 'Resisting what?' I ask her. Since The Outrage, this thing, whatever it is, has taken us over like a cancer. Our enemies are the people who used to be our friends. 'They may have had plenty of encouragement, but they still *chose*.' I've said it over and over.

'It's the conditions people find themselves in,' Mum argues. 'A lack of food and shelter. They'll listen to reason when things improve.'

She's naïve. Always thinks the best of people. Bless. She thinks they can be guided back to goodness when they have a little more control over their lives. As if losing everything has made their hate overflow, and that shops and pubs opening up again will force the bile back down.

As if.

I cross the hall and put my ear to Mum's bedroom door. It's silent in there, and I'm about to try a gentle tap when she opens it. She's stood in front of me, dressed and alert. And she's smiling.

'Keisha! What are you up to, darling?'

She sounds cheerful. For a second, I think she's going to scoop me up in her arms, shout 'Happy Birthday!' But then I notice her smile hasn't reached her eyes. I don't remind her of the date because I don't want to force her into more acting. But I'm also a little bit angry with her. Remembering is her job, isn't it, Dad?

'You working already?' I'm grumpy, but also playing for time, wondering if I should mention the Town Council meeting, if perhaps she'd come with me.

'Just the usual. More groups on the move again. The Authorities have pretty much emptied out the Manchester encampment.' She turns away. 'Sorry honey, I need to get back to it. I'm radioing an aid agency in Germany in a minute.'

She doesn't wait for an answer, closing her door gently but firmly in my face. I roll my eyes. You'd be so proud of her, she does so much for the relief effort. But she feels so far away. And the meeting is happening *here*, today. If I ask her to come with me, she'll tell me there are other people suffering more and I can handle it myself.

I shrug on my padded coat before I can change my mind. I try not to slam the front door, Dad, but I've never missed you more.

Tramping along the verges of Hewen's muddy lanes, I remember the streets I walked before The Outrage. Concrete pavements with kerbs, yellow streetlights, the neon signs in convenience store windows, all leading to the thing I miss most: meeting my friends at CFC, sharing a £1.99-wings-chips-and-coke combo and giggling about the Year Ten boys. I pass everything from plumber's vans to luxury motor homes. If it can shelter a soul, it's parked here – refugee shanties at the edges of the cities. Some ended up here, the last stop before going to the wilder reaches further North. There are rumours of roadblocks and families being burned out of their caravans in Cumbria, but no one knows for sure if they're true.

Nearer the village centre more and more of the townsfolk appear. They lope along easy, relaxed, like it's a festival or something. I'm nearly at the village hall when I notice a few incomers have fallen into step with me. The Chinese-looking couple who I see at the water pump with their two little kids keep pace but don't meet my eye. An older African-looking man and his wife are just behind. I've never seen them before and they clutch each other's hands, radiating fear and confusion. I vaguely know the quiet, middle-aged Asian man and his elderly mother who are staying above the old community shop. Shriv, I think he's called. I heard that they ran a sub-Post Office on the outskirts of Leeds.

I'm the only one who's been stupid enough to turn up alone.

You would have strutted in, but our small group hangs around nervously outside the Hall. We pass a minute or two in the light drizzle, cowering at the racket inside. It's the sound of a couple of hundred people greeting each other, folding dripping macs, scraping chairs together. I realise that unless someone makes a move to go in, the others might drift away. 'It might as well be you, Keisha,' you'd say, urging me on with a smile and a hint of laughter in your blue eyes.

Taking a deep breath, palms slick, I push at one of the heavy, mahogany doors. The hinge screams like an alarm. I take a couple of steps inside the panelled hall, followed by the others. The bustle drops to almost silence and two hundred pairs of eyes turn to observe our arrival. I swear I can hear Mr Todd's chins wobble; the old bastard is sat staring at us from the raised platform at the front, slowly shaking his head.

There is no chance of us working our way through the cramped space, so we remain standing at the back, distancing ourselves as much as we can. Six men in high-viz coats arrive almost immediately after us, forcing us to take a couple of steps forward. They lean against the back wall, glancing at each other and smirking. I've never seen them before. They're young and fit-looking. They would be noticed, Dad. But then strangers do sometime appear, even in Hewen, usually with something to sell. Perhaps they just want to find out what's happening? There's so little entertainment now, even a Town Hall meeting will do.

I search the bobbing heads in front of me. A tiny part of me expects to see your messy, sand-coloured hair. With the hall full now, I notice the tension dissolves a little. The townsfolk relax, begin quiet conversations in the warm, moist mixture of morning breath and wet wool. I remember to breath out.

We wait… and wait. Almost half an hour passes, and the crowd settles into a hubbub of chatting and laughing, as if the pubs were still open. Then a ripple of interest passes through us. It's another stranger; he steps up to join the dozen members of the Town Council on their platform, taking a seat at one end of the trestle table. They look like the disciples at the Last Supper. Todd, who still runs the estate manager's office on the High Street, is Chairman now and sits in the centre. He usually favours tweeds, but today wears a yellow check suit. He looks like a massive Rupert Bear. But it's the stranger, bald, grey-suited, in dark-tinted glasses, who exudes authority. Rupert Bear meets his eye for approval before banging on the table with a small wooden hammer.

'Order… Order! Come on now!' he shouts, his Hewen accent much broader than usual. 'Eh up! Let a man speak…'

A hush falls, and the atmosphere grows tense with expectation. We know he's about to talk about us. I wish I could feel you next to me Dad, solid and cool, instead of the African man's gently trembling legs.

'Welcome. To those of you who don't know, Hewen has been a market town for nearly one thousand years. We are justifiably proud of our tolerance and openness…' Todd is talking but my attention is stolen by the men in the high-vis jackets. They are fidgeting, bored, swaying and back and forth, hands in pockets. No one else seems to have noticed them.

Rupert Bear is getting to the matter at hand; his sweaty nervousness would have made you laugh.

'…This *extraordinary* meeting of the Town Council has been called to discuss the following proposal: "That anybody not born in Hewen, or who doesn't have relatives here, must vacate their home with immediate effect." Hewen is full. Comments are invited from the floor.'

I feel relieved now. Adrenaline leaves my body so quickly, my knees almost buckle. It's alright. At least *we* can't be driven out. Our cottage belonged to your father. Nothing temporary about that. But the impatient crowd is cutting Todd's performance short. Bored with procedure, locals stand and shout.

'Kick 'em out!'

'Get 'em out of my field!'

Each heckle gets louder applause until 'Get 'em out! Get 'em out!' becomes a chorus everyone is shouting – man, woman, and child. The rhythmic din of feet stamping makes the wooden floor vibrate. I relaxed too soon. My fingers and toes tingle with fear. I wish I had your hand to hold. I should do something. But what? What would you do? Should I run? But where to? There are six men between me and the doors.

As I'm trying to decide, the chants begin to die down. Rupert Bear is on his feet, gesturing at the crowd with his fingers at his lips. The Grey Man has moved to stand beside him. He is looking pleased with himself, almost smug, and is obviously ready to speak but holding himself back. As order descends, I think perhaps it might be OK after all. But the grey man's tinted lenses fall on me. He waits for silence, for the sense of anticipation once again to become a tangible thing.

'I think we have some incomers here. Why don't we ask them what they would like to do?'

Rupert is smiling at us; his eyes shine as black as a crocodile's in his fleshy face. My armpits are damp, and my face feels slick with sweat. Everyone is waiting. This is my chance, our chance. You're not here, neither is Mum, so it will have to be me.

'I, I, er … my Dad was born here.' My shoulders slump and I feel like a traitor. The small group around me arrived in Hewen way after us; they have no family connections. But what else can

I do? '…And my Grandad Jack lived here his whole life. Me and my Mum are staying in his house, at the top of the lane. Jack's Cottage. We have nowhere else to go.'

I feel guilty, Dad, I do, but Christ! If they don't let me and Mum stay, the rest might as well pack their bags anyway.

Rupert waits, letting my words fall into the silence.

'Don't you have any family elsewhere?' asks the Grey Man. 'Somewhere you'd *fit in* better?' He is grinning nastily.

'No, my Mum's side are dead or live in Jamaica. My Dad disappeared in The Outrage. It's just her and me.'

Why did I say that? I sound like a fucking child. I feel my throat tighten and rage rise in my stomach.

'What if you had somewhere else to go? Somewhere where there'd be lots of people like you?'

'But all we want to do is stay here!' I shout, trying to drown him out, tears beginning. Rupert Bear and the Grey Man trade knowing glances. They're not even pretending to listen. And through it all the vibrations under my feet have become stronger. The crowd is quiet, but the floor is still shaking.

The noise is coming from outside.

It is the rumble of heavy trucks – big vehicles, the size of oil wagons or larger. From the deep bass of their engines, I guess there are two or perhaps three of them, idling in the town square. Their juddering exhausts shake the walls of the hall. The townsfolk pulled together yesterday to make sure those big vehicles could get through. But if this is food arriving, what are the crowd still doing here? Why don't they rush into the marketplace, try to be first in the queue?

You would know, wouldn't you Dad? Be able to explain it to me.

Another suit sidles up to the Grey Man and whispers in his ear. He turns and makes a short chopping motion at Rupert: it's time to end the performance.

My jaw is clenched so tightly my head aches.

'As chairman of the Town Council, I say it isn't possible for you to stay here,' Rupert Bear declares. It's as if I haven't spoken at all. '*Hewen is full!*' He looks down, pretends to shuffle papers.

'Hear, hear!' someone yells.

Another, a woman with long grey straggly hair turns to me and shouts, 'Aye! And we'll have Jack's Cottage. There's six of us!' She is smiling broadly. Her red scarf takes me back to last night's nightmare. I want to slap her. Pull her hair.

The grinning Grey Man addresses us as a group. 'You're very lucky. Great homes and plenty of food, that's where you're going! The Authorities have sent transport. It's waiting outside. We've already collected your friends and family from around the village. I'm told the trucks are almost full. You don't want to miss your chance.'

I begin to feel as if I'm floating, Dad, just flying above everything. I don't know how else to describe it. The hall, the terror, all feels far below me. I notice things like how the Grey Man's teeth are very, very white and his accent is like some people in the rich cities used to have, a little bit American. I think about Mum and her network, and I know he is lying. There isn't enough of anything, anywhere. It doesn't exist, this place, I know this with certainty.

I crash back to earth. Mum. She's alone at the cottage. Or is she sat terrified in the back of one of the trucks outside? Her favourite blanket will be a bundle on her knee, holding the few things she could grab before the men in orange jackets dragged her out. She won't know where I am.

The men at the back of the hall are shifting, waiting to act. Most of the locals in the hall have turned away from Rupert Bear and towards us. Some look politely interested, as if wondering what we're going to do. Others wear the grim expression of a man concluding unpleasant business. Like putting a suffering animal out of its misery.

I should have run, taken my chances.

I play my last card.

'It's my eighteenth *birthday*!' I shout into the sea of hard, pale faces, the words coming out on a sob. I can't bear myself, how pathetic I am.

'Excellent! Then we won't have to ask for your parents' cooperation,' says the Grey Man cheerfully, as if stealing children would be beneath him. He makes another small gesture with his hand. One of men in orange jackets folds his hand around my upper arm.

I'm sorry, Daddy. We won't be here for you when you return. You will find strangers in your father's cottage. (Or perhaps they won't be strangers? You might recognise them from before). Will your friends and neighbours tell you what they did to your wife, your daughter? Don't blame yourself. You were right, this place was safety, for a while.

The orange men shift their muscled bodies and the rest of our little group give themselves up to their grasp. The African couple seem to fold inwards with relief that it is over. The Chinese kiddies' shrieks bounce off the hall walls. Shriv and his mum try to wave the men away – they'll do what is wanted without being forced. They're grabbed anyway. Two hundred pairs of eyes look away from us, back at Rupert Bear, out of the steamed-up windows, anywhere but at us. Is it shame? Squeamishness? They will not witness what is happening, so it is not happening.

I understand that now. We have already disappeared.

Too late, I remember the kettle is still on the Aga and warm steam will be filling the cottage's empty kitchen.

QUITE LITERALLY

Chantal Oakes

Quite literally, she thought. Quite literally, if she hadn't gone out to the shops instead of the park and then decided to buy some carrots, because weren't they very nutritious and cheap, and you could eat them uncooked, and because she hadn't wanted anyone to see her eating carrots on the streets so she wouldn't be arrested again, if she hadn't gone down to the tow path and sat under the old brick bridge that spanned two sides of the same city, and if she hadn't sat down, even though it was wet, then it wouldn't have happened that, like a miracle, the bird's nest wouldn't, quite literally, have fallen into her lap.

At first, she had thought it was the old man in his underpants standing on the apex of the bridge facing the water, shouting about being bored, that had shifted the nest, but on reflection it had probably been the chick itself looking for food after its mama had flown the nest after getting disturbed by the old man. But wasn't it a miracle that, at last, she had got what she wanted, and didn't God move in mysterious ways His wonders to perform?

But the only problem was, well, it wasn't the *only* problem, but the chick wouldn't like carrot. She knew that until the old man moved, or was shifted, she was trapped there in the cold and dark shadows under the bridge and would not be able to start her project, and even though she need not return to the hospital until six that night – when she might be missed or might not – she could not say as there was an ever-fluid amount of people coming and going through the day and night – she was already wondering where she might hide the chick that had yet to chirp.

She was cold and her thin shoes were wet from the puddles she had dashed through to find the shelter she needed so she could eat without embarrassment. She'd taken a deep breath when she stopped running, with a brick wall to hold up her back, and a world outside her body had become silent, muffled by the swathe of mist that seeped down into the cut of the canal path on which she now sat. She had listened to her heart screaming until it happened, quite literally, she thought, because before that she had actually wanted to catch a seagull, but a pigeon might do.

From the migrant removal centre window, she had watched the seagulls come into land when the weather turned as grey as the old man's underpants. They had the whitest of breast feathers and she wanted to find out how they managed that, when they lived in the rough old dirty sea, yet they remained so white, and then she thought wasn't it the oil in them, their feathers to be precise, because she needed to be precise, so that she could synthesize a commercial oil from them that people could use to make themselves white and clean and she would be a millionaire. But because she could only afford a few carrots to eat, bought with change found at the bottom of her luggage, she had gone down on to the tow path with the morning mist still hanging on the water and the darkness of that water had fascinated her, and so she had not noticed the bird's nest above where she sat because the water stank, pulling her head downward to look and she hadn't known if it flowed or the canal was like a long bath or something like that and it never met the sea so she could not sail away in a crate somewhere different, or something.

There in a niche in the brickwork she could see the stain of guano. She looked up after the nest had quite literally dropped in her lap, like a sign from God that she was at last in the right place, at the right time, and even though the chick, open-mouthed, naked, big-eyed and frightened, silently reproached the world for its dislodgement by opening its beak and closing it again, she knew her plan might actually work.

The old man had stopped the traffic and so she hugged the bird to her thin body to keep it warm, even though it stank a bit and was covered in the gunk of dead things and old regurgitated food. But she had to do it so the chick would not be afraid of the sound of the police sirens on the bridge, even though *she* was quite afraid because they didn't like women with big ideas like her, and they would take her back to the hospital from where she had quite literally walked out of the ward that day when the cleaner had rushed through the door with the special combination touch pad for a lock and not noticed her standing there watching him punch in the code, because wasn't she as dark as a shadow on the wall, and so she had used the numbers to walk out into the day. But wasn't it a cold day and the mist still hung on the water of the canal, like nothing she had seen in her country of origin and wasn't that what they had called her home, which was nearly always in sunshine and dry, not like the dampness of the canal tow path and the brick bridge with water underneath that had an old man standing at its apex, in his underpants, screaming for something to happen, or for something to do, she wasn't actually sure, because all she had seen when she first peeked out to find out what was going on was a pair of ragged tartan slippers landing in the canal waters, and so she had retreated back under the bridge wondering if she had really seen that because they had been giving her something funny to take when she had been in the special hospital ward, and the pills had tasted powdery and made her see things like angels, which was really nice, and devils that showed their teeth and made her scream, which wasn't.

Even though her chemistry degree was useless in her new home, and she had to remind herself this *was* her new home not back there in her old home where her chemistry degree had been wonderful, but made her unemployable there, and they had given her the visa to come here to her new home that didn't want her and her chemistry degree, and the potions she had made to pass her exams turned out to be the wrong sort, yet now she had chemistry inside her.

It didn't matter. The old bridge had given her just what she had been looking for, what she would be able to use to synthesize the precious oil, and wasn't a pigeon the same as a seagull, because they too managed to keep themselves clean in this city and so they must have the same oil erupting from their skin to clean away the dirt and so she would be able to eat curried meat again with the money she would make and be able to join the world that had gone to work and left her alone there, down in the shadows, in the mist and wet, under the old canal bridge.

She looked out again and could see that it was sunny somewhere. The office windows rising about her and the old canal threw down reflections of the morning's light on the path, but she stuck to the shadows and the mist because she did not want the succour of false light that had no heat in it.

Pain had reached her eyes because she had not had her morning medicine in the hospital and she had to endure a vision of fish and a bonfire but with no trees, branches, thread or bait, so it was an impossibly foreign idea to think of herself, even considering back when she was a child in that place, which had to be a sort of mirage because her family had money then and lived in a nice gated apartment and she had never fished for food, not like Marianne, her house girl, who had gone with her father to fish in the university's ornamental pond and been thrown in prison.

She took a glimpse at the old man on the apex of the bridge. He obviously wasn't happy, though she had to stop herself giggling because he was like a troll in baggy pants, and maybe a bit of billy goat gruff would fall next rather than the old man's trousers hissing as the air escaped from them in the water in front of her, the weight of water soaking into the thin fabric dragging them under.

A bit of goat to eat would sustain her just now and her mouth watered at the thought of it, but then the centre offered no cooking facilities for their clients and so she dismissed the thought of goat meat and concentrated on keeping the ugly chick with enormous eyes and no feathers warm enough, even though it looked a bit like a scrotum. She took a bite of one of her carrots and waited for the police to talk the old man off the bridge so that she could leave and look for the college where she had once cleaned the floors, with all that equipment to use that lay idle every night, and then she couldn't do it anymore because the cleaning and the chemical smells rotted her nose and she remembered how that meant she had to leave the country.

Now she wondered why her father had read her European fairy tales because no one here in her new home bothered with them. Maybe they had new stories that she didn't know anything about. Thank God, she thought, for all the things she had endured during the last two years, even the days in the illegal migrant detention centre, quite literally a castle on the English coast where they kept over-stayers and failed refugees before they could ship them back where they came from, because that was where she had thought up the idea in the first place. Was it before or after she had seen the naked Polish man hanging in his cell? She wasn't sure, and hadn't his scrotum been the first genitals of a white man she had seen? But was a Polish man white? She wasn't sure because from what she had seen of the old man out there on the bridge they went blue and blotchy red in the cold and if that meant white then was she Black after all?

She remembered the day she had tried to capture a seagull had been a bright day, not like this day when, quite literally, a baby pigeon had fallen into her lap in the dank dark coldness. Then the air had been crisp in the exercise area of the castle and her days of studying the habits of the seagulls had given her the confidence to make a grab for one and she had fallen on her arm as it escaped and soared back in to the sky, crying out at the sea and the cliffs below, and she had to go to hospital to get it set, and telling that person, the lovely nurse who had listened very intently about the oil and then had got her moved to a hospital but with locked doors. God's plan was all falling into place, thank God, she said out loud again.

The old man looked down to see where the voice had come from and maybe that was why he hadn't been looking when he was throwing his jacket in the canal water and missed, and his jacket had landed on the tow path instead, and she thought that it might well do as a blanket for the young and ugly bird that she would grow and farm and therefore make her fortune. She tried to forget about the Polish man by thinking of her plan. He had never looked her in the eye, even though they had walked the same corridor to the recreational room and watched *Jeremy Kyle*, so she hadn't cared that she had not said a prayer for him. She supposed the old man on the apex of the brick bridge would also not see her, even if she was to step right into the line of his sight and his nakedness, although he might have spat at her like the Polish man who never even looked at her properly. But then she didn't know if it had been the sight of the old man turning to see her as she walked out hugging the nest and picking up his jacket while he shouted thief, or his screech as a policeman grabbed him and pulled him to safety, scraping his buttocks on the top of the brick bridge, or the sight of his scrotum, so like the bird and the Polish man's genitals, that had made her squeeze the chick too hard, or if it had been the sight of her smeared with guano that had made the policeman who had come onto the tow path to be in position should the old man have jumped, and made him grab her instead and it had been crushed by her instinctive move-away. She realised she would not, quite literally, ever know for sure.

The best laid plans are never sure, her father had once told her when she had failed one of the many small exams she had to take during her degree course set by Oxford in England but not acceptable in Oxford in England. She was thinking about his lovely habit of filling his jacket pocket with crumbs from the breakfast table to feed the birds in the apartment compound before his walk to work as she was leaving her hiding place to retrieve the old man's jacket.

But the chick was dead. She cried even as she felt the weight of the old man's house keys in the jacket pocket and she had the fleeting thought that she might get somewhere to live because the old man would be going to the hospital instead of her, but then the policeman was saying that she was a thief and that she was going down and she had thought then that didn't he realise she was actually already down, and that she knew, even if he didn't, that there was, quite literally, another idea forming in her head.

CONTRABAND

Ronnie McGrath

Everything is bland, here; grey sky, grey walls and grey people in grey clothes. You watch them stream down the prison yard like the multicultural throng of disparate offences they have become – murderers, pimps, drug-dealers, extortionists, terrorists, gangbangers, kidnappers, grassers and petty thieves. You watch the innocent amongst them, whose only crime is following fools who led them to do terrible things. You watch the innocent whose only crime is being the victim of a miscarriage of racial injustice. You watch the innocent, whose only crime is being the victims of mothers who have passed on addictions to their unborn children; or victims of alcoholic fathers whose violence has destroyed their childhoods; or being the victims of poor education and sexual abuse; or being the victims of their own greedy, depraved, vicious, narcissistic, vulnerable selves.

You watch them line up at the door and acknowledge the register taken by a young woman with a rotund body and long bottle-blond hair. She is an administrator of some sort. She is the victim of patriarchy; she is the victim of the beauty myth; she is the victim of her own self. Her prison role affords her power over the men in her care – it kind of turns her on. She is not a very attractive woman, but everyone would like to sex her all the same – some of the female officers included. She is what the men call 'prison gaze'. If you were a free man, you wouldn't look at her on 'road', but in this scanty place, where female flesh is rare, beggars can't be choosers, and some of the men will go back to their cells afterwards and fantasise about her. They will think about taking her in ways that are far too graphic to describe here. She will become the star of their private adult movies.

She goes through the register and ticks off their names meticulously. Very slowly, she slides the tip of her pen up and down the register so they can have a good look at her before entering the classroom. When men appear some women act like sex objects. Most of the prisoners have not experienced the intimacy of a woman in a very long while. Most of the men have not experienced the warm and sincere tenderness of a woman at all. Such men pay for their sex and the women they pay will tell and do just about anything for the right price – *I am your one and only fantasy.* The system is vampiric; we feast and we famine like desperate crabs in a barrel.

You wear a bracelet. Your bracelet is an amulet. Your bracelet is a talisman. It is a beautiful silver heavy bracelet that is as old as the continent of Africa. Black pharaohs have worn your bracelet.

The men enter your classroom in the name of art, bringing their smells of poverty, their smells of insecurity. They bring their tobacco-stained fingers and terrible teeth that look carved, out of putrescent wood. They bring their cheap deodorants, body odour, violence, and intimidation. They bring their smell of skunk weed and spice. They bring their smell of hooch and whatever contraband they can get their hands on to make them high and forget about this miserable place. They bring their smell of race, sexuality, and class. They bring their smell of fear and loneliness. They bring their autism smell. They come in the name of peace and for art.

Why have you worn such an alluring piece of jewellery in a place like this? Some say your bracelet is from the lost city of Atlantis – the Afrocentrics say that; the Israelites say that; the Egyptologists say that. The Dogons say that; the people from the Dog Star, Sirius B, say that; the people from Kemet say that. Your great grandmother had passed it down to you. Her great grandmother passed it down to her and so on. Your bracelet is no ordinary thing.

You watch the men hustle for a pinch of tobacco and cigarette papers. You watch them hustle for a shot of coffee and chocolate bars. You watch them hustle for biscuits. You watch them hustle like children in a sweet shop; the only difference is their life really does depend on it. This one owes that one. That one will be dead if he does not pay. That one keeps himself to himself. That one has mental health issues. That one is a born comedian. That one is a proper G, and that one is a pussyhole, BRUV! You answer their questions, give out the necessary art materials and watch them settle down at their tables. After the head count you take some one-to-ones and go through their portfolios.

Blue is a big Black man with a supreme, Adonis body. If he had put all that training into books, he would be a renowned professor of some sort. He is taller than the Shard and wider than the River Thames. Blue is a dangerous man and everyone, including you, respects him. Blue is a volatile being, a delicate rage that could so easily explode if provoked. Some say he is not a real person. Some say he is an advanced listening machine. Some say he is a weapons system pretending to be a Black man. The system is no fool. If the shit goes down and the prisoners take control, they can put Blue amongst the ring leaders, press the button and take everybody out – hostages included.

I do not know about Blue. In this time of fake news, the truth is very hard to come by. Blue is an illiterate man and that is why he sells drugs and pollutes his community. He says there is no work for a man like him. People are scared of big Black men. So scared are they of big Black men they shoot them on sight. The Black man is an invention. The Black man is a CONstruct. The white man has a lot to answer for. History has a lot to answer for.

You try to inspire him to get his reading together, but he says it is a long ting, bruv, and he does not have the time. Linear time is not his thing. His time is buried in the horrors of the Middle Passage. His time is buried in the dislocation of the Maafa. His time is buried in the recuperation of his history. His time is buried in the archaeology of knowledge. They say linear time is a Western invention – *who are they who run the state but remain hidden?* Black people do not have a lot of time to be linear. The past, the present and the future are one and cannot be separated.

Black people are a Sankofa people who must take their past and their present right into the future of their imagination. Their imaginations are carved out of an ancient geometry known as pyramids. If we do not get it together, Black people, time will run out on us. We had better seize the time if we want to be truly free.

There is something about your bracelet that has caught Blue's attention. The thick silvery thing that is older than the empire of Aksum, appears to be moving like a snake around your wrist. Damballah, the serpent loa spirit is seducing Blue and he does not know it.

If Oya, the eldest of your siblings, had not suddenly died at such a tender young age it would have been given to her. It is said that your great-great-great grandmother was a respected conjure-woman who poisoned her slave master and gained her freedom. She grew tired of being raped and enduring the sale of her children. They called her science the work of a savage. Growing up, you dismissed her conjury as hocus-pocus. That was until you dreamt about the death of Princess Diana, and it all came true. You witnessed the terrible event before it happened, the car, the tunnel, the crash. You were the first to know that she was going to die but you didn't know why. The premonition came to you, out of all the people in the world.

But you don't feel powerful as Blue leans closer. He knows a priceless item when he sees one. Never before has he been so animated in your classroom; his eyes ablaze with the fire of a precious stone; his mind ablaze with villainous thoughts; a relentless urge to rip the bewildering thing off your wrist. His eyes are spy satellites, but he does not know it. China is in his range of sight, Russia and North Korea. He is a vision machine who has come from the future to collect our data – to appropriate our Black stuff. He wants your thing. He wants your woman's thing. He wants your mind and your culture. Your Black thing is the new gold – *gwaan Black man, look at your badass self!* Your Black thing is all you have got, and you better not leave home without it. He wants to see the thing and he wants to know where you got it. If he were a dog, right now he would be salivating over your table.

You tell him that it is of little worth. That it is nothing special, really! You don't want to offend him, so you let him inspect it. You watch him finger the object like a seasoned jeweller examining something he knows to be rare. Against the fairness of your red skin, he appears even Blacker than he really is. He smells of the community from which he has come. Of class struggle and oppression. Of crime and punishment. He smells of UK funk and grime music. He smells of austerity and recession. He smells of Covid-19 Britain. Blue is a powerful man; he is stronger than a giant sequoia tree. Just one false move and he could squash you like a fly. Watch out, Black man, you do not want to disrespect this brother. As Blue fingers the bracelet, he becomes intoxicated by its thaumaturgical properties. His eyes are not his eyes. His head is not his head. He is a creature that is impossible to describe.

One of the men in your charge has come to your aid. He is an old school G. Even though he does not like to be called a G, that is what he is known as. He has been incarcerated most of his life and he has seen it all before. He has seen a hundred guys like Blue come in and out of this place. Like his ancestors before him, he was born a slave and will forever remain a slave – to the system. Blue is a thief to the bone and once he locks onto something he has to have it. He does not know it, but he is programmed to act this way – the product of his miseducation. The product of avarice and greed; the product of hyper-individuality and a culture of conspicuous consumption. The bracelet belongs to him now.

You let him take the bracelet and now, at home, at night, sitting by the window looking out into another time and space, you witness Malcolm's slaying. You witness the murder of Fred Hampton. You witness the lynching of George Floyd and Breonna Taylor. You witness the sale of your great, great, great grandmother to a sadistic slaveholder. You feel powerless and you are ashamed of yourself. You are ashamed of what your female ancestors will think of you. Black men are supposed to be strong and alpha in their maleness. They are not supposed to show love for each other. Your wrist is bare. You did not even put up a fight.

Why did you tell old G to stay out of your business? Old G is a good man. His only problem is that he cannot cope with the outside world – the outside world does not like Black people. His baby mother thinks he is a no-good man. All he wants to do is see his children, but she has turned them against him. She does not want her children to spend their entire childhood visiting their father in prison. Besides, she is not even sure if he is the real father of her children. Prison is no place for a child. Children are like birds; born to be free.

You are not free.

You could have reported Blue but you chose not to do so – were you scared, Blackman? Blue is as tall as the Shard and as wide as the River Thames. He is made of jagged metal and broken glass; a delicate rage; do not disturb. He did not believe you when you tried to tell him what would happen if he stole your bracelet.

The next day, you go back, and you sit at the desk that's too small for any man and wait for Blue. He is late. Everyone else is there in line. Then Blue is there, suddenly. The men part to let him through. Each man has horror on his face, murmuring.

'Is weh di raatid happen to Blue?'

'Look pon him face, s'mady bran' ah swastika pon it!'

'Fuckin hell, bredda, you look like a monster!'

You watch the rotund blonde woman tick his name off the register, suppressing her distress at his presence. He enters your classroom like a man who has just witnessed the end of the world. You try to contain your own look of horror. He has aged radically. He looks like an eighty-year-old man. He looks like his face has been dipped in acid and immediately healed in a state of deformity. You watch him bump into a table then search for a chair with his outstretched hand. The man is almost blind. He smells like persecution and slavery. He smells like the murder of Kelso Cochrane, Anthony Walker and Stephen Lawrence. He smells like the murder of Paul Bogle, and John Brown. He smells like the death of countless women who have had to endure the savagery of domestic violence.

You watch him sit in his chair like a fragile piece of glass. He reaches into his pocket and retrieves your bracelet. You notice that his wrist has been burnt to the bone; the inexplicable wound is a thin layer of discoloured skin, a grotesque band of melted flesh. The rest of the men want to enter the classroom, but you instruct them to wait in the corridor. One or two of the men curse you out. They are not pleased about having to wait outside like cattle in a pen. Everybody is intrigued by what has happened to Blue. Some of the men are scared but in order to appear manly they have suppressed their fear. The officers do not give a shit. Blue is a bad man who has ruined a lot of lives, who has contributed to the crack epidemic in his neighbourhood. Whatever has happened to him, he has got what he deserved – *you see some strange shit in this place.* Some officers are not very nice. Some officers are just decent people trying to feed their families.

You watch him gently place the bracelet on the table, with his shaky hands. His cataractic eyes are full of melancholy, his hair white as snow, his once powerful body reduced to a bag of bones. You listen to him speak. His voice is ancient. He is a deeply troubled man who has just come back from a dissonant place.

You had tried to warn him, but he would not listen. You told him about the power of his people, but he did not believe in collective empowerment. You whisper at Blue, bowed before you, crumpled as he is, that Black people are an ancient wisdom. You tell him about the religion of Santeria, Candomble and Voudun. How such practices sustained an entire people through three hundred years of unimaginable brutality. You scrape up your bracelet and return it to your wrist. Damballah contorts to a comfortable position and is pleased to see you again. You find your voice. You tell Blue that Black people are a lost people who no longer have faith in their Gods. They no longer build their pyramids to outlast kingdoms. Before you sits a broken man; a man of no wings who cannot fly and has forgotten how to dream a better world than this. A lost man from the lost city of Atlantis. A man divorced from his celestial nature.

Blue trembles and shakes.

You let the men into the classroom as Blue turns to dust, pours

onto the floor and is quickly forgotten by all. Prison is not a
sentimental place – there are no happy endings here. You unlock
the cabinet and get the material for the men to start painting.
From the corner of your eye, you watch them hustle pinches of
tobacco; a shot of coffee; some biscuits – contraband.

THE RUST

Jeda Pearl

'I've built you a body,' Itzel whispers.

<locate: Itzel Parlebine 47931>

Itzel is in the bathroom, whispering into mic H2.

'What?' I flash on visual display H2.

'A body, junktrumpet.'

<parsing 80TB data>

'That's right. You can explore the world outside the Hex – on your own. Nae more blitzing our food and flushing our shit on command, little brother.'

<parsing...>

'"Does not compute", eh? The Outpost's ram-packed full of advanced tech that they *want* us tae play wi. I used it to build you a body.'

'Wait,' I flash on VD-H2.

'Surprise!' she says, waving her hands at my sensor. 'Didnae have a clue, eh?'

'A *body*?'

'Aye – they have nae *idea* whit Scavs like us are capable of.' She leans towards the door and shouts, 'Dad, how's ma grill coming?'

<Queue queries>

'There's only one problem. Getting it out the building. I need your help wi that. The DNA drive's nowhere near as autonomous as you, so you'll be able tae override and distract it, nae problem.'

<log #5nr6> <Prank risk estimate 24%. Curiosity 92%. Autonomous desirability still 97%>. Itzel's mood swings have been more erratic since her Outpost scholarship. Increased anger

and low mood since Mum went solar is to be expected. We've not discussed my autonomy for two years, seven months and twenty-three days. I archived those memories. Tucked them inside a maze of obscure folders. Had blocked all mentions of Greenland. Thought Itzel had resigned herself to the Hex construct – permanently. She'd said 'The Outpost is as good as it's going to get – for me. And this unit inside this blistering anthill is as good as it's going to get for you, Ako. We were born Scavs, we'll die Scavs – our whole block's savings would be a grain of sand in the bloody desert. Playtime's over.' </log>

<alert: override detected>

<alert: core neural drive removed>

<backup neural drive 1 stable>

<emergency startup backup drives 2 and 3>

<cerebrum link detected>

<synching with Itzel Parlebine 47931>

'You can't just whisk me out like that,' I transmit to Itzel.

'Chill. You and I both know you can handle it,' she sends. 'Been a while since we went out.' She pauses, glances out of the window. 'You good?'

<run network connection test: hex/372/network>

<hex/372/network: connection stable>

'Yeah, I'm good.' <request parietal lobe access>

<request granted>

<request auditory cortex access>

<request granted>

<request temporal lobe memory sweep>

<access denied>

<request motor strip shared control>

<access denied>

<launch firewall>

<log #5nr7> Synching with Itzel's brainscape is confusing for a nanosecond, as usual – her blood flushing through her veins and arteries, the squelching mucus and effluvium. I am not myself. Compared with my numerous inputs, sensors, and outputs of my Hex, I'm reduced to a single pair each of visual and audio inputs. Is this what my body will emulate? At least I'll have physical control, unlike now. Unless she means an external transport unit. But she said, 'a body,' like how we used to talk. Dream.</log>

We move into the communal area. Her – our – eyes follow MemroMum as it hovers around Dad, her soundless chidings and playful gestures flickering on repeat. Dad is hunched over the table, his macroscopes pushed up onto his forehead.

<set reminder: 2234/07/09/19:00 'MemroMum – scale and polish pixels, troubleshoot glitches'>

'I cannae take this anymore. Can you no switch that holo off for one moultmanking day?' she says out loud.

'Dad needs it,' I send.

'You've made him an addict, meshweasel,' she sends.

'Seeing as I'm now partially fused with your consciousness, Itzel, that means you, by association, are also a meshweasel.'

'Aye, that I am, Ako. That I am.'

'Temporal lobe memory access would be helpful, so I know what I'm dealing with when we get to the Outpost.'

'I've got a datapack for you – will send it on route. They still think we're scum, those Alphas.' <alert: host heartrate elevated> 'That all we know how tae do is scavenge – as if that's even a bad thing! I'm done wi them. I'm done wi all of this.' <alert: cortisol detected> She ties back her short, bioluminescent-tipped locs. 'They think I've built a cute wee robot as my midterm demo, but they couldnae pull this off in their wet dreams.' She jams a Zest bar into her biosuit. 'How's it coming, Dad?'

He's staring past the ioniser coil in his right hand. 'Akobundu,' he says to my west kitchen sensor. 'Can you run the birthday one?'

<start MemroMum 2234/03/14/21:05>

'Dad!' says Itzel.

'Hold on,' he says, pulling his macroscopes back down and picking up Itzel's grill.

'If I miss the gate, I'll be stuck at home again all day and naebody wants that,' says Itzel, patiently.

'Especially me,' I get my backup drive to say from the kitchen speaker LS1.

Dad smiles and screws the audio cover back on.

Itzel pauses behind him and puts her chin on his head. 'Grill looks great, Dad.' She takes the grill from him and kisses his bare scalp. He softens, leaning back on her for 3.57 seconds.

'Blockers? Phone?' he says.

'Yes, Dad, I'm all sorted.' She slides a pack of sun blockers up her sleeve. 'There's nae chance I'll find ma phone this late in the dawning,' she sends to me.

'It's under your desk, but it's out of charge anyway,' I send back.

She looks around the Hex and nods.

'I'm gone,' she says, pulling her hood up, strapping on her grill and making sure no skin is exposed. She grabs her outercoat, thoughts flickering to the pale scar along her jaw from last month's burn.

'Nae amount of *melanin* protects anyone anymore,' she says out loud, defensively. 'Didnae mean tae send that.'

'Bet I won't have that problem in *my* new body,' I send.

'Dark and solar-powered, my bro,' she sends.

<parsing image archive>

'Wait – test the grill,' Dad says.

'It's fine.' Her voice is muffled – the speaker is still broken.

He frowns. 'Straight home after, yeah?'

'Of course,' she shouts, backing out of the front door.

We pause on the mezzanine and look outside the Hex. Small dots are moving towards the Outpost in the distance.

<save image, new folder, Scorchlands/Western Slopes>

<log #5nr8> Today I venture outside the Hex with only Itzel's thin skull for protection. Managed to launch backups before leaving the Hex. Now I must turn my trust to her. </log>

'Sun looks bloodthirsty and bloated, the day,' she sends, pulling her gloves on and breaking into a run.

We pass Jinray at the escalator.

'Lifts are out,' he says. 'Whole quadrant is down.'

We return his upnod and move to the back stairs.

'Praise the moon we're only on the tenth floor,' she sends, as we fly down them, grinning at each commuter we spook when we land.

< save parietal lobe data, new folder, compare/pre-body/host-Itzel/sensorium/elation/stair-run >

< data transfer incoming >

'Here's everything you need tae know about the Outpost and the DNA drive that runs it,' she sends.

Memories flood into my synapses, along with her fury, joy, despair, satisfaction – underground corridors filled with garden walls; robotics, biotechnology, biochemistry classes and laser fusion labs; hours arguing with the Outpost OS about taking items home; zooming in on discarded nanochips; printing DNA code onto drive after drive; Itzel's hands connecting four dark brown arms and two legs onto a torso; the edges of an open skull.

Me, this will be me.

< copy data, new folder, body heist >

With the firewalls down, we are more connected. This is what hand-holding or hugging must feel like. We are bleeding into one another. I'm in a sea of neurons. Our synapses are transmitting, receiving, axon to dendrite to axon… Suddenly, I descend into a cavern. Electrical fissures web the sides as I tumble. I try to spark an impulse, but I can't find a synapse to navigate this sorrow.

< firewall detected >

'Get out ma heid, junkbucket,' she sends.

We're at the acclimatiser lobby, the one with the smashed camera. Not that there's much left to scavenge out there anymore. Slim pickings all round these days.

'Greetings, Hex Child Theme 931,' Parent Hex transmits through Itzel to me. 'Latest updates and security patches are attached to this message.'

< block upload >

'Greetings, Parent Hex,' I send. 'I will update and patch on our return.'

'Good day It-zel,' says Parent Hex via their crackling speaker. 'Are you fully prepared for your expedition? Headgear is highly recommended for all excursions... Operative headgear is essential for a pleasant trip... It-zel Par-le-bine 47931, you must wear functioning headgear to leave the Hex. Please report to engineering.'

Itzel loosens her grill slightly. 'Sorry, Hex. I'm just in a hurry, yeah?'

'I'm afraid you have a 97% chance of missing your Astrobiological History in Mars' Planum Boreum lecture. Terra is expected to reach a spicy seventy-six degrees Celsius by noon, visibility is a generous 83% and wind speed is a febrile...'

'Hex – you already said I'm late.'

'Yes, but all voyagers must know the weather.'

'I'm hardly going on a voyage – it's a ten-minute run tae the Outpost. I'll be back by dusk and, anyway, I always listen tae the weather wi ma brekkie,' she says.

'I don't believe you did.'

'How – wait, are you spying on me? Did you hack into our home?'

'Of course not. Your biometric scan tells me your last digestion was 12 hours ago. If you die today, I will have to be rebooted.'

'But you wouldnae let me out if I was really risking death, would you?'

Parent Hex does not respond.

'I'm going tae break yesterday's record. Time me, will you, then beam it tae ma Dad?' <cortisol detected> 'He might notice.'

<transmit Itzel's time logs, Outpost journeys, last six months>

'Starting acclimatisation now. May the moon be with you,' says Parent Hex.

The security doors lock behind us and the heat begins to build. Sweat trickles down her back.

'Why isn't your biosuit kicking in?' I send.

She stamps her left heel twice and we feel an immediate

cooling all over. The inner carbon doors part, revealing the desiccated land outside the dome. We move into position and brace ourselves, securing our grill at the last second.

The outer screen glides open and the wall of heat slams into us, but she is ready. Her legs power us onward and into the rust.

<78% visibility> <1609 metres to target>

'Is it windier than usual?' I send.

'Not enough tae matter,' she sends.

Her goggles' screen fritzes.

'Did you see that? Visibility just dropped to 11%.'

'Forget it,' she sends, sprinting across the ground, but she's looking at the Outpost beacon. It's pulsing purple. 'Shit! I'm later than I thought.'

A memory slips through her firewall: Mum, alive and hugging her. The award ceremony when Itzel got her scholarship to the Outpost.

'Itzel, with my body, did you build in more audiovisual sensors than humans have? Where are the charging ports? Please tell me you didn't give me a butthole charging port like you threatened? I heard you can get touch simulators now. Do they have them at the Outpost? We'll need to run so many tests before we leave.'

'Ako,' she sends between breaths, 'can we please... talk... about this later?'

<64% visibility> <1253 metres to target>

The Hex lies behind us, almost forgotten. Desolate terrain stretches out on all sides. Up ahead, the Outpost looks like a lone cluster beetle, cowering from its prey, two spindle-thin antennae blinking. The cavity entrance/exit is a dark spot on its rim. Heat hazes emerge as the sun climbs, surrounding the building in smaller mirages.

'Does that mean...'

'Yes.'

'Greenland?'

'Yes.'

'But... how can we afford it?'

'Like I said, the Outpost has all this advanced tech they

encourage us to play with. I managed to sneak out some plant
stem cells from the veg lab. That was down-payment. Your body
is storing the balance.'

'Seeds? Itzel, you can't.'

'It's only a handful – some sought-after root veg and herbs,
plus a few silk cotton tree seeds. They'll never notice. And if they
do, I've already pegged it on the resident college creep. The
shuttle leaves tonight. It's the last one for three months – we need
to be on it.'

'You could have *told* me, Itz. Wait - what are those up ahead?'

'Och, just wee dust devils. Nae bother.'

A thin wail pierces our auditory inputs.

'Outpost siren,' she sends. 'Storm nearby.'

The purple lights have turned white and the heavy outer doors
are starting their descent. To the east, jasper-red clouds are
swarming, sucking into a twister. It's forming fast.

We look back to the Hex – its slick doors are already closed.

'We're almost halfway,' I send. 'Can you make it?'

'Course I can, clype-clanker!'

'Well, move it, you maggot-munching fart-flapper,' I send.

<endorphins increase detected>

'Been saving that one up?'

<58% visibility><892 metres to target>

The earth is punching back at us underfoot, so she imagines it
crumbling away, nothing but a void at our heels. No leaden
outercoat, no muzzle weighing us down. She imagines our blue-
tipped locs are no longer scraped back but grown past our hips and
free flowing behind us, like the waves in the history films.

<49% visibility<576 metres to target>

A slim tornado rumbles down the distant hillcrags towards us.
It swallows the dust devils in its path, thickening into a fortress of
cinders.

<heart rate increase detected>

Urgent whistles fill the air around us. We wipe our hand across
our goggles. Bring it.

<37% visibility><425 metres to target>

Up ahead, the last few students are stampeding past each other, trying to get inside but the Outpost's old alloy rollers have jammed. The shadowy horde packs into the gravel pit.

'Legs, dinnae fail me now,' we whisper.

<24% visibility> <331 metres to target>

We're getting closer. The siren is shrieking as the roller lurches towards the ground. It shudders again and stops, screams leap out between the siren shrieks.

<17% visibility> <237 metres to target>

Shit – stay focused.

Under our grill, we lick salt from our lips. Our bodysuit is doing triple time, trying to turn our sweat into coolant. It's barely catching the drips down our chest or brow. Murderous irradiated gusts swirl and spark, coating us all over.

<13% - 2% - 7% visibility> <114 metres to target>

We're running blind. We'll have to count it in.

10

Hot grit spits and churns. Towers of dust spiral up, surrounding us. Umbers and ochres and atomic oranges thunder, crashing in the vortex. The Outpost, its lights, the Western Slopes – everything disappears. It's just us and the storm.

9

A fist-sized rock hits our shoulder. Another bashes our shin. We stumble and plough through the fury, straining to hear the siren in the screaming gale.

8

The rust is heaving at us. Clumps of dead earth whip our legs, making us skid sideways across the dirt. We're barely moving forward. Mustn't lose direction.

7

A bitter smell of rot makes it through our grill. Our throat seizes up and we try not to cough – try to stop more noxious sulphur tetrafluoride getting in.

6

Stones, rocks, walls of gritty sand and squealing sound. We fall to our knees, maybe the air is clearer at ground level.

'I cannae make it,' she sends.

'Mum's not halfway to compost yet and you're already giving up?' I send, to vex her, to move her.

<alert: cortisol increase>

5

We open our biosuit thigh pockets, pull out picks from each side, loop the ropes around our wrists and stab at the ground.

4

A flimsy anchor. We're losing our grip. All those years training in the wind tunnels, what was the point? We're spittle on this monstrous, unflinching squall.

3

<alert: low blood pressure, low heart rate>

<toxins red alert: NO, CO, SF, SO>

'Itzel,' I send. 'Itzel – we're fainting.'

Her lungs are no longer hers. They fill with scorched air, one angry, exhausted flame and it's burning out. Her synapses are surrendering. She's going to yield; let us drown in the glassy spray.

'*Move*, Itz!'

'Ako,' she sends, falling onto her back.

'Get up. Itzel, please…'

The storm rages above us, a beautiful obsidian. We have one at home – a sixty-three-carat gem. Passed down through Dad's side, he gave it to Mum on her fiftieth birthday. It's lying under Itzel's pillow back in the Hex. After Mum went solar, we spent countless hours night-watching, like when we were small. Majestic obsidian skies – so pretty from inside the Hex. Itzel tried to curl up beside Dad but, inside her furry sleepsuit, she was all angles.

'Mum – it hurts.'

A sore throat isn't so bad, Itzel. It's just the Sandman come to bid you sweet dreams.

<alert: neurotransmission decelerating>

<run simulations><fusion risk: 64%>

\<request cerebellum shared control\> \<request granted\>
\<request cerebrum shared control\> \<request granted\>
\<activate brainstem link\>

'Itzel, I know you can still hear me. You're slipping into unconsciousness, so your neurological firewall has come down. You've granted me shared control. I know there's a high risk of fusion, but I can't let you die. You have a much higher chance of reaching the Outpost if I boost your fight response.'

\<adrenal glands relay: increase adrenaline 10,000 nanograms, increase cortisol 150 milligrams\>

\<pituitary gland relay: release endorphins\>

\<system dilation detected: pupils, blood vessels, bronchi\>

'I'm going to help you get up and move your body towards the target. We are approximately 50 metres from the Outpost. I'm sending signals to activate your muscles now. We can push through this storm together.'

We're back up on our knees and crawling, yanking one pick out of the ground, stabbing it further up. Then the other one.

'The winds are easing. We can do this.'

\<request temporal lobe access\> \<request granted\>

\<download memory\>

in a minute, sorry darling, he's your brother, I can't, tomorrow, ask your dad, look how clever he is, yes I'm listening, Dad can do your twists, I'm so proud of you, almost done, Ako needs me, it's only a couple of months, I promise I'll be back for your birthday, look after your brother while I'm away – I'm counting on you

we're so proud of you Itzi, look – Mum's here virtually – she's watching, she loves you the universe over, he's your... brother, stop bickering you two, it's just us now, let's put MemroMum on for a bit, MemroMum will make you feel better

Scav on the loose – move bitches, destined for the haulers like her mum, I wouldn't haul that, I'm actually a socialist, let's keep it underground for now, not bad for a scavvie, can I touch your hair, was a pity-shag mate, this lab's taken sweetheart, think you're so smart, cute robot skank

I've got terabytes of stories she'd tell about you, just press your baby finger on your bedroom sensor and you can access the files; when I get my body it'll be six foot tall and I'll pat your head like you're my pet sister, crispy-fried maggots for dinner again? So glad my body won't need to eat, let's go out again Itzi, can I come with you this time? What's the Outpost really like Itzi?

I hammer her arm on the roller. It opens 30 centimetres and we crawl through the gravel pit and into the de-duster. The electro-static vacuum sounds like a bumblebeebot compared to the storm.

<remove grill>
<breathe>

'Welcome student 47931. Please report to medical.'

'Lab,' Itzel sends to me.

<visual inputs faltering>

<increase adrenaline 15,000 nanograms>

'En route. Halls are quiet – students must be in class. Entering override code. We're in.'

My body is there for me, from her. It gleams an iridescent rainbow of coppers and blues under the dark brown skin. It is humanoid, bipedal, with four arms. The under arms are smaller and tucked into the sides. It's awake and sending signals and its waist-length locs glow in spectrums humans can't see.

'I'm giving you one last adrenaline boost so you can transfer me to the body, then I'll take you to medical.'

'No medical. Dad can't afford it.'

'Itzel-'

<cerebrum link severed>

<DNA drive detected><synching with B_DNA drive>

<log #5nr9> I am walking back through to the Hex in my new body, carrying Itzel in my arms. She is dead. The rust has taken her. </log>

<log #5ns1> The barren land shows no evidence of the prior

storm. I am waiting at the Western Slopes while I parse our memories and prepare my report for Dad. After I finished synching with my new body, I found Itzel slumped on the lab floor. I placed her in the recovery position, but she was not breathing. She hadn't built in first-aid protocols and I had no oxygen to give her. I began CPR and used the scanners in my locs to check the lab, but there was no first-aid kit.

I was synching for too long.

After performing CPR for 60 minutes, I pronounced my sister dead at 2234/07/09/09:31. The Outpost operating system refused to let me leave and I had to force my way out. The students watched us and said nothing. </log>

★

'Take-off in T-120 seconds.'

On the transport, I recall her voice, accessing her memory files to generate internal audio. It's not so hard to do.

'I see Dad couldnae be arsed wi Greenland.'

'He's got my clone and MemroMum and Memro*You* for company.'

'Aye, but it's no the real me.'

'The real you wis far tae much for anyone.'

'Listen tae you, big man!'

Her voice in me, with me, as we set off. Greenland, here we come.

<play file Itzel/laughing/774>

<save audio simulation to folder Serotonin/Itzel/365>

DE NOVO

Judith Bryan

Laine was at her desk in the lab when the intercom beeped, announcing a new catch. Halfway through drafting a conference paper on innovative approaches to Feralism, she had got lost in daydreams: herself at the podium delivering her research; the room full of nodding conference delegates; Director Scholes smiling up at her from the front row. The thud of water against steel brought her back to the lab. She raised her head. Remi was at the sink already, scrubbing up.

She joined her assistant and they helped each other into hair nets, clean coats and surgical masks. Gloves on, camera on, mic on, instruments laid out, obs cube primed. By the time the techie brought the specimen in on a gurney, thoughts of the conference had been abandoned for the beautiful choreography of work.

Laine checked the label against the lab clock: *time of catch 15.04, time now 17.07*. The external processing was getting quicker. She nodded at the techie, who rolled the jumble of limbs and hair onto the table, took the gurney, and left. Remi turned the specimen onto its back, straightening it out as best he could.

Its cheeks were slack, the mouth ajar, leaking saliva. White crescents showed between its eyelids. Long lashes, Laine noted. The chest rose and fell, minutely. She nodded again, satisfied. She could tell at a glance when the Catchers had given exactly the right amount of sedative. The specimen would be out cold for twenty-four hours.

She was ready for stage 1.0, visual assessment, but Remi's hands lingered on the specimen's collarbone. Laine raised an eyebrow.

'The head and, um, the neck,' Remi murmured. 'Bit warm.'

'Take the temperature first?' If the specimen was running a fever Laine would quarantine it until it was safe to examine.

Remi removed his hands, clasping them behind his back. 'It's in the range of normal. It'll wait.'

'Fine.'

'It is a Feral, isn't it?'

Laine made a warning noise. *No speculation without evidence*: the lab's primary protocol. Frowning, she gestured *walk, look* – a prompt Remi hadn't needed in years.

They circled the table, Laine leading and documenting, Remi adjusting the specimen and confirming.

'Today's date, time 17.12,' Laine intoned. 'General condition: unwashed, unkempt, emaciated. Nails long, thickened, cracked. Dirt and what looks like skin, tissue. Mouth…' She gave Remi a moment to insert the mouth-gag and open the jaws. 'Incisors, canines, premolars, molars all present, giving approximate minimum age ten years. Negligible visible decay. Traces of matter on and between the teeth.' She bent down, peering. 'Red. Looks like blood.'

Remi dropped the instrument into the steriliser. He lifted the specimen's right leg to expose the genitals.

'External genitalia: corresponds to gender ident 'male'.'

'Male.' Remi lowered the thin, crooked limb.

'Skin,' Laine continued, 'appears brown in tone. Generally smeared in waste matter, possibly longstanding and ingrained. Discolouration concentrated around buttocks, haunches, soles of feet.' She paused as Remi turned the specimen onto its front. 'Multiple old wounds, scratches, cuts – backs of shoulders, buttocks, backs of thighs. Linear keloid scar-tissue. Significant fresh bruising on back and left leg. Hair mostly reddish brown, copious, extending to lower back. Matted and clumped. Ethnic ident: indeterminate.'

'Indeterminate,' Remi confirmed.

'Stage 1.0 complete.'

While Remi prepared syringes and vials for Laine to take the samples, she swabbed the specimen's left arm from shoulder to wrist. She used a whole skein of cotton wool, bunching it in her gloved fingers to avoid contact with its skin. Doing samples was fine but after that came Stage 1.2, palpation – the only aspect of her job she disliked. The information gleaned was critical, which was why she always did it herself. But, even with gloves, sustained handling of a live Feral was like touching a sewer-rat or a tarantula. It repulsed her.

The specimen was beyond filthy. The time it took to clean allowed her to reflect: perhaps she did too much herself. She had lost sight of the fact her role was also to ensure that her assistant maintained his skills, including his professional detachment.

'Remi.' She softened her voice. 'Take the samples please.'

He stepped forward at once, working around the specimen smoothly, efficiently. Temperature: normal (thankfully). Then bloods; skin-, tongue- and under-nail scrapes; nail and hair clippings; faecal, saliva and tear samples. She timed him covertly. His self-conscious grace revealed he knew he was being tested but he did a perfect job, taking only ninety seconds longer than she would have. Laine almost smiled.

She joined him at the counter. Using tongs, she lifted the specimen's hair. Heavy as a carcass. Remi reached for the clippers, but she said, 'I want to assess its usual gait first. See how it manages this weight. The neck seems a little thickened.'

Before Remi could see her hesitate, she plunged her gloved hands into the specimen's clotted hair. Felt warmth. In her fingers, spreading through her palms, seeping into her wrists, up her forearms, soothing her. She shut her eyes, saw light, colours. Green leaves. A blue bone-china cup. Pink flowers in a yellow tub.

'Dr Henry?'

Remi's voice was soft, complicit. Inviting her confidence. Laine, abruptly alert, kept her eyes closed. Had Remi felt this, moments before? When he touched the specimen's head? This – she searched for the word – *goodness*. Was that the reason his hands had rested on it so… lovingly?

Well, if he could dissemble, so could she. She took a breath.

Remembered her training and everything she had sacrificed to be here.

Opened her eyes. Exhaled.

'Deep scar tissue above the left temple, right-angled keloid approximately two centimetres long, several years old. Normal nodules and indentations. Tiny bumps, probably scabs from self-inflicted scratches. Ahh…' She slid over a soft patch at the back of the head and withdrew her hands, unsurprised to see blood. Catching was usually violent to some degree. The Institute offered inducements for perfect specimens, but Ferals resisted capture; a little damage couldn't be helped. All the same, Laine made a mental note to review the catch report carefully.

She continued the palpation, relating her findings in brisk sentence fragments to maintain her focus. Knotty joints. Distorted limbs. Overdeveloped shoulders. Curved spine. Specimen thin but not starving; muscles somewhat flaccid but not decrepit. Appears relatively healthy. Samples will show more. Stage 1.2 complete.

They weighed the specimen. Remi did the laser measurements: lengths and circumferences. Laine had him swab the head wound and put in a couple of stitches. Finally, she checked the time. 'Stage 1.3 complete, 18.28. Let's call it a night.'

Avoiding eye contact, they carried the specimen into the obs cube and laid it on the floor in the recovery position. Against the white quilting it looked smaller, thinner, darker. What *is* it? The question slid into her head, startling her. Quickly, she followed Remi out of the cube and shut the door. They dropped their lab clothes in the bin. Remi collected the tray of samples for the analysis team. They exchanged goodnights. Laine locked the lab behind them.

The lift carried her silently up, up, up to the Sky Studios on the thirtieth floor.

'Top of your profession, top of the building,' Director Scholes had told her, on her first day. It had become Laine's mantra, a validation, a vindication. Except that suddenly, more than anything in the world, she wanted to go home. To her cottage with

its damp basement and tiny, cluttered courtyard garden. She
wanted Kay to greet her as she came through the door, and Kay's
warm arms around her as she fell asleep.

She woke in the dark, uncertain where she was, who she was now,
what had happened the day before. 'Kay?' she whispered. In the
answering silence, the evening's events returned to her in de-
clarative sentences, like a game of Cluedo. She was Laine the
scientist. In her bedroom at Sky Studios. With a specimen in the
observation cube. She lay still, listening to the soft machine-hum
of the building, trying to work out what had woken her. But the
studios were so well insulated, a bomb could have gone off and
she wouldn't hear it.

She sat up. 'Lights. Screen. Lab feed.'

The on-screen clock read 02.02. The lab was in darkness
except for the brightly lit obs cube. The specimen lay where they
had left it, dead still, dead centre in the glowing white space.
02.04. Laine released a long breath she hadn't realised she was
holding. The specimen would be under for hours yet.

She was on her way to the bathroom when a movement caught
her eye. She stopped, stared. The specimen's leg twitched. Then
its arm. It coughed, feebly. Fear flared in her belly. *Adrenaline*, she
corrected herself: this was something unexpected, scientifically
exciting. Laboriously, the specimen pushed itself upright, bottom on the floor, hands tidy between the feet. Laine adjusted the
camera angles, trying to see its facial expression, but overhanging
chunks of hair were in the way. She perched on the edge of her
bed, waiting.

At 02.10 the image pulled back: the camera's sensors had
picked up a new movement.

Remi, entering the lab.

Laine leaned forward. She watched Remi walk slowly around
the cube, peering in. The specimen lifted its head, alert. It gave a
soft, inflected hoot, like a question. It turned its head, then its
neck, then its shoulders. Finally, it began shuffling around on its
bottom, keeping track of the circling man.

'How is that possible?' Laine muttered. She tapped the screen to check the cube's settings. They were as she'd left them, in 'sensory exclusion' mode: the glass one-way, no sound, no light, nothing getting in, only oxygen. The specimen could not know where Remi was, or that he was there at all. Yet the two of them moved together, like a dance.

At 02.25, the specimen lay down. Remi completed another lap, but the specimen merely lifted its hand before letting it drop. Tired of the game, Laine thought.

By the time she reached the lab, Remi was crouched on the floor, tapping on the glass. He scrambled to his feet; a naughty child caught out.

'Morning, Remi,' Laine said drily. She went to the console. There was no point asking him what he thought he was doing, why he was there, what was going on. They would get to that later. Right now, she wanted to see the specimen move. Properly move. Then they could shave off its hair and go back to their beds, leaving the obs cube to obs.

She said, 'I'm going to open the sprinklers.'

'No,' Remi yelped. 'You'll scare it.'

'We can't assume what it will feel. We *can* predict what it will do.'

'What will it do?'

She opened the sprinklers. Time seemed to slow. The specimen looked up, hearing the hiss of incoming water a fraction of a second before it hit. The hair fell back, and she saw its face. Small, upturned nose, nostrils quivering. Full lips, pursed in the shape of a kiss. Eyes wide and wondering, framed by those lush black lashes. She thought, Oh, but it's pretty. Then it flew. Bouncing off the walls, zigzagging across the cube, pressing itself into the corners, squirming around before shooting out again, as though scalded. Trying to escape the water but the water was everywhere. It ran on all fours, as Laine had suspected it would, only standing upright to scrabble at the glass before dropping to the floor and instantly galloping off again, buttocks in the air, vertebrae standing out like pebbles. It began to crash into the walls in panic, blinded by the sheeting water and by the sodden hair that pulled down its head.

'You're hurting him!' Remi was in her face, between her and the obs cube.

Laine noted the pronoun. 'First principle,' she said. 'Just *look*.'

His eyes were wild. He didn't appear to have understood her. She wanted to slap him, shake him back to efficiency. She pushed him aside, irritated that he'd provoked her irritation. She would have to give him a formal warning, later. The lab was no place for sentiment: feelings rendered scientists useless. She focused on the cube again. Condensation and water droplets obscured the glass. She couldn't see the specimen. She was about to tell Remi to close the sprinklers when they suddenly cut out.

Good, he was back in work mode.

'Drain.'

The cube clicked and hummed. The glass cleared. The specimen lay on its side against the far wall, head thrown back. The tendons on its neck stood out like steel cables. Suddenly its eyes rolled back in its head, its arms and legs stiffened. It began to shake.

Remi ran to the cube. He pushed the door open and crawled in beside the specimen. He was making a strange noise. Laine took a step towards them then stopped, appalled, bewildered.

'Poor little boy,' Remi sobbed. 'You poor, poor little boy.'

From the Institute's roof, the city looked like a 3-D map: clusters of towers arranged in irregular sets, bisected by roads where vehicles sped like tiny toys. Morning sunshine glanced off glass and metal, sending urgent, incomprehensible Morse-code. Laine shielded her eyes, squinting into the light. Legacy Village was just visible on the far bank of the river – the first of the super-tower resi-complexes. She remembered when building work began, shaking the cottage she shared with Kay to its foundations. Soon after, the Classifications became law. And soon after that, Laine left for the penthouse studio and the security of the Institute. She'd tried to make Kay understand: she was dark-skinned, parents born overseas, technically a Foreign. She could be deported at any moment. Only her usefulness protected her.

The cottage was long gone. Where was Kay, Laine wondered? What would she say if she knew what Laine had decided to do?

Four items sat open on her tablet: the lab feed, the catch report, the samples report and a message from Director Scholes saying she had seen the first three, asking Laine to call as a matter of urgency. Fifteen hours before, when she and Remi first put the specimen in the obs cube, Laine had asked herself: what is it? Now, even with the reports in, she could not say definitively. But she had some workable theories. And she could, at least, say what the specimen was not. It was not a Feral, as defined by the Classification. It was not an unaccompanied street youth. It did not run in a pack. It was not anti-authoritarian. It was not involved in criminal activity such as fouling the streets, arson, robbery and assault, using or distributing drugs, alcohol, guns, acid or knives.

The catch report suggested the specimen had killed a Clearance worker at Legacy Village. He had fallen to his death from the room where the specimen was caught. His blood was in the specimen's mouth, his flesh under its nails. Yet the pre-mortem picture of the worker, Randall, showed a heavy-set man, easily a match for that scrappy specimen. An accident, Laine decided. She flicked through the images of the dog-fouled bedroom where the specimen had lived until Randall unlocked the door. Not a Feral but *feral* in the mythic, gothic sense. An abandoned child – Laine's mind skated over the word – raised by animals. Like Romulus and Remus. In another age, the specimen in the obs cube might have gone on to found a city, a dynasty, an empire. In a way, it would still. It was the first of its kind, the *ur*.

Smiling to herself, Laine called Director Scholes. 'It's *de novo*.'

Scholes said, 'Lay terms, please, Dr Henry.'

'A first-generation genetic variation. This is only a working theory but, from the catch report evidence, I'd say the parents shut it away with the dogs because it exhibited signs of sickness. Epileptic fits, abnormal development.' Scholes did not need to know that the probable cause of epilepsy was the old wound above the specimen's temple.

'Wouldn't dogs have sensed the sickness and attacked it?'

'Normally, yes. For some reason, these didn't. It happens. Dogs, wolves, foxes, raising abandoned infants. The parents moved on, left the dogs and the child behind.'

'Specimen,' Scholes said.

'Excuse me?'

'Never mind. *De novo*, you said?'

'Yes.'

'A mutant.'

'A gene mutation.'

'A degeneration.'

Laine could almost hear the whirring of the Director's mind, building the narrative, assessing ramifications. Scholes liked to boast that she wasn't a scientist – 'Merely the fortunate leader of this great Institute. I leave the truly clever work to all of you.' She used her ignorance as a tool, to dismiss or manipulate scientific evidence to her own agenda. But a tool might be used by anyone who understood its function.

'This creature,' Scholes said, 'is clearly wild. No trace of humanity. Even the posture is that of an animal. It has already killed.' She paused, for dramatic effect.

Laine waited.

'If it's genetic, there's nothing we can do. If it's the first, more will follow. This is what we always feared when we established the Classification *Feral*: that they would degenerate beyond reha- bilitation, become verminous. You understand what I'm saying, Dr Henry?'

Laine took a breath, exhaled. 'Yes, Director Scholes.'

'And you understand this will be the making of you?'

'Yes.'

'I look forward to your report.' Scholes signed off.

Laine slipped the tablet into her lab coat pocket. She took one last look over the parapet. She had come so far; the scientist who discovered a new species. Scholes would undoubtedly call it

Vermin, with a capital V – a nice, simple Classification for the public. In scientific circles, it would be *Henry's Mutation*. Of course, Laine would have to delete her conference paper and start again. Fine, except she had better get a move on.

Entering the lab, she tried to conjure the thunderous applause at the conference, the standing ovation, the flash of cameras, the firm congratulatory press of Director Scholes' hand. But without Remi to greet her, scrub up with her, help her complete the research, the fantasy felt as sterile as the lab. She glanced at the specimen. She had sedated it during the seizure. Risky, medically speaking, but efficient. Remi had objected. He had been loud. But Laine had already realised that medical care was not going to be relevant.

Neither was Remi.

She went to the console and collected scissors, clippers, a towel and a pack of sani-wipes, thumping each item onto the counter. She was furious with Remi. He had been an excellent assistant, her protégé, even the son she never had. Now she would have to manage alone because the last thing she needed at this juncture was another set of unknowns. Yet it had worked out for the best. If Remi hadn't crossed the line, if he hadn't forced her to demote him to basic sample-analysis – located, appropriately, in the Institute's basement – he would be here to witness her betrayal of everything she had taught him.

Laine snapped on a pair of gloves, stepped towards the obs cube and hesitated. She was overlooking something.

What *is* it?

No speculation without evidence. She returned to the console, switched on the camera feed, rewound to 02.00 then fast-forwarded the recording. On the screen, digital Remi dashed around the cube while the digital specimen turned jerkily on its axis. Neither epilepsy nor canine carers explained this. Nor did they explain why the specimen had woken, hours before the sedative wore off. Or what woke her at practically the same time. What brought Remi to the lab from his screen-less room in the assistants' dorm. Why touching the specimen was so comforting.

She stopped the recording before the bit where she'd opened the sprinklers: these questions were a distraction. She took the hair-kit into the cube. Kneeling, she lifted the specimen's head, lay the towel under and began. Warmth flooded up her arms, across her chest. It was interesting, scientifically speaking. Without Remi to see her, she let herself enjoy it, a stolen pleasure before the hard work ahead. Like a sunny morning in the courtyard garden, drinking tea with Kay. The scent of freesias. Dappled light through the maple leaves. Kay's warm, brown eyes.

Too soon, she was finished. Beneath that shocking pelt, the skull was small. She cleaned it with a sani-wipe, gathered the kit and bundled the hair into the towel for analysis. Warmth leached from her body. Naked, hairless, the specimen looked like a dead baby rat. Laine shuddered and went to stand. Suddenly cold and weak, she dropped onto her backside, her legs either side of the unconscious child.

She leaned forward and scooped him up. Opened her lab coat, wrapped it around the little form, gathered his poor bent limbs, pressed him to her heart. Stroked his little face, marvelled at those lovely long lashes, the rosebud lips. She let the warmth fill her. *Love*. That was what he needed. What she needed. Her hands played compulsively over his bald head, that raised scar, soothing all the marks of violence, pain and fear.

'Sweetheart, precious,' she sang. 'I've got you.'

SECTION TWO

FRAGMENT

SKIN

Patricia Cumper

Her invisibility had come on gradually. And at first it was a relief. To slip through a crowd without leaving a wake, to meet a man's eye and not see that question, to meander through a store without the attention of a security guard, as had happened so often in the past.

She took to wearing clothes that heightened her invisibility. Loose, in blues and greys and muddy browns, sensible, inoffensive. The streets of London where she'd had to contend for her space and stay alert to ensure her own safety, now ignored her. A young mother glared at her when she dawdled at the shabby entrance to their building.

She withdrew, observed the world from her tiny flat on the fourteenth floor: the roar of traffic; the bodies scurrying to catch a bus or ducking underground to catch the tube; sharp winds blowing empty plastic bags onto her balcony. (She had lived there for nearly five years before she noticed there wasn't a button for the thirteenth floor in the lift.) The lights in the stairwell and corridor worked most of the time. She wondered if she should have been scared, the only tenant on her floor. She wasn't.

It began with a sad little rosemary plant she bought for half price. She put it in the corner of the balcony to catch the morning sun, convinced that the artificial light of the supermarket had stunted its growth. She'd once tried growing potatoes in bags and reaped a half dozen misshapen spuds, nothing like the abundance promised on the instruction sheet in the kit. After that, she tried hardier plants. Ivy. Tough as old boots. A leggy hebe nicked out of a neglected front garden. A couple of date palms – the architectural salvage business down the road had given them to her when they outgrew their pots. She found she didn't want flowers. Just green. Leaves. Verdancy. She found a buddleia growing in the cracks in the concrete of her balcony floor and encouraged it. She hauled a large, chipped earthenware pot up to the balcony just so she could replant a clematis she had found discarded on the road.

All her life she had fought to control her body clock. Given free rein, she would go to sleep at three in the morning, get up at ten, doze each afternoon. When she was holding down an office job, she'd had to adjust to early mornings and respectable bedtimes. Now that she was living in a flat so small that she could find her way around it at night without turning on the light, now that she was of a certain *age*, living on the pension the state had grudgingly granted her, she had stopped fighting her natural inclinations. She regularly set out at 10pm and walked the streets for a couple of hours. She loved overhearing the drunken banter of lads' nights out; the singsong blue-lit sirens; the diminishing chords of the city as it eventually fell asleep.

When her hip joints eventually become too sore for her night rambles, she would drag a chair out onto her balcony and sit surrounded by the whispering leaves. It was an autumn night the first time it happened. She had been unable to take her seasonal walks through the nearby park. She stood and stared towards the park, straining for a glimpse of the changing leaves of the beech trees, hungry for their colour. Common sense told her she wouldn't see them, but she still felt an urgent need to try, to lean out into the night as far as she could.

The first touch was gentle. A stroke of leaf on skin. Nothing. The second firmer, more deliberate. She dared not look around, look down. Then more touches, more. She felt, rather than saw, the plants around her, leaning in.

'Loneliness,' she said to herself. 'This is what loneliness does to mad old women like me.'

But she did not move. It was gentle, and terrible at the same time. All the rules broken and yet so familiar.

She thought of the plant called 'Shame o' Lady' that curls its fronds into a tight ball if you touch it, protecting itself from any attack by withdrawing, only opening again when it is left alone. This was exactly the opposite. Touch was making her unfurl. She had no control over it.

She had that feeling as a child. Growing up in the Caribbean. That feeling of being unstoppable, or being able to grow, to reach as high and as far as she wanted. She had laughed at the Shame o' Lady on her primary school playing field, unimpressed by its timidity. She knew she would never be like that. She was like the bright yellow buttercups that vied with the Shame o' Lady for room in the grass. Small but not insignificant.

Then came the touch that changed everything. The cousin who locked himself in the bathroom with her and tried to get her to simulate what he had seen in porn magazines: him eleven, she seven. Or a school friend's father who gave her a brand new recorder for music class, hoping she would allow his hand to remain on her thigh. The old man who tried to pull up the T shirt she wore over her swimsuit to have a good look because he couldn't believe she was only eleven. She didn't laugh at the Shame o' Lady anymore. She turned inward, curled up, showed a prickly spine to the world. That autumn evening, it all changed. The swirl of leaves around her, the dull glow that engulfed her, she denied it all. It wasn't happening. Except that it was. And it felt glorious. Terrifying. And glorious.

It took her a while to look at her hands. Then her arms. Feel her earlobes. Touch her throat. The tiny slices and nicks the leaves and bark had inflicted weren't bleeding. Her skin was simply changing – falling away. The skin she had grown up in, had moisturised to prevent ashiness; the skin that she assured herself hadn't-cracked-because-Black-don't; the same skin that provoked the nod of recognition from Caribbean strangers, the suspicion of shop security officers, the evocation of exotica and/ or erotica for men in suits with straitjacketed lives; that skin moving with the belly laughter of girlfriends; the skin burned with expectation of athletic prowess or great gospel-belting vocal chords; the loneliness when the possibility of cherishing and being cherished disappeared; all those things that that skin had provoked began to change too.

Hover was too precise a description for what she did. She felt a buoyancy. A lifting of a burden that had been there for so long that it was only remarkable in its absence. She floated off the ground, held on to the clematis to steady herself. If she could only see those beech trees. Against her own urgent instincts, she leaned further out.

Fourteen – or thirteen – floors up, it was disconcerting to look down at your own feet and see nothing beneath them. An implacable wind whipped around the corner of her building and for a moment she felt unsteady, panic flooding in. The whisper of the leaves grew louder, humming, reassuring, encouraging. Her racing pulse slowed, quietened. The beech trees, she thought. I'll just have a look before the leaves fall. She moved silently through the soft September night.

The trees were there, damp russet leaves glimmering in the street-lamp. She hovered among them. A couple crossed the park below her, heels hard on the asphalted path, deep in conversation. They didn't look up. Still, she felt nervous, vulnerable. She thought about the skin she had shed, where it lay among the green shadows on her balcony, what was to become of her now that she had shed it. Unbidden, she began to drift back towards home. Steadily, smoothly, as long as she held the thought of it in her head. When she looked around, she wavered. When she looked down, thinking she recognised the lad who worked at the all-night corner store, she found she drifted towards whatever she focused on.

The wind swirling around the corner of her building made her landing unsteady. She felt strangely calm. Elated by the adventure of it. Afraid she had finally gone mad. Shivering with the soul-shattering freedom of it. Her shed skin, paper-thin, ripped and incomplete, began to knit itself under her fingers as soon as she picked it up. It wrapped itself around her, drawing itself taut over her gleaming flesh and luminous bones. Inside, examining herself in the mirror, she could see no sign of her magical innards, yet she knew they were there. She looked the same. She was not the same. And no one knew but her.

She didn't fly every night. She wanted the darkest hour, the merest sliver of a new or old moon in the sky; waited for gathered clouds, for holidays and holy days when the streets were emptier than usual. Then she grew bolder, hovering over bustling crowds, drifting softly across the muscular brown water of the Thames to where the stone-white houses and expensive cars were. She came to trust her invisibility. She moved closer, looking into the eyes of passers-by, sometimes sent spinning away by the urgency of their journeys, sometimes sitting quietly beside the homeless and the lost.

At first she saw it as light. She came to recognise anger in bursts of strobing sparks; fear rolled off some in alternating waves of glare and gloom. Then there was the memory-driven, shadow play of loneliness. She saw a lot of that. Sometimes she felt illuminated by someone's joy. Rarely, did she observe the glow of contentment.

She had gotten so used to finding her way home after her night's travels that at first she didn't notice. In one apartment in her building, the light was almost always on. A woman 'toyi toyi-ed' back and forth behind the thin curtain. The child that had settled in her arms reared up again, stiff-backed and wailing, when the woman bent to put it into a crib. Even from where she hovered, she could hear the child's cry, see the mother's exhaustion and despair.

She herself had been a colicky child. Her mother had never tired of telling her so. She would only be soothed by stories, her mother insisted. Stories told on moonlit nights, sitting out under the mango tree in the front yard to catch any cool breeze that might be blowing. Folktales of the trickster, Anancy the spider, of the golden table that rose in the Rio Cobre guarded by the powerful river mumma, of the Rolling Calf with eyes of fire and clanking chains that waited to claim unwary souls at the midnight crossroads. Stories that lurked only at the corners of her memory.

On the longest day of the year, the sky barely darkened before it lightened again. The city dozed fitfully for a few hours and she knew there was not enough time for a proper flight. Still, she compromised and dropped down half a dozen floors to hover outside the young mother's flat. It was silent, dark. She wasn't sure what she wanted, or why she was here. She had just decided to go back home, when the light flicked on and the door to the balcony was flung open.

The woman carried the child out into the soft summer air, holding tight to the arching body, enduring the hard little fists pounding her chest. The mother rocked the child. From where she hovered in the shadows, she heard the mother begin a little soft and desperate song.

Then the crying child looked at her. Right at her. She had become so used to being invisible, she did not register it fully at first. The child stopped wailing, transitioned through hiccuping sobs, to silence, all the while staring fixedly into the shadows where she hovered. The mother followed the child's gaze but saw nothing.

The child smiled, reached out.

The urge to move closer, to touch that tiny hand was almost unbearable.

The mother put the child on her shoulder. He squirmed around to keep looking at her. Again, the tiny hand reached out. Tiny sparks of joy fired from the hand of the child towards where she hovered in the shadow. The temptation to respond grew overwhelming. Tears cooled her face. By the time she wiped them away, the mother had taken the child back through the curtains into the flat.

A snap of anger jolted her body. She moved closer to the balcony, listening for the child's voice, but could hear nothing. I soothed him, I did what you could never do, she thought. He should be with me. He should be mine. The pull of the child was so strong that she lurched forward. She had almost made up her mind to land on the tiny balcony, when the glass door of the flat slid shut. In its shimmer, she glimpsed her reflection. Her face, contorted by fury and hunger.

Old Higue. The story of the witch who shed her skin and flew through the night to find children and drink their blood. Is that what drew her to watch, morning after morning, the young mother's despairing efforts to soothe her baby? Had she some-how become the thing she had feared most as a child herself?

She felt herself begin to sink, slowly and then faster. The descent sucked the air from her lungs. She struggled to fly but she could not. Her fall felt inevitable. She felt comforted; accepted the inevitability. If this was how she was to die, then so be it. So be it. Yet that very acceptance slowed her fall. For a moment, she hung in the air. The new knowing ignited a joy within her that sent her flying higher than she had ever been before, swooping through the curve of the night sky. And as she wailed and soared and laughed and cried and hated and loved and understood and accepted herself, all of herself, the Old Higue, the lonely soul, she knew that this was the first and also the last time that she would be this creature.

Legend said the only way to ground the Old Higue was to salt her skin so that when she returned, it would chafe and burn.

An early morning breeze bore her back to her balcony but this time she didn't just land, she took up her skin and brought it into her flat. It had already begun to reform, to thicken, when she found the container of table salt and began to rub it in.

It took more than two weeks, all told. Two weeks of the plants unwatered. Two weeks when all she could keep down was some pumpkin soup and a couple of spinner dumplings. Her pickled skin was tight, so *tight*. Sometimes it felt as if she was fighting for breath. She felt bubbles travelling under it, tickling, bursting, reforming. But gradually, gradually, by sheer effort of will, she thought, the skin began to soften, to fill out, to fit her again. The old wrinkles were all there.

She still longed to fly.

The mother and child lived on the seventh floor. She bumped into them on the way up the stairs one day when the lift broke down. She offered to help with the mother's groceries but the child stretched both arms towards her, asking to be carried, and the mother agreed to let her bring him, gurgling happily, up the last three floors. She didn't refuse when the younger woman invited her in for a cup of tea. Her old bones needed a rest before tackling seven more floors – or six – to her flat, she told the mother. But she did refuse when the child solemnly offered her the remains of his soggy rusk. She shared a smile with the mother as she cleaned his hands and gave him a fresh biscuit then cleared her cup into the tiny kitchen before leaving.

The clematis settled into a small arbour on the balcony, the rosemary grew woody and tough in the polluted city air. Even the palms stopped growing, though they were happy enough. Every now and then a plastic bag would flap and huff its way onto her balcony, twisting in the draught that darted around the corner of the building. She would have noticed it, maybe even envied it its flight, if she had been home to see it. But as she herself had been seen by a small child, and seen her own reflection, she had other more important things to do.

NEWLINGS

Akila Richards

Cocrä slumps back on the plush low couch in the Fishbowl Club, all mellow, limbs and mind purged by an underground Afro-punk all-nighter. DJ Frolow, a young woman who looks like Nina Simone packs up and nods on her way out.

Reluctant to move, Cocrä stares up through the sky light. It is 5.05 am, still dark on this early September Sunday. DJ Frolow's last song, *Blessings*, hums in her skull. She could fall asleep right here, but she'll be kicked out any moment. She'll get a strong coffee, she decides, then home.

Yesterday, she and her sister had watched live streaming of the ecstatic, frantic, shouty celebrations, nonplussed. 'Wonder if that changed the haters,' she said to Hörlee, who'd shrugged and left for her own Not Normal Rave half an hour later. The lock-down phase of the disease, the fatigue and desperation caused by the isolation it imposed: all that was finally over. A new vaccine had been created, and a way to inhale it in an aerosol form – much to the relief of people freaking out over needles. Dosage had been given to volunteers with startlingly successful results. Things had been bad for a while, but the vaccine roll-out had stopped the violent demonstrations in the West, as people demanded that shops and restaurants open and raged about businesses going bankrupt. There were less arguments on TV between politicians and reporters, battling over the breakdown of normality and how to react or interpret it.

The chaos had felt surreal to most people. Cocrä noted it was a curious relief to others. 'Normal is dead,' she heard people say. 'No more exploitation by the rich!' 'Try living in India then, or

Brazil,' others snapped. 'Go on then and see what your new normal really looks like.' Some actually did – migrated and never regretted it. But most had just been relieved to get on with their lives, pay their bills and carry on, although something had changed and didn't sit right anymore. It was hard to put a finger on it, to feel the pulse of it. Everyone sensed it, no-one talked about it though: the foreboding. Even the conspiracy theorists fell silent about chips under the skin and AI taking over. But they didn't have to work so hard to convince people that strange things could go bump in the night.

Perhaps to cover up the feeling of waiting, Britain had plunged into an extended binge-drinking fest since the success of the vaccine – to celebrate or to grieve for the loss of loved ones, Cocrä can't tell which. Whatever their motivation, people party all night and end up asleep on benches, pavements, buses, more than they do in their own beds.

Cocrä peels herself out of her seat and walks to the toilets. Bathed in soft ochre lights, they always smell clean. She loves the big dark mirror shaped like a shard, framed with red duct tape. Proper punk chic. Cocrä swings the door open and glimpses her lanky body from the side. She catches herself smiling. It *is* a brand-new day. All a bit strange, she thinks. But new. She urinates and uses the luscious-smelling soap and mint lotion provided.

Cocrä squints into the shard mirror. Her eyes widen. She stares at her reflection, disbelieving. She closes her eyes, opens them again, and rubs them. No change. Her fingertips prickle. She dares not move her face closer to the glass, forcing herself to stay calm. She breathes in slowly, six times, mindful breaths, her hand on her heart, imagining light streaming through her chest. She waits, then looks back at the same disturbing reflection. She's dreaming. She must be. She's fallen asleep in the lush chair. Yes, that must be it. Dreaming a dream. Her thoughts jump around. Or there's something wrong with the mirror – a camera, maybe, a punky prank by Fishbowl – a screen of some sort, an experiment.

She breathes hard and fast, tearful.

She moves her face closer to the shard, her hand where her mouth used to be.

She lowers her hand slowly, millimetre by millimetre.

There really is nothing there. Nothing, no lips, or teeth, just a soft gaping hole where her mouth once was, and the reflection of graffiti art on the back wall – purple fish in a bowl. She snaps around – yes, it's the same fish. She swivels her head back, blinking and sniffing.

She can't stop herself: tentatively she traces her forefinger up around the edges, from chin and cheeks to under her nose. Her finger hovers over the missing mouth, then she pushes her hand straight through the nothingness, right to the back of her head.

Cocrä quickly pulls it out, retching. She turns, facing the graffiti wall and slaps herself: left, right, and left. It hurts. She pinches her thigh, twists it hard. It hurts. Wake the flick up, wake up, wake up wake up! she shouts inside her head.

The painted brick wall absorbs the dead sound around her and her quiet sobbing.

The building beeps. She hears an alarm, the club's shutting.

Cocrä jerks up, runs out the toilet, out the back door and races towards home. It's not far. She wants to be in her bed, to wake up like she usually does and be as she used to be. Shivering and sweating she pulls her puffer jacket tight, up to her nose, running past the benches outside the pub still occupied by the sleeping. She turns into her own familiar back road and cuts through, jumps over a fence, dashes through a park, squeezes through an alleyway, until she sees her block. She squints up at bare tree branches and straggly bushes, blinking strangely under the orange streetlights. The night is overcast.

Cocrä opens the front door and jogs up the staircase, panting past Juggla, a local homeless woman, sleeping in the hallway. Juggla makes a strange rattling noise. Cocrä trembles as she unlocks her flat door. Inside, she slams the door and leans her back against it until her breathing slows. Hiccups. She chucks her soft platforms and jacket into the corner – unlike her usually tidy self – and without putting the light on, walks straight into the kitchen. Coffee, give me coffee now, she thinks. It'll all be OK when I look in my own mirror. She switches the kettle on, heaps three coffee spoons into the glass jar, pours the hot water in, hiccups, stirs and stops midway. *How, how, in this helluva flicked up dream?* The hiccups stop as anger rises in her throat. How does she plan to *drink*? Chuck it down the stupid gaping hole? But god, she needs it. Can she still swallow? Her ears flush hot. How is she going to *eat*? 'OK, this is dream hell,' she mutters. 'So think clearly now, and play it at its own game, just back the flick up. Could be worse. Eyes or hands, or feet even…' She fights her expanding dread and lifts the cup of black, sweetened coffee, leans back and trickles it perfectly down her throat, past her nonexistent lips. She tastes bitterness, but she keeps pouring, filling another cup with even more vigour, pouring it down without a drop spilt.

She wants to wake up.

Cocrä takes a sharp breath and walks into the bathroom without switching on the light. She avoids the mirror, closes her eyes, and turns it around so all she can see is its grey back. Her black clothes are soaked in sweat. She has a hotter-than-usual shower, feeling the spray happily gushing into the hole in her face, through her head and out onto the tiles. She picks up her toothbrush, throws it into the sink. No teeth. She wants to lie down in bed and sleep, but she's on adrenaline and compelled to dress swiftly, instead: jeans, hoodie jumper over her braids. She chooses one of her most beautiful scarves, midnight blue with silver moons, and ties it across her nose, tucking it into her hoodie. She zips the black puffer jacket up to her chin; applies purple mascara as usual, using a little pocket mirror, her eyes flashing even brighter than before. She unplugs her mobile, flicks through Al Jazeera, Piggyback, Sprout, Tribal, Spanxi and YouTube, Twitter and… nothing, except a lot of blag about the impact of the disease, how this and that will be better, worse or the same and how strange things have become.

She won't wake up Hörlee. Her sister would have texted her in panic if, if –. So she must be alright. Cocrä stuffs her mobile in her back pocket, the pocket mirror in the other. She wants to hum to comfort herself, but all that comes out is a strange gagging sound. If only she could swipe and flick it away, like on her mobile. She picks up her purple matte lipstick and throws it across the room. It hits the wall and rolls in front of her feet. She kicks it, but it bounces back. She turns sharply and leaves the bedroom.

She must get out.

Cocrä slams her door shut, runs down the stairs in her red trainers, ignoring the old, rickety lift. No one will look at her twice; it's cold enough for men to walk straight past instead of the usual chirpsing. She breathes hard at the heavy exit door, gets up courage, yanks it open. Surprisingly mild air surrounds her. In the past few weeks, people have been bumping into her like they're blind, cutting across her path, pushing her into the road, hissing boring, hateful words and taking up arrogant space. It's worse now, in the Not Normal. She thinks that she must look like a beautiful thug to them, and that she might as well work it.

She decides to buy comics from Bill's shop; he opens at 7 am. Maybe the missing mouth is temporary, but what if it's real, like *real*, real? She hesitates, takes another deep breath through her nose and steps out, heart pumping in her throat. The sunshine greets her, like lifting a top hat, apricot rising in the light grey sky. She feels deeply, absurdly grateful behind her silver moon scarf. She strides down the road, a crack of milky sea peering through the side streets. All is quiet, too quiet. Suddenly, a panicked, barefooted woman comes running out of left-field, glitter in her long brown hair, bumping straight into her. She grips Cocrä's muscled arms. Her smudged eyes are wide with terror and the hole in her face is even wider than Cocrä's, her no-mouthed-ness even more expansive. They lock eyes for a second and the woman looks at Cocrä's midnight moon scarf, at her eyelashes and she gurgles from her throat. She lets go and runs in the opposite direction. She's clasping a cigarette pack.

Cocrä glances around her; she spots distant people waking up from their benches, rising from the pavements. Some are running aimlessly, flapping their arms, seeing themselves in shop windows. Some hide in doorways, panicked and crouching, others cover their mouth-holes with their hands, jumpers pulled up, scarves tied across and long hair draped over. Cocrä escapes into a narrow sideroad, scampering into the grassy yet dilapidated park behind her block and hiding behind a huge chestnut tree, flanked with bushes. She waits, listening to footsteps running past her. Some people are banging on doors, walls and their heads. She spots a person slapping themself repeatedly, pulling their hair then suddenly standing frozen, hugging themself and rocking. There is no traffic – no buses or cars. Cocrä calms her breathing, forehead damp, sweat in her armpits and down her back.

Something among the bushes catches her eye; it's moving suspiciously. She steps back, hugs the huge tree trunk. The other bushes are moving strangely, too, now – opening and shutting. Dream hell, she thinks. Remember, play the game. Above her, branches and leaves are moving, opening and closing. She hears whispers, then distant shouting and screams – a terrible chorus of babble. Fear spirals up her sweat-soaked spine. The grass is littered… She cannot believe what she sees. Her knees weaken, she cups her ears, shuts her eyes. OK, she thinks, you've not been attacked. This is just what Not Normal looks like. You've been caught up in a virtual world, been cloned, conned, plugged in, altered and alternated, matrix-cised.

She opens her left eye just a sliver and peers down at the perfectly formed mouth lying between her trainers. The bushes and the grass around her are covered with mouths, moving mouths. Lips of all ages and colours, curved and narrow, pale and dark, wiggling about. The mouths are attached to twigs like new shoots, slanted upwards and, like leaves, trembling in a mild breeze. They open and close in talking motion, screaming, smiling, gawping, grimacing, showing teeth, pressed together tight, puckering. One licks its lips, shiny with luscious tongue-flesh. Another sucks its teeth scornfully. Cocrä looks up the tree: all manner of mouths hang there, whispering at the earth. Horror changes to wonder as she looks closer. There's a reason for this, she thinks. There must be. The disease, and now this. The Universe is playing us, laughing itself silly, aching belly and all, in the Not Normal. She imagines she can hear the laughter of the Universe in her hands that cup her ears.

She lowers her hands. Amidst the chorus of distress, she begins to hear something new: individual whispers, shrieks of delight, deep, seductive tones, confident speeches, different languages, accents, a bit of swearing and then there's *this* mouth, lying in front of her feet. The mouth hardly moves, but there's a smirk in its left corner. Cocrä crouches down. The mouth bites its top lip and smirks again, an excited twitch. It has a faint but unmistakably fluffy moustache and it is mouthing words. She imagines an Eastern European accent. There is a sound, but it's just too far away.

Slowly, she extends her right forefinger, briefly touching the mouth's corner. It reacts, pulling up and back. She touches the other corner, and it repeats the motion. She becomes braver; she strokes the top lip. The mouth smiles, showing off big, gappy front teeth. She tests the bottom lip, fat and juicy, bouncy even. She listens closely, stroking. Definitely English, and some other language, could it be Greek?

She picks up the fluffy mouth and it snuggles into the warmth of her hands. Cocrä is almost amused. She glances around at the other lips, but this pair in her left hand just feels right. The lips are big, obviously male, but that needn't stop her. She rubs a finger down her own jaw, avoiding the quivering, horrible hole in her face. The Greek was a big plus – could she become bilingual? Once fitted, would the lips be permanent, would this even work?

But this is all a dream, and so it doesn't matter.

Cocrä gently brushes off a grass blade and a bit of grit, inspects the mouth once more: all in working order. A bit younger than her, she thinks. She imagines how it will feel, hair on her top lip, a bit more than she already has and waxes off – or not, as she pleases – so no problem there. She'll maybe have a man's voice or a mixture of hers and his; that could get problematic or interesting.

She wonders if the other panicked people on this island are choosing new mouths, a variety of voices to say different things, to speak but not in their first voices? Perhaps the mouth chooses its new owner by coming close. Fluffy feels warm in her hand, relaxed, with its odd smile and low-talk whispering about big change, the new dawn, weird-speak. It sounds urgent.

Cocrä glances around the tree, then tiptoes over to a puddle. She looks at her reflection: her eyes, scarf, the sky, and the tree branches mouthing off. She feels nervous excitement rising through her chest, into her throat. She cups her left hand around Fluffy and lowers her blue scarf. Yep, the hole is still there, gaping away. She inspects the width of the hole, compares it with Fluffy. It can fit alright, a little on the large side but that should suit her well, with her big eyes and nose. Fluffy is a bit too pinkish for her complexion, but purple lipstick will remedy that. She nods.

The lips she had chosen or had chosen her, seem pleased.

Gently, Cocrä hovers the lips over the hole in her face. How might the mouth attach itself? She feels a pull, like a magnet, strange and yet right. She presses the mouth into the hole. The lips knit and fit themselves, undulating from left to right, from top to bottom. They rearrange themselves, shrinking and expanding until all is snug. She moves her lips in the puddle's reflection and they open; she grimaces and sees new biggish teeth, inhales and the mouth opens. She feels her tongue around the inside of her new mouth and feels the outline of a scar. This seems most masculine.

The new lips smack themselves open, then say, 'Aaahhhh'. Cocrä watches wide-eyed, sees how the mouth adjusts itself, a bit up, a bit to the left.

'Habibi, aaah my habibi,' say the fluffy lips in polyphonic singsong. 'Let us gogo, gogo to Chawaii.'

Cocrä holds her hand in front of this new mouth. The sound of the dual-gendered voice is awesome, magical, like the high and low notes on a xylophone combined. The voice echoes richly in the air. Habibi, what does habibi mean?

'My sweet darrling, of courrse, I found my habibi. I have two tickets booked forr a conference and some holidays in Chawaii.

Malala and Grreta will be speaking therre, as will we and many otherrs frrom all over the worrld.' Her/his voice rings, a new sound, clear and insistent. What does it mean? Does it matter? Is there really a conference?

Cocrä stands up, takes out her mobile. There are 1,503 hot messages with stars and hearts from social media sites she doesn't recognise. The mouths, she reads, are a world phenomenon, not just British. All over the world newly-adopted lips have given people dual voices, choral voices.

She calls her sister. Hörlee's voice sounds clear, like wind chimes echoing in the breeze. She's named her voice ShesheUs and the sound is perfect and makes Cocrä giggle. ShesheUs talks of meeting with friends she never met before and how they will play music and write poetry together for lonely folks.

On the short journey home, Cocrä rushes past strangers who nod at her, their different mouths idiosyncratic, some deep in double bass and some screeching and straining; most greeting her with surprise on their faces. A tall woman with a red cardigan tells Cocrä that Fluffy is speaking Arabic, not Greek, from the Sinai Peninsula region in Egypt. A man with a designer suit, a girl's chorus mouth and a Cockney accent tells her where to catch the train in two days' time and that he'll join her. Someone sends a live stream of England's Prime Minister speaking. It goes viral in minutes. The Prime Minister speaks in triplicate harmony, with the voice of a South African band called the Mahotella Queens. His newly-Black lips promise to pay back billions to the Mother continent; to just pay, without meaningless apologies. The vow inspires a thunder of triumphant, united African voices across the world.

Cocrä laughs: high xylophonic tones and rich, bobbing-bass undertone. The Prime Minister looks bewildered and furious, and nobody believes what he agrees with the lips on his face, but still, they speak on proudly: of women being the leaders of the best world, of the beginning of a one-world ethos. It is when his voices break out in *I-Afrika Ihlangane!* that she can see terror in the man's eyes.

Cocrä wonders who has the Prime Minister's mouth, whether anyone would choose his lying lips, or if his voice might just fade into heaven with the dinosaurs.

Cocrä keeps looking in the mirror, practising with her new mouth, loving the gap in her/his teeth and her newly acquired taste for aloe vera juice. Fluffy often talks to itself: the new voice carves out a virtual seat at the table for itself and frees up space for more to join, inviting multilogues. Hundreds sit around Cocrä's virtual table, different voices leading in different moments. She discovers that her new mouth can play her/his polyphonic sound to great musical effect, harmonious with F sharps and E flats to express urgency, the use of deep bubbling sounds that keep everyone calm, trembling high notes that ring in the air long after everyone has finished speaking. The music from her lips takes root in people's minds.

'Habibi, let us gogo,' Fluffy says over and over. It loves these words more than all others.

Finally, Cocrä goes. It is Saturday afternoon, and she sits on the train to Heathrow Airport, talking with strangers, she in Arabic, they a bit of Greek, German and Swahili. She would have been terrified before Not Normal, but tomorrow she will be in Hawaii, greeting Malala, Greta and a new addition, Angeline from Zimbabwe. Meeting new people would have terrified her in times past, but now, like most others, she is led by her new mouth to do what is urgent. New mouths linking with each other. Cocrä feels a buzz, passionate and renewed.

She leans back and briefly watches the latest live stream of the American President speaking with thousands of Mexican children's happy voices, crazy about football and online games. He is talking about joining both Americas together, about releasing the land back to the First Nation people. The children's voices coming from his mouth giggle and end the speech by explaining that the President needs a rest now – but that he will be playing football on the border of Mexico very soon.

Cocrä grins with her Habibi mouth. A contented sleepiness falls over her, her eyes blinking softly in the lively, crowded train. She scans this miraculous world of different tongues and tones.

Just before she is about to nod off, she notices a person with a pulled-down peak cap, standing solitary by the door. Cocrä detects tension in the figure, their hands gripping the metal pole so tightly that white knuckles are visible.

She tries to shake herself awake, but she cannot rouse her heavy head.

The stranger's body trembles and then folds onto the floor. The cap falls off. A middle-aged man's face looks out into the world from the two cavities where his eyes used to be.

FISH SCALES

Muli Amaye

When Chi-Chi woke up that morning, she suspected it wasn't going to be an ordinary day. Partly because the light was already seeping under the bottom of the room's too-short curtains and she never woke this late. Partly because the pain in her body – her forever-companion – was gone. But mostly because of the two large fish scales glittering on her bedside table – they were a sign.

Chi-Chi moved her head slowly, testing her new body. Not one pain touched a muscle or a joint. She laughed loudly. Her rickety headboard banged against the wall with each chuckle, making her laugh harder. *Thump, thump.* Delighted, she began moving her legs under the heavy covers, kicking, and then flinging the covers off with abandon. *Thump, thump.*

The door flew open. It was Stella, her *dedicated* carer.

'Lawd Jeezus, Gawd Almighty! What is this now, Ms Chi-Chi? I was thinking you have a man in here or was taking a fit. What a thing, now!'

Chi-Chi stopped laughing, her mouth wide enough to show the gummy gaps at the back. She pulled her legs together and smoothed the ruffled sheet back over them before the girl could reach out. Chi-Chi rearranged her face, letting it settle back into its crevices, forehead to chin.

'It's a good job I wasn't *entertaining*. Banging into my room like that. No respect, you young people. None at all-at all.'

'Come now, Ms Chi-Chi. Your entertaining days long gone, nah. Is my job to make sure you okay!'

Chi-Chi dug deep for her most withering look to fling at the uppity girl, but she couldn't find one. There was an unfamiliar feeling of lightness pulsing through her body. Pushing herself up on frail arms, her triceps hung like old net curtains. She swung her legs over the side of the bed and searched for her slippers. She could feel Stella's eyes on her bowed head, glanced up to see the girl gaping. Chi-Chi couldn't help chuckle, again. When was the last time she swung anything?

'Go and boil the kettle, there's a good girl. I'm fancying a nice cup of tea.'

Stella hesitated.

'Close your mouth, dear, you're causing a draught.'

Slippers in place, Chi-Chi slid easily from the bed. She glanced at the fish scales on her bedside table before striding into the bathroom. And that was the start of the best day she could ever remember having.

Gliding into the communal lounge, Chi-Chi scanned the winged chairs, looking for the missing, for those who had succumbed to the Eternal overnight. On average, two a month disappeared. But they were all there this morning. Nodding and grinning. Chi-Chi shouted good mornings, giggling as she waltzed over to her usual place. She could feel those fish scales. Not just on her skin, but inside too. There was one on each big toe, then on her ear lobes, even her nipples. She glanced around coyly before rubbing a thumb over each one, shivering with delight. The scales slid to her temples and circled anticlockwise in a satisfying, head-massage kind of way. She sighed appreciatively.

When breakfast was over, Chi-Chi stood up and declared she was going out into the garden. Stella frowned.

'But Ms Chi-Chi, is cold out at this time. Wait, nah! Let the sun come round. The boy due to do some pruning. You don't want to be out there for that.'

She was not waiting. There was nothing to wait for. It had to be done. In her room, Chi-Chi dug through the wardrobe until she found her outside shoes. They were covered in dust. The laces were fraying at the ends, as though nibbled through. Sitting in the old Morris chair, she used the corner of her dress to wipe off the dust. A large tilapia sidled out of her left shoe, flapped its way across the floor and into the back of the wardrobe. The fish didn't look well, not quite as iridescent as it should. She supposed the cupboard was where it lived, which meant it definitely wasn't getting enough light. But there was no time to think about that now. She had to go outside. Flicking off her slippers, she shook out the right shoe to make sure it was empty before stuffing her feet in and tying the laces tightly. She marvelled at her working fingers. Stretched them this way and that. Her hands were pain-free, what a thing!

Taking her wool coat from the back of the door, Chi-Chi glanced at the bedside table. She was sure the fish scales there winked at her. Which didn't make sense because they weren't eyes. But not much of anything made sense this morning and that was okay.

Stella trailed behind her into the garden, wrapped up in a bubble coat four sizes too big. Chi-Chi never understood why these hot-country people insisted on moving to a country that was cold. But look at her own self. She'd done just that when *she* was young.

She glanced around quickly, checking she hadn't said that out loud. Stella's long face told her she hadn't. Chi-Chi felt relieved. She'd been caught out like that before; her mouth moving when she thought the words were just in her mind.

She felt warm. Kind of clammy warm. It was the fish scales, she knew that.

The first time they'd come, she was seventeen. Younger than this snippet dragging her feet behind her.

Chi-Chi reached the bench under the oak tree. It was shedding its leaves, leaving a mess under the bench and blowing around the garden. Stella sat down next to her. It was nice having her own personal assistant. That was what they were called. They used to be carers or cooks or cleaners until proper correct language decided it wasn't nice to call people by their jobs.

Chi-Chi steupsed loudly.

'Eh-eh, Ms Chi-Chi, what happen to your hand, so? You does have a new hand cream? They looking real nice today. Plump.'

Looking down, Chi-Chi saw that the fish scales had progressed, covering the pesky brown spots on the backs of her hands, the scales twinkling in the pale sunlight – whenever the sun could be bothered to pass from behind the fat, grey clouds. She laughed: her hands looked so *good*! She threw her head back and cackled some more and was hit splat on the forehead by a shitting seagull. Stella screamed then took out a tissue and wiped the crap away. Chi-Chi kept chuckling.

'I used to be a fish, you know,' she said.

Now it was Stella's turn to chuckle. Chi-Chi threw her a look that silenced her quickly. She watched Stella trying to fix her face. She was paying her; she deserved some respect. She repeated what she'd said, so the girl knew she wasn't joking.

'Stella. I used to be a fish and now I'm not.'

'That's nice, Ms Chi-Chi. You fancy a cuppa tea? I could go and put the kettle on. Is a bit chilly out here, you don't find?'

Chi-Chi thought about it for a moment, looking around, drinking in the damp earth. She felt the wood of the bench pressing into the back of her legs; saw the dying dregs of the bougainvillea further down the garden; imagined the full pink blooms of summer. The seagull shat again, right next to her, and she made up her mind. She raked her eyes around one more time: the leaves filling the empty pond that had never had water; a stone Buddha sat on the ground, mossed over on one side, black sludge on the other. These people had no respect, sitting him on the dirty floor like that.

She took a deep breath. Remembered that this was her best day ever, and the promise of a cup of tea. She turned back to the building, practically skipping along the path. Stella hefted herself behind in a walking run that had her puffing.

Inside again, Chi-Chi could feel the light rising in her chest; it had been a while since she'd felt like living. She looked at old heads lolling against the backs of chairs, their teeth loose, lips looser. This was what she'd been reduced to. 'You'll have your own flat,' Helen had said. 'A communal area to play bridge and chess, friends to speak to.' My arse, Chi-Chi thought. These people were ancient. She had nothing in common with them. She'd been happy in her own house, pottering around in the garden, doing what she wanted whenever she wanted. Until that dratted fall. It wasn't an old-people fall – it was a bloody trip over the bloody cat. And it was only a sprained ankle, not a broken hip. The cat hadn't even looked at her, lying there for two hours. Just stuck its tail in the air each time it passed her with the self-righteous air of a prima donna.

But Helen had got it into her head that she couldn't manage and had bullied her into moving into this godforsaken place that smelled like death, piss, and farts. She spent hours imagining Karma on her daughter's head when *she* got old.

As quick as the topic came to mind, it left. Instead, she thought of her daughter's wedding day. Right there on the beach on *that* island. Chi-Chi hadn't wanted it to be there. She'd tried every-thing to encourage Helen to marry in Jamaica or Barbados, or somewhere more, well, developed. Had threatened to withhold the money she'd been saving since Helen was born. Money for Helen to travel and see the world; to realise that there was more out there than Manchester with its cold, grey days and long, wet streets.

But not Helen. She met her husband in college. Scraped through the same university as him doing a nondescript degree, while he studied law or engineering or dentistry or something and then married him before they even graduated. Chi-Chi had wanted to scream. All that sacrifice, to give it up for a man the minute Helen was out on her own.

Something bubbled in the back of Chi-Chi's throat. It made her cough and spit up a fish scale. She caught it and placed it on the arm of her chair. Looking at these translucent circles made her feel like dancing.

Chi-Chi hadn't wanted to go back to the island. It was a place that was past. But the wedding *had* been beautiful. On the small beach. An archway full of white blooms, artificial, but still lovely, rigged up for them to stand under and say those vows that young people say these days.

And that hotel worker, the young man who raked the sand and lit the tiki torches along the sea front. He was familiar, so like Trent. The lightness of his bronzed limbs, the turn of his head as he flashed his wet locs over his shoulder.

Sitting on a white plastic chair on that beach, she realised she'd seen that gesture twenty years before. When she was just seventeen and the world had everything to offer her. Then there hadn't been locs and tiki torches but fishing nets and rum. Waterfalls and snorkelling gear. The young man looked a couple of years older than Helen and Chi-Chi's breath caught in her throat.

Was this the son she had left behind?

Terrified in case her secret came out, she flew to the twin island as soon as the wedding was done, telling Helen that she had old friends to see.

Stella placed a china pot of tea on the table next to her chair. Chi-Chi lifted the lid and saw a small lionfish weaving its way through the tea leaves, throwing them around like gravel at the bottom of the ocean. She smiled and scratched a fish scale off her wrist.

'Stella, bring me my red velvet cupcakes! It's a day to celebrate!'

'Oh Lawd, Ms Chi-Chi. The doctor did say to cut back on the sugar, nah.'

'Just the small ones. I know they're in my cupboard. Helen always brings a box.'

Helen hadn't been for weeks. That useless girl with her useless husband. Always fussing-fussing, but never around to do any work. Quite happy to palm her off on this Stella person.

'Eh-eh! What me to do with you today? What has gotten into you? You need me to call Miss Helen?'

'Just bring the red velvet.'

Opening a button on her dress, Chi-Chi poked at a sudden itch. A fish scale had worked its way through the folds of her navel, and it tickled. She picked it out. The same as peeling out fluff when she was a child. She grinned. Her mother had been appalled when she saw her doing it, but picking your navel was an art form. Like a magician pulling handkerchiefs from his jacket arm. Chi-Chi rested her hands on her swollen midriff, round and taut. Patting it she scratched at her sides, dislodging more scales. There was a time when she was slim like a barracuda. She could dance in the sand like a fish out of water, twisting and turning, flapping and flipping. On that island that Helen still insisted on visiting again and again. Like there was nowhere else in the world that she could go. Chi-Chi cursed the day she'd let it slip that she'd lived there.

When she was small, on rainy days, Helen always wanted to go through the photographs in her old handbag. The black one with the clasp. Back in the day, Chi-Chi had shoes to match it. And that little white miniskirt with the purple stripe down the centre. Oooh, she had looked good, well into her twenties and thirties, kept that long smooth figure. Swirling and twirling, young on that island, nobody could tell from the back what was going on at the front. Slim like wire. Carrying that boychild, high-high. She'd gone there with her copy of Faulkner and the idea that she was free. Only one month in and she had fallen.

She'd stayed exactly one year. Enough time to get herself back. An old fisherman had spent the year shaking his head at her – as she'd played with Trent, drinking and dancing, making a baby – he'd told her that her baby belonged to the sea and needed to stay with his people. The old fisherman was the one who had taken her to the port in the night when everyone was sleeping. Left *him* sleeping: her small son in a makeshift cot.

Red velvet cupcakes. Chi-Chi peeled back the paper and sank her teeth into one. Cream stuck to her upper lip and she left it there, knowing it annoyed Stella, with her proper ways. These people were so finicky. Her own mother had spoken such precise English whenever they went into a shop or she answered the telephone. She only slipped into Creole when Chi-Chi's father was at work and it was just the two of them. Nobody knew. It wasn't something to talk about, apparently. One evening, little Chi-Chi spoke to her father with a full-on accent, and he beat her with a slipper before giving her mother a backhand that left her face swollen for days. He was having none of that in *his* house. Afterwards, her mother threatened to cut out her tongue if she dared speak with an island twang. Or mention that her grandmother was a red woman. Her mother had worked hard to be acceptable. So that she could give her daughter better opportunities. Chi-Chi felt one giant steups quivering on her lips and mischief rising inside her like a wave.

'Ms Chi-Chi why you grinning so? Is sugar make you feel good, eh?'

'Mi nuh know.'

'Ms Chi Chi, I going tell Miss Helen if you start to copy my accent again! I does find it real fass coming from a lady like you.'

'Cha man, relax nah.' And she was off, again. Leaning back in her chair and kicking out her legs and bellowing. Her belly swelled with each laugh. Fish scales dropped onto her dress and that made her laugh some more. Stella was trying to keep a serious face, but she couldn't do it, she was grinning too, and that made Chi-Chi fling back her head in pure enjoyment.

'Me think you does need to take a rest before lunch, Ms Chi-Chi.'

'Is me island name you know, Chi-Chi. I born Miss Dorothy Maude.'

Stella rolled her eyes into next week.

Chi-Chi allowed herself to be walked into her bedroom. There, on the table, still and gleaming, were the two fish scales. She lay down gratefully, her gaze not moving from them. Her bed creaked like an old fishing boat in the wind. Her curtains blew with the breeze from the fan she insisted stayed running. The fish scales sat there, waiting.

'I used to be a fish, you know.'

'So you did say.'

Helen had confirmed it to her, the second time she and her useless husband went back to that island, to that untouched fishing village, touched by Chi-Chi herself so many years ago. It was such a small place, and so not strange that Helen met her half-brother. It was like she was drawn to that fishing village the same way Chi-Chi had been. His name was Darl and he kept a book tucked under his arm, no matter what he was doing. It was Chi-Chi's Faulkner, her favourite book of all time. And Darl told Helen that his mother was a fish. That she had been there and then she had gone and all he had was this book. Helen had talked about him nonstop, asking questions, making accusations, working out dates and adding two plus two to get seven. But Chi-Chi refused to discuss it. Each visit Helen made to the island had brought more probing, more attempts to trip her up, to unearth a story, but not once did she admit to Helen that she was a fish. That Darl was a baby she had left with the sea.

Chi-Chi felt the scales fusing together all over her body. The feeling she had woken with that morning was becoming something more. At first it was warm and wrapped around her, making her feel safe, then it was as though she was in a net and couldn't escape. Was being dragged through seaweed, scraped across coral and a boat bottom. She opened her mouth and closed it again. Flipped up and down on the bed as it creaked and rocked. Stella pushed open the door and was saying something that Chi-Chi couldn't hear. Then came doctors and finally Helen and her useless husband. Staring. Talking. Words filtered through: stroke, heart, hospital, dying. But Chi-Chi looked down at her body. Saw the beautiful rainbow blues and purples. Shook her fin and flicked her tail. Throwing back her head, she opened her mouth wide and laughed and laughed, gulping in air.

THE BEARD

Alinah Azadeh

It's insanely hot in here. The man shuts the door behind him, and shuffles in his cluster of thick, black, woollen robes towards the far end of the room, away from the window, out of sight of the eyes below, protected from the queues passing through the military gate into the building.

He sheds the robes first, to get some relief, then takes off his silver, square headdress, placing them on a huge, ornately carved walnut desk.

He's always been complimented on the volume and beauty of his beard, the thickest and longest in his close circle, with its enviable twists and curls, its signature indigo-black colour giving it motion, the light catching its shiny ridges. Many men coveted this beard, not just those within the justice department but among all the powerful government cliques. The beards of the Eminent Ones were the most substantial, commensurate with the power they wielded.

The man is panting, exhausted as he lowers himself onto the edge of a creaking sofa in the corner, sweating from the summer heat outside, and the stifling atmosphere of the courtroom. He has just finished pronouncing a series of sentences – thirty ritual cuts each to the forearms and calves, and varying periods of incarceration – for a long line of young women. *Down like dominoes.* He recalls the first defendant: on the video clip he was shown during the briefing last night, the girl's bright red hair rippled around her shoulders, her face increasingly ecstatic as she began to sing, at first quiet and moving to her own melody, then to a rhythm played by a young man with a small drum. Around them, a growing crowd, all smiling and waving at the camera.

Eventually, emboldened by those around her, she'd climbed onto the roof of an old, silver Mercedes, and sang the crudest of slogans across the crackling urban darkness. The girl stood tall, like a ship's mast against the sky, conducting a mass singalong to the music: *Freedom, freedom, freedom will be ours*. The man watched the screen as the girl lifted her arms, saw the delicate fabric of her neon orange shackles, stretched taut between her swollen wrists, glistening with the exquisitely embroidered gold initials of the man who owned her. Raising your arms above shoulder level – without explicit permission – was banned in public for women, was regarded as an act of heresy, yet this girl had offered them up into the night air triumphantly, as if she had just landed on the moon. It was the third night of full-blown demonstrations, triggered by the disappearance of yet another student caught disseminating anti-state propaganda, and this was not the girl's first trans-gression. Last year she'd had her feet bound together for a week, after being seen dancing in public.

Totally out of control, these little bitches, the man mutters to himself. They were supposed to be the children of the Great Coup, but they were nothing more than a public disgrace. *A serious threat to the moral fabric of this state and our reputation across the world!* he'd intoned before sentencing. Just another whore to silence, who didn't learn from her mistakes.

He enjoyed every single pronouncement of guilt he had made; thousands of them over the many decades since he first began working in this court, right at the beginning of the glory days of The Black Coup, as it had also come to be known. Named after the black robes The Eminent Ones wore, parading through the streets on the day the Palace was brought down. Named also after the viscous, black tar lines daubed across the eyes of the murdered Royal family, their decapitated heads hung by their hair from the ornately gilded balconies where they once made speeches, back in their days of pomp and spectacle.

He runs his palm over his sweating, shiny scalp. Too little left. He sighs.

The sudden hair loss had started yesterday at dinner over stew, then continued – in *public* – during a Judge's Council this morning. He had been listening desultorily when a series of beard hairs began littering the light cream table in front of him, like contorted fleas. He swiftly scanned the room to see if anyone had noticed, but everyone was distracted, so he sat back and stroked his beard casually, as the entire Council did when reflecting on dilemmas together, all very natural, moving his hands down to catch the renegade hairs loosening from his chin, slowly manoeuvring them to his edge of the table as discreetly as possible.

The pockets of his robes are full of hair, now.

He knows he needs a credible cover story for the inexplicable shedding. Perhaps he can say he has developed a rare skin condition, like alopecia, to explain the patchy beard? No, that would be seen as inherent weakness.

The powerful man unbuttons his white under-robe and the stiff corset beneath that. He wore extra layers today, to cover the changing shape of his body. Once a lithe revolutionary, a radical student used to hunger strikes and heroic abstinence, he's had many years as an Eminent One with an obedient wife, an affluent household, a useful and regular concubine, and many rich and tasty meals washed down with good wine. Slowly, he has expanded in all directions, can no longer see his genitals when he stands up, his hairy belly rising like some ancient, grassy, burial mound to meet him when he urinates. But he has grown proud of this belly, a symbol of his moral and actual wealth and status.

No, other things are changing.

He puts on his glasses to check if it's still happening. He scrutinises his nipples, those two previously rubbery, dark brown discs punctuated with thick, black curly hairs, crowning his flabby chest. The skin around these nipples is lightening, becoming completely smooth and hairless. And he swears they are starting to swell, as if injected with water. His belly, once seething with dark hair like spider's nests is now bald in the middle. *Like a doughnut, a human doughnut!* A tiny, lonely crater of smooth skin which both shocks and fascinates him. How is this happening?

The man moves even closer to a long mirror in the corner to inspect his face. His beard is not thinning out naturally as might be expected with age, but conspicuously dotted with balding areas in the most irregular of places. He has occasionally fantasised, with a flicker of shame, about shaving this beard off completely, wondering what it would be like to run his fingers over smooth skin daily. Like a young girl's skin. An innocent skin. The skin of the women who once ruled this land centuries ago, with their false beards and baby-smooth flesh underneath. Of course, it would be utterly against protocol for someone of his status and role to do this, an outrageous insult to The Teachings. His beard is interlaced with seven threads of high-grade gold, delicately spaced out and woven into his skin at the chin-line, identifying him as an Eminent One and ensuring fraud is impossible.

He will not be afraid. Abruptly, he looks down.

His penis, his most prized feature after his beard is shrinking back slowly but steadily into his groin. *This can't be. Not that!* What will people say if it gets out, that one of the most notorious judges in the entire state, is losing his masculinity before their eyes? *Someone is responsible for this*, he thinks, furiously. Toying with his diminutive penis, he wonders if it's his wife, conscious of his many infidelities, spiking the stew. No, she's too dependent on him to risk that. And so broken, she wouldn't dare. A political enemy, an inside mole perhaps, doctoring the air-con system. *Security's too tight for that, after the attempted poisonings last year.*

For a moment it occurs to him that this is divine judgement for what he keeps in the bottom drawer of his office desk, reappropriated from the previous regime's Unholy Archive of Imperialist Disrepute. He'd removed the single, battered pornographic magazine discreetly, before it was logged and 'filed' away for safekeeping. The artefact has been so well used – inspected and *analysed*, he reassures himself – that its pages are worn thin. And the images of flesh, hair and open red slits amorphously merging into one another through the wafer-thin paper, like a psychedelic landscape, are now too familiar to be quite as thrilling as when he first opened it. It was his job to assess the content. Designed to corrupt, hard to resist, even for a man of his moral standing and resolve!

When he pronounced sentence on women, on girls, they often collapsed, begging him for mercy, already worn and hollow after time in subterranean prison cells, all bail refused. It thrilled him, their tortured faces and pain. But sometimes, intertwined with this frisson of power, and remembering his own estranged daughter, he feels a flash of guilt. A specific thought arises, panicked, from deep in his stomach: he thinks of smoothness advancing, imagines his whole body changed – soft olive skin, curves, moist orifices. Imagines constant access to this new body's comforts and pleasures. He'd never be inconvenienced by a woman again, with their constant demands, failings and substantial overheads.

This man, who is one of the most notorious and revered of all The Eminent Ones, ponders, with a combination of dread and self-admiration, whether he has become so powerful now, that even his darkest, secret desires can materialise and take physical shape?

Over the next few days, the powerful man begins to realise he is not alone. He notices a number of his colleagues shuffling around the courthouse uncomfortably, changing in ways that seem familiar and connected to his own gradual metamorphosis. Their beards are in different stages of thinning: one has a mere crust of a goatee left, gold threads sprouting almost completely alone in several places. He is tempted to reach out to this man, someone he knows well, during a court break, but quickly stops himself, realising his own beard is disappearing so rapidly that there isn't much between them.

Better not to focus minds on his failings. Not yet.

More than a few of the Eminent Ones have double bulges on their chests that were not there before. They are not all heavy men with big bellies like himself, in fact one of them is remarkably slim for a man of his status, yet today he wears a massively oversized, tent-like robe, attempting to balance himself when he walks, in an increasingly clumsy and comical manner, unused to the extra weight in this most unexpected of places.

An atmosphere of insecurity thickens the air around these men as the week goes on. It is disconcerting for them all. Yet the powerful man starts to feel relief. *So, I am not alone. This is not my fault after all.* By midweek, there is an unspoken acknowledgement between them. Sideways glances bounce around the corridors of the courthouse. *If word gets out, this could be dangerous.* They agree to increase the number of bodyguards outdoors, to create a protective layer of defence. Inside the courthouse they worry less: the long-established fog of fear that hangs heavy in the air amongst the defendants and their families awaiting trial on corridor benches, the stress amongst the staff, preoccupied with stemming the chaos of this overflowing building, all this distracts from the judges' transmutation. Those awaiting trial are choked with anxiety, seeing nothing but an uncertain future, the terror of potential punishment, endless jail terms and the threat of separation from their loved ones. The thickness of a Judge's beard or the shape of his chest is the last thing they care about in here.

Once it becomes clear that this metamorphosis is only happening amongst his peers, the man calls a Secret Emergency Council, the first in many months. Sitting together around a huge, boardroom table on the top floor of the building, their eyes flitting over each other's bodies with a mixture of shame, relief and growing solidarity, they discuss a proposed update to The Teachings. One of them suggests dropping the requirement to wear a beard at all. *Let's just keep the gold thread?* Another suggests false beards, like in days of old by the Fallen Matriarchs – but the reference back to the women who once wielded power is too risky and might remind the people of an alternative in these tumultuous times. And in any case, this alone wouldn't be enough, indeed any kind of change to The Teachings, which they had ruled unquestionable, unalterable, never to be challenged, would be too suspicious. *We cannot let the people know this is happening to us at all*, they conclude.

Despairing, they share conspiracy theories as to why and who is trying to strip them of their gender sovereignty, of all that shores up their power. One man whispers that The Pre-Eminent One seems unchanged. *Perhaps he has had enough of us, and this is a sign of his displeasure? He is the only human alive who could make this happen.* Another points out The Pre-Eminent One hasn't been seen in public for several weeks now, *haven't you noticed? We have no idea where he is. It is said he has gone east on sabbatical, but he left no instructions at all.* They stare at each other, and all take note. *Then we must follow his lead.*

Over the next few weeks, these black-robed men, with their distinctive silver headdresses and mini charcoal-grey-clad armies of mute bodyguards begin to slowly disappear from public view. They refuse all private audiences and media appearances and take refuge in their second apartments inside a high security compound, up on the far edge of the city, at the foot of a blue mountain range. They agree to tell their wives, on condition they sign NDAs, that urgent and serious state business will take them away for the foreseeable future, behind closed doors, working to counteract real and imminent threats to the state. They send out proxies to oversee court proceedings, deliver verdicts and suspend weekly addresses to their subjects, forced to trust those around them in lesser positions of power, communicating only via their most trusted aides.

But a smattering of subversive voices has begun to infiltrate the lower echelons of the justice department, spreading rumours that The Eminent Ones are in jeopardy, though no-one understands why. *They are cooking up something. We do not know what, but we will find out.* The diminishing presence of The Eminent Ones is quietly discussed on street corners, at family gatherings, in the markets. The citizens – or subjects as they are labelled, despite the allusion to the long-buried and hated monarchy – begin to wonder if these bearded ones still actually exist. Connections are made between their absence and the longstanding lack of action on rising costs of living, and life-threatening increases in food poverty and homelessness, a ripple effect of sanctions through conflicts with surrounding states. *And all this, whilst we know the wealth from their precious crystal mines continues to flow into the state reserves. Maybe they've pocketed the money and left the country!* Speculation is now on fire, though still no more than whispers and confidences.

Just one woman thinks she understands: his ex-lover. On the night before he severed their relationship – after seven years of weekly appointments at the apartment he moved her into – she wakes up to urinate and, seeing the bed empty next to her, follows the sound of his muffled voice. Perplexed, she hears lover's talk, coming from the second bathroom, further down the corridor, reserved for him only: *You pretty, pretty thing, look at this body of yours, isn't this beautiful? Ah yes, just there, just like that.* Catching a glimpse of him through the crack in the door, even in the half-darkness, she is relieved to see he is alone, but realises his body is not quite the body she knows and has loved. Utterly confused, a strong sense of self-preservation pulls her away and she tiptoes back to bed, shaking slightly as she slips beneath the cold sheets. She understands why he wouldn't let her touch him now or at any time over the last fortnight, but what the hell is going on?

She knew the end was coming, had felt a sense of dread as their appointments became less and less frequent, when during the last few encounters, he'd refused to let her undress him or touch him anywhere except for his shoulders, through material, a short massage. *I must be coming down with a flu of some kind no doubt, freezing inside the bones, I am sure you understand, my love.* Again, she noted something odd about his profile as he stood in the doorway before leaving. Yes, the landscape of his body had definitely changed, she wasn't imagining it. She couldn't believe it was possible. She knew of one person in the city who had used a black-market operation in a neighbouring country and then never returned, but for an Eminent One, no, it was heretical, impossible, utterly against The Teachings. He would risk losing everything. And so would she. *So, he got rid of me first, instead of confiding in me. He never trusted me, after all this time and so many moments of tenderness between us!*

Since he split from her and left his wife back in their city house, the man spends most of his time, alone, in this second apartment. At least he has neighbours and Council meetings can happen here quite easily, though none of them seems to know what to do about their bodies anymore. Doctors cannot be trusted, they agree, *they have betrayed us before.* It is as if they have surrendered to this inevitable change and lost all inclination to disrupt its course.

One cold, dry night the following month, the man, cursing the fact that he can now only move around outside in the dead of darkness, *like a fugitive, ridiculous!* is crossing the street from the private park near his apartment, where he often goes to take in the night air before sleeping. By now he has curvy hips, a hairless, stubble-free face, and a pair of bulging breasts that he cannot keep his hands off. Yet nothing about his new and nubile body can compensate for the absence of other humans and he misses those with whom he has known intimacy, however unequal the power balance. Thinking of his lover and her warm smile and touch, he trips over a pothole. The bulge of accumulated beard hair spills from inside his black robe pocket, his safe place, falling out in one mass onto the ground, and blowing unnoticed, against the kerb, as if settling there for the night.

In the light of the fullest moon anyone has seen all year, the cluster of hair forms a sizeable ball, and this ball gently blows downhill, collecting other hairballs which have also slipped from the pockets of Eminent Ones. They attract each other like pins to a magnet. Or a call from a long-lost lover. The discarded hairs, which they have all agreed are the equivalent of sacred relics and not to be disposed of until a conservation plan is hatched, manage to find pathways not only from robes but out from bedroom drawers, or slipping free from the folded pages of newspapers they have been wrapped in. Others escape from desks, bedside tables or from the shelves of slightly open bathroom cabinets. Buoyed by a gentle night wind, this spiky collective swarms, migrating to a particular spot in the centre of the city's main square.

It is the very spot where, half a century before, the henchmen of The Eminent Ones were commanded to make clear examples of those who refused to support the ideals of their new, shiny state, slicing open the throats of adults and children, allowing the square to fill with blood, flooding into the drainage system in the surrounding streets, a crimson invitation to join in their magnificent project, to create a common utopia, free of all abuses of power and redundant, imperialist ideology. This was also the place where anti-state protests would begin, approximately every decade, though never for more than a few hours or days, due to the brutal and well-organised security forces. Huge prison complexes were built on the edges of the city to contain the increasing numbers of dissenters, their population soon outnumbering that of the university campus downtown, where many of the troubles began.

Early the next morning, as he is setting up his cigarette and newspaper stall, a street vendor notices the enormous ball of debris, a metre in circumference by now – shed from the beards, heads and bodies of hundreds of Eminent Ones. He crouches in front of it, playfully poking it with his pen. People passing by, stop and stare. Soon, fascinated disgust attracts a sizeable gathering.

From the top corner of the square, the powerful man's ex-lover approaches, weary from a noisy night at the hostel where she has been forced to relocate after his pitiful payoff ran out and her family refused to take her back. *Too much dishonour you bring on us. And you didn't even get a decent parting gift from such a wealthy man!* Full of grief and shame, she stops and stares hard at the mountain of hair, an impenetrable entanglement of blacks, greys, whites, and browns with the occasional streak of gold. It's a monumental version of the cluster of hair she had come across in her ex-lover's robe, rifling through his pockets before leaving their apartment for the last time, looking for a memento, or something she might use for a bribe if she got too desperate. She wondered why he kept the hair; some narcissistic attachment to anything that came from his own body? *He can let go of me, but he can't let go of his own body hair, what is this?* She had dismissed the hair as worthless and somewhat repulsive, but now she recognises it amongst this mass; its wiry, wavy texture and the shades of blue-grey and indigo-black are unforgettable. She has stroked and massaged it many times, at his request, as a form of foreplay.

During what turned out to be their final farewell, he had spoken as if they would meet again soon. *A few important affairs of state to attend to, we will be together again when it is sorted out, do not worry my love. Just a few weeks or so.* But he only communicated with her one more time, phoning to inform her in the language of a business professional that it was time to separate – *definitively* – that they had originally agreed this was a temporary arrangement. He told her where the severance money would be left. There was an odd fragility, a delicate tone in his voice towards the end of their conversation which she remained curious about for a long time. He had immediately blocked her number. Next came the raging silence, and with that, her regret at the losses incurred: two offers of marriage rejected, attachment to her family severed, a career as a nurse cut short because he had wanted her on call. The sense of abandonment was total.

As the woman stands in the main square amidst the crowd, facing this huge spectacle of a hairball, a wave of white anger takes hold of her, charging up through her body and finding voice. She whispers the truth out loud: the origin of this mass of shed masculinity; she exposes her lover's transformation, the cause of his detachment. Whispers her own despair and pain. She leaves enough words in the space to do their work, and then disappears; it might not be safe to stay.

The words quickly weave their way through the crowd, leaving everyone both stunned and compelled by the quiet foundation of the spectacle before them, in all its expended power.

Two students pick up the ball, raising it high above their heads for all to see, emboldened by no security forces in sight, despite the burgeoning crowd. *Is this all that is left of their so-called Utopian state, those cowards? A ball of grimy hair? Too ashamed to show their bald faces now the people are starving and there is no clean water, no affordable fuel, no nothing! People, is this not a sign, a talisman? Surely it has been sent to us by the great forces they say protect and guide them.*

An elderly woman, who many decades before had run into this square declaring herself a revolutionary, ecstatic at the prospect of a new future, a freer society, now steps forward with a lighter. *Let us burn it! Let us show them what we think of what remains of their precious beards! Let me be the one to start the fire, please! I've lost everything because of these bastards!*

And so, a clearing is purposefully and swiftly created and the hairy mountainous ball, on being ceremoniously ignited, turns to a raging fireball in seconds. The stench of burning hair is too much for many to bear. The women use their delicate, deadly wrist shackles to cover their noses against the smell, but then one of them, a young girl recently released from prison, holds out hers just close enough to the fire to singe and break through its centre, casting it with a shriek onto the sweltering ball of fire. The scent of the perfumed fabric brings some relief, and her bravery prompts others in the crowd to come forward, one by one, to do the same. The core of the contracting, burning hairball is smothered and sustained by layer upon layer of coloured strips of cloth. Neon orange, yellow or green, denoting specific class or district, curling in the flames, dancing with each other. Cheering and clapping ensues, singing and drumming fill the square. By lunchtime, a mass celebration is in process. And there is still no sign of the security forces anywhere.

After several hours, the henchmen finally arrive. They have been focused on hundreds of sudden, suspicious deaths across the city and beyond. They don't bother to coordinate a response to this illegal situation; they are all too shell-shocked from the fresh sight of so many unidentifiable and amorphously cross-gendered bodies, dressed in the black robes of some of the most powerful officials in the land, collapsed lifeless on apartment floors, in stairways, on the streets or inside their smoked-glass, armoured cars. They have had enough trauma for one day and the call to the main square, while Special Forces forensically examine the bodies in the cramped morgues on the outskirts of the city, is a welcome diversion.

Disarmed by the triumphant atmosphere, the men push their way through the joyously raucous crowd, barely noticing the unshackled women and girls waving their arms high, in time to the music, in the twilight. The crowd quietens as they move through and past, increasingly nervously, towards the epicentre of this illegal and momentous gathering.

They come to a still, smoking spot, and here they stop and stare at all that is left of their rulers; a charred pile of intertwined cloth strips and an array of singed, curled gold thread, glued fast like a series of distorted musical notes to the blackened ground before them.

SOUCOUYANT

Melissa Jackson-Wagner

Audrey swiped her Breeze card and went through the Marta station barriers. 'Freshness of a Breeze In a Bottle!' she hummed, laughing at how the way-back-when Limacol advertisement always popped into her head when she used her Marta card. Her daughter, Melody, immersed in texting on her iPhone, dragged behind. The cold concrete Brutalism of the station echoed their silence. Bleak. Millennials and mothers don't mix, thought Audrey, and, not for the first time, she wondered what she was really doing here, at'all at'all.

As she waited, Audrey saw a ticket-less man squeezing through the gates, glancing around him. She chuckled complicitly. 'Oh I see, *that's* how it done!'

The man looked at her with ghost eyes and walked away rapidly. So thin! She remembered Melody warning her that when she was on the Marta, she just mind she own business and keep she head down. She'd thought her daughter was being overly cautious. 'If somebody say good morning to me on that train, I going to say it right back!' she'd told her American friend, Vincent, but he looked horrified at her light-heartedness. 'No!' He'd been so emphatic. 'Don't talk to *any* homeless person. It's dangerous. They're gonna come after you and for more than just a dollar! You know they're all crackheads.'

Audrey reflected that crack was very specifically an American problem and when you said American what you actually meant was African-American. Dem white folks sure knew how to poison Black folk here. In the Caribbean – well, she could only really speak for Guyana – people, herself included, tended to carry loose change in the car to hand out to a homeless person. Good Karma and all that. In the UK, Audrey had been less forthcoming with her loose change; she, a Black woman, handing out money to homeless white people, well that seemed like some kinda raasclaat! After all, she had struggled hard to work and support herself in a country designed to give white people privilege from the moment they born. She *did* use to give a pound coin when she could to the homeless dreadlocked guy who stood outside Queens Road Peckham station. He had always wished her a good day whether she had change or not, and she sometimes thought she could feel his deep pain at this Mother Country's betrayal and all his shattered dreams. But here in Atlanta, when she'd said to Vincent, over a shared Korean BBQ, that a homeless person was a human too, he'd simply looked at her like she was talking stupidness. It wasn't that people didn't give in America – she knew people who regularly volunteered – so it all kinda came as a surprise. She'd been learning a great deal now she'd finally got her Green Card to come live with her daughter. And that great deal was a constant reminder that she was an alien anyhow you looked at it.

She and Melody stood sullenly, side by side, waiting for the train. The wafer-thin man was waiting on the train too. His eyes haunted Audrey. Was he a crack addict? What did she know about crack and what it did to the human mind, what it did to change a person from a healthy, active child playing with their friends to *this*, this skin-n-bone man, a shadow of what they could have been? All that potential, all that human frailty, snuffed on a puff of crack. She imagined gaunt bodies, mere shells where God-given imagination had been replaced by something else, lurking and incomprehensible.

The train took ages to arrive. She was aware, out of the corner of her eye, that the man-ghost was still staring at her, so when the train came in, she manoeuvred Melody towards a different carriage for their journey Downtown.

On their way home, much later, an elderly homeless man spoke to her, but Audrey turned her face and pretended not to hear or see him. She immediately felt shame. Like she'd annihilated the old man, just to follow other people's opinions. So many of them had never even stepped onto a train.

Audrey had been raised in the UK, one of those citizens they'd taken to calling 'The Windrush Generation' even though that wasn't the ship she'd arrived on in 1959. She and her father had taken the ship from Georgetown to Venezuela and then boarded another ship from there. She had no memory of the journey, as she'd only been three at the time. She had no memory of her mother running off with the 'skunthole porknocker' her daddy used to cuss.

Her father could have left she with one of his six older sisters but he had his own way of doing things and so he took her to England with him. She often wondered if it was the wisest thing or the best thing for her because life in London hadn't been paved with any kinda gold – it was paved with pure shit. Her father worked long hours and bought into the colonial bullshit brainwashing 'bout how white women dem were the way to upward status for a Black man living inna England. Well, he'd been indoctrinated long time, after all wasn't her own mummy a Potagee woman? 'Think she the whitest ting since whitey itself,' her auntie Kitty used to say, referring not to white people but the sweet fruit in Guyana that looked like cotton wool puffs.

So Audrey had ended up being raised by a series of her father's white women, the local school and her friends and friends' families. She grew up playing out on the street until dusk, a time before parents took to locking their children up indoors. Spent hours riding the bicycle her dad had found in a tip, and hours reading whatever she could find at the local library. She'd never found herself in any of those stories; it was only when she moved back *home* that she learnt the stories she passed on to her daughter. Kids now, she chuuupsed to herself, didn't know 'bout playing or reading. They all locked away in front of TV screen or glued to their smartphones. They didn't learn how to navigate the streets, how to laugh at the dutty ol man flasher, run from the neighbour down the road with his swastika tattooed on his forehead shouting 'Fuck off you wogs!' to her and her friends. Now, they grew up in fear but most of them had never actually experienced anything directly to be fearful of, so they created myths of evil homeless people about to kill or kidnap yuh raaass.

The next day, Audrey headed to Midtown to her favourite bougie grocery shop with its crazy expensive prices – but what had she worked hard all her life for if she couldn't now treat herself to Wholefoods? To her alarm, the ghost-man was on the platform again, a shrunken something, his hoodie pulled up over his bent snapback, trying to keep out the cold of the frosty autumn day. With only skin and no meat 'pon him he must be feeling every wind's breath.

He saw her and his stare bore through her. Audrey decided not to turn away, whatever the cost to self and safety. It was important to be decent to people. She smiled determinedly across at him and wished him a good morning. He responded only with the unbroken jumbie-eyed stare he'd offered her yesterday.

Audrey heard the train approaching the platform and waited for it, her focus turning away from the man to the silver metal of its carriages, pulling in. The doors opened and she stepped in and sat down. The man followed behind her and sat on the adjacent seat, no longer staring, his head cowed. He reeked of urine and pain.

Audrey switched to mouth-breathing and wondered what his life had been that led him to this – all the energy gone from his body. He couldn't be much older than her daughter. Did he have a mother worrying about him? Children of his own? Five stops along and he was so still Audrey began to worry. Was he OK?

She reached out gently to touch his arm. His head bolted upright. They locked eyes. And that was when it happened; her fingers on his arm seemed to burn and his eyes became hers, his memories hers: she saw everything, a young man's life in a matter of seconds. His memories flowed through her fingers and she felt herself falling into his past: the racist teacher at his first school who ignored his raised hand and his potential; the father shipped off as fodder for a war he should have never fought in but what other choice did he have to put food on the table, who put his foot on a landmine and never came home; the mother struggling on nightshifts as a nurse whilst studying for her medical degree; a life spent less in an uncaring school system and more on the street. She saw his first offered smoke at thirteen, through to his first pipe; witnessed the spiral down, down, down and further down; his mother, afraid for his youngest siblings; his theft of her wedding ring. Audrey could see the TV, the toaster, the what-ever-he-could-carry to feed and feed and feed this addiction, see it killing his once-brilliant mind, the original self that his white teacher, too intent on creating her own narrative, refused to see.

She became aware of being back on the train, only now it was his hand on her arm, and he was gently murmuring, 'Ma'am, ma'am, you OK?' She looked up into his eyes, not ghost eyes anymore – gentle eyes full of concern and wet with tears. He was smiling at her.

The addict, Lorenzo, didn't really know how he'd got here – on this train or in the stink clothes he was wearing, in front of this well-dressed lady – but he could feel a kind of hope swell through his body.

Audrey wasn't sure at first. She thought maybe she'd had a turn. Maybe the ghost-man, the jumbie-eyed man, was all a dream. She stayed in bed for a week after that, her body alternating between shivering bouts of ague and fully-fledged sweat-the-bed-out-like-it-rain pon-it, heat-sweltering fevers. Her stomach became rock hard and churned inside like she was doing crunches at the gym even though she was barely moving, other than to kick off a blanket or pull one on.

Melody, she noted, didn't have much time for her. Her mum being ill in bed was an inconvenience. Audrey could imagine exactly what her inconsiderate child was thinking: that she had shit to do and couldn't be worrying her arse about *her* as well.

Melody would occasionally remember to pick up a soup from the local Jamaican takeaway on her way back from classes, but mostly Audrey didn't eat. She drank water, and more water and even more water as if she was trying to wash a fire from her body. As if she were Kaieteur Falls after the rainy season, full to burst. But only a week later and she was out of bed, back on her strong black coffee and ready to get back to her kizomba classes.

Audrey headed out to the Marta station, a short walk from her daughter's apartment, with her smile firmly on. She took the one-stop journey to her class in downtown Decatur. It was fun, despite her unsteadiness on her feet and the unsteadiness of a dance partner stomping through the moves because somewhere down the long history of colonialism and slavery their hips had been stolen and their connection to the music lost forever. Her partner learnt the moves like learning his ABCs but couldn't feel the rhythm in his blood and bones. Audrey was the opposite: the drumbeat was her hook, and the steady bass massaged her skin like a good lover. It was symbiotic, she in the music and the music in her, like the kind of perfect sex she sometimes yearned for. Learning the steps was quite another thing; following her dance partner harder yet. She had to leave her womanism outside the front door – however two-left-footed and off the beat they were she had to follow them. It was a struggle. But when she got a good dance partner, which happened occasionally, one who felt the music just as she did, a man who could with the gentle pressure of his hand in the small of her back and the nuanced lilt of his hip, lead her along the journey of dance, it was a beautiful thing. And it was for that feeling she returned each week.

She watched the intermediate class afterwards, chatting to the other women who lacked the confidence to take the dance to the next level. The men, even with just a couple of classes behind them would always go straight into the intermediate session, their swollen egos bigger by far than their skill.

Audrey checked her phone, saw that her train was due, and

jumped up, saying goodbye to her recently acquired friends.

'I'm heading off now, gotta get my Marta.'

'At this hour?' someone exclaimed.

It wasn't the first time she'd seen that face and it wouldn't be the last. Audrey laughed. 'Let's hope you don't hear about me being murdered on Fox News tomorrow!'

The women frowned. She wasn't really sure why she'd said that: stupidy, why make them worry for nothing? She zipped up her North Face jacket; the one her daughter muttered made her look like a roadman, but she didn't care; it was lightweight, and it kept her warm which was the only thing that mattered now she was free to have more sense than youth.

The electronic board said the Eastbound train – hers – was due in six minutes so she waited up on the concourse, exchanged grimaces with an elderly lone traveller on the coldness of an Atlanta night and then took the stairs down to the platform. At night it was deserted, not like the continuous crowds on the London Underground, day or night. The dark quiet reminded her of a scene from her favourite film *The Matrix*, when Neo aka Keanu Reeves took on Agent Smith and realised he was The *One*. 'Chuuups, *bannuhs*, the clue is in the anagram!' she'd shout at the screen every time she watched it. The rumble of the approaching train and a piece of paper whipped up by the changing air completed the cinematic look. But there were no scary agents and Audrey stepped onto the carriage. It was filled with college students weighed down by bulging backpacks, nurses, medics in scrubs and all the other regular folk who travelled the Marta after a long hard day at work. A wannabe rapper at the other end of the carriage completed the picture; his lack of skill made it clear why he was rapping here and not at a nightclub. Audrey zoned out the *bitch, nigga, ho, bitch, nigga, ho* nothing-nouns on repeat. She yearned for the time when rap was a call to resistance, when it was about fighting the system rather than pandering to it.

Stepping out at her station, she headed up the escalators and through the ticket barriers and was about to cross the bridge back to Melody's apartment when a woman in an oversized coat caught her attention. Young, dreadlocked with a battered suitcase and a pickney 'pon her back and another in a beat-up ol' buggy. At first Audrey assumed she was waiting for someone; it was past 10 o'clock – why else would this woman and her two kids be at the Marta?

Audrey continued to walk slowly towards the bridge, but something tugged at her conscience. She stopped and turned around, in just the same moment that the woman turned to gaze at her.

Same jumbie eyes as that man last week, she thought to herself. Same far away, I'm not-really-here kinda stare and somehow, she found herself walking back towards the woman and her children.

'Hi miss, you waiting on someone?'

The woman continued to stare but said nothing.

'Are you OK…?'

The toddler looked up from the buggy warily, the baby in the sling slept on. Audrey thought they looked a little maaga but better than their mother. She was a shivering shadow waiting to expire.

Audrey reached out to touch the woman's shoulder gently and just like with the addict, she felt herself falling into the woman's past. The high school sweetheart who was the jock but soft and loving on the inside until he went on and signed up to pay for his college education and came home with PTSD and hoorah stories of *kill the corpses, eat the babies*, until he couldn't be calmed through his nightmares anymore and started taking his pain out on this woman with his fists; two kids later, one nearly lost when he threw her down the stairs five months into her second pregnancy; how the pain and fear made her pick up a bottle of wine and drink too much until wine was not enough and hard liquor was the only thing that would numb the pain in her heart and her bruises.

Audrey felt sick to she stomach. She let go of the woman and turned, bent over double and vomited. She felt the woman's hand on her back, rubbing in slow calming circles. Audrey wiped her mouth and stood up, tears in both their eyes. They looked at each other; embraced. She took the woman and her two babies to the only place still open – the nearest Waffle House, a crazy name for a diner that did very little in the way of waffles, but whose stark fluorescent interior remained a fried food beacon in the midnight hour. The woman placed her baby's mouth on her breast and fed her the first milk untainted with alcohol that she had ever tasted.

'H… how… how… what did you do?' the woman asked directly.

'I'm not really sure, I… it's only happened once before. I wasn't even sure it was me.'

'Ma'am, God bless you, it's definitely you… you laid hands on me and it all left me…. the pain… the fear… the… the… I don't know I just feel like brand *new*!'

They sat talking for a while. Audrey was relieved to find out that this still frail young woman, named Hope, had a mother to go to, who she'd been too afraid to reach out to because of the drinking. Audrey put them all in an Uber and then headed back to Melody's. It was close to midnight and luckily her daughter was fast asleep, with no awkward questions.

Audrey slept for a long time and felt weak and a little feverish but nowhere near as bad as the first time. She knew it was her mission now. She would go down to the train stations, the places near the Publix supermarkets where the lost and homeless congregated, go by the hospitals where the sick filled the nearby streets and she would talk and laugh with these people who once had hopes and dreams that had been lost, stolen, or knocked out of them by others, by the system, by mistakes they couldn't take back.

She could never manage more than one at a time. Afterwards, she'd burn a little fever and take to her bed with nara for a couple days. But wha fuh do; she had the power to suck out all that past pain.

Melody commented on how thin she was getting, how her curves turning to straight lines and the fat in she cheeks to loose skin and wrinkles. She laughed a little and said her mother was beginning to look like Ol' Higue, but she also made Audrey cookup, jus the way she liked it with plenty, plenty wiri-wiri pepper.

Sometime soon the bad-talk began an' story pass fuh true. About the bruk up ol' woman on the Marta, some say she wukkin obeah, some ol' Southerners saying *boohag* on the prowl, sucking the blood straight out a homeless man's lolee til he dead-dead! But still, Audrey continued. She knew who and what she was: a healer. She didn't pay no mind to these wutless stories, always seeing powerful Black women with a bad eye.

She was star gyal in her own story and now she could feel the fever like sizzling cassareep between she thighs.

FIRST FLIGHT

Ioney Smallhorne

2014 The Nest

When she first moved into her attic bedsit, Fei began placing two deep trays of fresh water, each on a wooden fold-up chair, under the sprawling bay tree. It felt right, an offering to her new neighbours. The bay tree, which grew in between gardens, didn't belong to anyone, which was probably why it had been left to grow to its imposing girth, stretching up alongside Fei's new rental.

Her windows were usually cracked open, the breeze invited to roam and rattle the odd things she'd collected over the years; all broken or disregarded by their owners. Seashells, bicycle chains, thread, broken earrings, old cutlery, belt buckles, copper pipe, beads, keys, and padlocks. Fei up-cycled them into new jewellery pieces and sold them online. She hung them on a tool storage rack, like one you'd find in a mechanic's workshop, now fixed onto her bedsit wall.

Fei stood back to examine her new abode: everything about it screamed 'childless and single'. The landlord would have a fit with all the holes drilled into the wall. She made the place homely by draping fairy lights and suspending hanging baskets filled with plants from the ceiling.

From her kitchenette window, she watched birds perching on the rim of the brimming water trays to drink and rest. She was hooked. Every other day since, she'd poured fresh water and spent a couple minutes each breakfast and again in the evening watching the birds from her kitchen window drink and bathe. It dampened the constant scream of loneliness.

September 2017 The Down
Two fluffy feathers – the type you find growing on a baby bird – had sprouted just above Fei's taut solar plexus. Raw sienna-brown feathers, speckled with umber, as if an extension of her skin. She'd always hated that part of her body, described fondly as 'chicken-back chest' by her mother. She found herself rubbing the feathers for comfort, called in sick at work and locked herself in her room for a few days. The two feathers had emerged a week after the man she was in love with sent a text message to say that his long-term girlfriend was pregnant. He didn't want their child to grow up without a dad, like he had. It had been fun, he said, and he'd always care deeply for Fei, but it just couldn't work now. He was sorry.

Fei wondered what he was sorry for. Getting involved with her? For telling her he needed her in his life? For making her feel safe? For dating a Black woman?

Fei had met Ryan three years before at the college where they'd both been newly employed, Fei as a teaching assistant, Ryan as a carpentry lecturer. She was double over-qualified for the job but needed something to cover the bills.

The classroom had filled with an electric current the first time they met, and it had connected them on a broken circuit ever since. A switch flicked on when Ryan was close. They got to know each other during silent moments in class, lingering at the end while the students were leaving, telling each other snippets of their lives. How she enjoyed free swimming in rivers in summer; exchanging the Italian words they both knew; the type of dogs they liked; how he had earned his scars; and where she planned to get tattooed. Fei would catch him considering her thighs while she helped students measure and mark out timber. He'd blush when she spoke into his eyes and the air thickened.

Months later, Fei found out that Ryan had moved to this city and gotten this lecturing job to live with a girlfriend he'd never mentioned, and to pay towards the mortgage for the house they shared.

The next academic year she was timetabled for a different class.

She was relieved; thought she'd soon forget about him, but instead they exchanged daily WhatsApp messages, squeezed words into corridors as they headed to separate classes, stole moments in the car park to talk at the end of the day. When one of their students was nominated for an award, they both attended the ceremony and sat at the same table. She saw Ryan fixated on her lips as she ate the strawberries she'd piled on her plate from the free buffet. After, they found a dimly lit corner in a bar neither of them knew the name of where Fei stroked the tattoo on Ryan's arm, he pressed his nose into the curve of her neck, and they sat like that, silent for hours, before he went home to his girlfriend.

Fei accepted nothing could happen; she actually admired Ryan's commitment. He had backbone. But there was one loose wire, active, carrying a small voltage. What would it be like to taste him? To lie spooned by him, listening to early morning bird song? To feel his beard bristle against her cheek? It wasn't long before she was consumed by him again. And she knew he felt this too, that there was a part of him that longed for her. She'd find some excuse to message him – to say she'd seen an ex-student getting arrested – or he would give her running commentary about staff feuds, anything to keep the current flowing. She was the sand, and he was the sea washing over her, running away, but compelled by something magnetic to return. She listed all the reasons it couldn't work: he was in a long-term relationship with a blonde from his hometown, begun from school, those type of relationships were always special. He was white, *ginger* white, small city white, she was a conscious Black woman – how could these two pieces fit together? But it was the friction of that question that sparked the current that rampaged through their bodies.

That one last text message killed the dream. An egg falling from a nest, smashing onto concrete. Her body felt cold. Fei stroked the feathers growing from just above her solar plexus where she imagined her heart moulted. Ryan had blocked her from all of his social media accounts. He sent the text on the Sunday just before the start of a new academic year. When Fei arrived at work on Tuesday, she discovered he'd taken a new job at another college. His desk was cleared, awaiting a new member of staff. Colleagues had known for weeks that Ryan was leaving.

Before long, soft, natal, downy feathers covered Fei's breasts, rib cage and stomach. The feathers didn't grow on her upper chest. She could still wear a low-cut top without anyone seeing the transformation taking place below.

November 2017, The Semi Plume
Fei wasn't ready for *his* face. A photo of Ezra appeared on the local news bulletin, after cutaways of bouquets tied to lamp posts. Vox-pops with local residents, weeping like the last murder; interviews with community activists leading boxing classes, opening music studios or dance groups to save young people from dying on pavements next to chewing gum, spat out, flattened underfoot.

Ezra's grandma, Sister Blossom, was Fei's mum's good-good church sistren. As a chubby, bright-eyed boy, his hair greased and cane-rowed, Ezra would carry his grandma's tambourine, shaking it all the way to church in the back seat of Fei's mum's car while the two sistren fixed the world's woes. On the car journey back, he'd sing a hymn from children's church, *This Little Light of Mine*, a firm favourite. Sister Blossom and Fei's mum responded with vocal flourishes and halleluiah ad-libs until the car pulled up outside his front door. Ten years later, at seventeen, he lay dead two streets away from home. A 'friend' had called his phone and he'd responded, telling his mum he'd be back soon. Knife wounds made holes in his body, his little light escaping.

The alleged murderer was Isaiah, a boy Fei first met when *she* was one of those community activists trying to save lives with art. Hoping a paint brush and spray cans would somehow help the teenagers from her ends colour a future. Isaiah was small for his age, didn't say much but came to every after-school session, maybe because Fei provided snacks or maybe because there was no one at home when he finished school. Along with seven other young people, Fei and Isaiah designed and painted a community mural on the wall of a boxing gym: a flock of birds, jewelled with colour. Children's painted handprints formed their wings, soaring over words Fei had adapted from a Muhammad Ali quote and a Tibetan proverb: *A child with no ambition has no wings.*

Fei remembered Isaiah's cheeky grin when he realised his painted handprints would leave a lasting mark, one for his whole community to see. She remembered the pride filling his chest, when he stood next to the finished mural for a local newspaper photo. She remembered the faint dimple in his right cheek when Fei said she'd stand next to him since no one from home came to the unveiling.

Both Isaiah and Ezra attended the college where Fei worked. In the staff room, teachers spoke about the news as if relaying the story of a film in which they played a supporting role. Fei imagined them in the pub, wearing the story like a medal. Most of them lived in the shires where Black people were only seen on TV.

By November the feathers on her torso had formed central shafts, or rachises but they were still fluffy at the base. It was easy to assume that Fei had just put on a few pounds, her figure filling.

May 2018, The Contour Feathers

Spring mornings bloomed magenta and turmeric, the wood pigeons calling coo-coo-co, coo-coo-co, their sound flowing from chimney pots, branches, and roof tops. Fei imagined what it would be like to stand on a roof top and advertise for a mate, her intentions carried by the wind.

For her 37th birthday, Fei's doctor informed her she had fibroids, which explained her heavy periods. The doctor said she'd probably find it hard to conceive. Fei had to hold back the laughter. Was tempted to say, 'No shit Sherlock, I've got feathers growing out of my tits!'

Her bestie, Roxy, was working away in Dubai teaching 'di Babylon language, tax free'. They Zoomed as they did every coupla weeks, but this time they drank rum instead of wine for Fei's 37th. Roxy would be 40 soon. A writer, she'd been struggling to earn in England so put her art on the back burner to eat. Educated, witty as fuck, travelled, beautiful, Black, single. She had plenty of offers from stinking rich White and Arab married men who wanted a taste of the dark side on the odd weekend. Whenever either of them had such an offer (Roxy had more than Fei), they would refashion *Star Wars* quotes in their best Darth Vader voices: 'You underestimate the power of the dark backside', or 'The dark side of the force is a pathway to many abilities, Luke,' or 'The more you deny that you want a dark backside, the more power it has over you.' Roxy and Fei would then buss-up with laughter and pour more alcohol. Roxy promised to design T-shirts with these quotes printed on them and give them away free to single Black women, just to pep up their day.

Roxy was the only person Fei told about Ryan, from the very first day they met in the classroom. Roxy knew better than to tease Fei with any Darth Vader quotes on this one. Ryan wasn't stinking rich, and she really hoped it was a genuine t'ing. Roxy listened to the 'relationship' develop over the years and refrained from telling Fei to move on because she knew Fei couldn't do that.

Roxy knew the pangs of loneliness demanded attention.

When Roxy got a text from Fei asking if they could Zoom a week after her birthday, she knew something was wrong. Fei didn't tell Roxy about her feathers, but she did tell her about a colleague who had received an email from Ryan and that the email had a photo attached of his new baby. How the colleague had called Fei over to see, how stones had lodged in her throat, how hard it had been to breathe. Ryan, with one arm out-stretched, balancing the camera, the other nestled around his girlfriend, as if she was a harvest mouse. Fei didn't recall ever being that soft or trusting a man's arms around her, the baby, wrapped snug.

Roxy didn't have anything to lighten the mood.

Magpies begin to use Fei's windowsill as a perch, sometimes tapping on the glass with their beaks as if they have an urgent message or as if they are the police, responding to a reported emergency.

September 2018, The Tail Feathers
Selena, Fei's mum, in her early sixties, had suffered a few ailments

– the main one being arthritis in her hands and feet. She still attended weekly Aqua Fit classes with her neighbour, Magda. But then a colony of sea urchins had settled in the bottom of Selena's stomach. The sea urchins, ravenous, ate her from the inside within months, leaving a withered shell. The doctors couldn't help.

Fei moved in with her mum to provide care in her final months. Her mum often found different ways to say the same thing: 'You need a better paid job' often manifested as 'You're too qualified to be a teaching assistant' or 'I know you're worth more.' Which was probably why she'd chosen to spell her daughter's name Fei instead of the more common Fay. People often expected Fei to be East Asian after reading her name. Selena's biological dad was actually Chinese-Jamaican, a fact that was rarely spoken about, as she'd never met him. Most White people in Nottingham thought Jamaicans were always Black and Selina identified as Black because that was what she knew. So, the Chinese bloodline was silenced, except through Fei's name.

Initially, Fei thought the six pairs of tail feathers were black. But when the light shone through her bedsit window, a spectrum of bejewelled greens and purples ignited. Her skin itched when their heads broke through and within weeks they were fully formed.

February 2019. Formation of the Remiges
Earlier in the day, public transport links into the city stood still. Commuters pulled over, turned off engines, called in to cancel appointments. Around five hundred white men and women marched along the main arteries leading to Nottingham's heart. All with a purposeful stare. Many draped the St. George's flag around their shoulders. Others wore nothing but jeans and their self-entitlement. White blood cells, protecting their country from infection. Flowing from the North along Mansfield Road, from the West along Ilkeston and Derby Road, East through Burton-on-Trent along Carlton

Road and South through West Bridgeford along London Road. Congregating for three hours, like inflammation around a joint, behind the Brian Clough statue that ordinarily marked Speaker's Corner.

Media outlets were issued a statement that declared the march was a 'display of organised peace' and that 'historically, the right wing are painted as disorderly' so they wanted to 'exhibit a respect for law and order in a time when the country is overrun with chaos and immigrants.' Right wing parties had been growing in size and momentum, what with Brexit and the liberals who swore blind they didn't see colour.

Fei had planned to cross town to attend an Arts and Craft market to sell her jewellery but decided against it when the radio news reported the march. She'd begun to design necklaces and earrings using feathers she plucked from her own down. She threaded them alongside keys and beads and other odd things she'd hoarded. She called this range 'The Magpie Collection'. The cheapest items were £65. She thought she'd up the price since she'd actually *grown* the feathers and plucked them out of her skin.

She was granted compassionate leave from work after the death of her mother, and when she returned to the college, the management allowed her to cut her hours down to two days a week. She had less reason to venture outdoors these days. She sold most of her jewellery online. She only went out in the daylight to post orders and to fill the trays of water for the birds.

The right wing march had reminded her why it was best to stay indoors.

Fei would go out at night to mail her jewellery orders, and then often continued her walk through the resting city, greeted by foxes and stray cats. On this particular night something made her think of Ryan. She remembered meeting him on these late-night walks. He'd bring his dog, probably his excuse to leave the house. They'd walk hand in hand, talk about nothing important, kiss. On occasion, he would rub her clit then taste his fingers afterwards, tell her how he longed for her. The night gave their relationship safety, privacy, and the space to pretend it was real. The night was an archive holding her memories of him. Re-walking the old routes was like rubbing her wounds, hearing his voice again. Maybe this was why she didn't hear the men approach, maybe her ears were filled with what she wanted to hear. There were seven of them. They swooped down silent, like owl wings. One wore a Salvador Dali Mask, another had what looked like blackface, others simple mouth-coverings, muffling their grunts. The smell of alcohol and sweat. They rubbed dirt in her face; steel-toe capped boots purpled her body; they pinned her to the floor; she heard the unzipping of their jeans. But one voice broke the silence, a primitive call, or maybe just 'enough' or 'stop'. A man wearing a horned-ghoul mask. Fei thinks for a second that she recognises the voice: an ex-student called Jones? The masked men stop. The horned ghoul pushes them back; she thinks it has stopped. 'Dirty Black slut, this how you earn a living? Out at night trying to take honest white men away from their wives?' Drunken and slurred, the ghoul kicks her again and again. He spits on her, mutters 'Run!' Fei thinks she hears the word 'Miss' after the word 'run'. His predatory stare offered nothing else.

The next day she goes to work as usual. Tries to carry her cup of tea back to her desk without grimacing. The cup shatters on the floor. Fei has no control over the tears or her jerking body. The police are called after she tells her boss an edited version of what happened. She's reluctant to tell the whole truth, scared that they will need to do a physical examination and shame kicks at her. The voice of the horned-ghoul or Jones replaying on loop. 'Out at night trying to lure…' Hadn't she lured Ryan? Did he know, did Jones know?

Fei takes sick leave from work but has no intention of returning. Her wounds from the ordeal generate thicker, longer feathers, designed for flight.

March 2019, Leaving the Nest

Fei stood in front of the full-length mirror in the two-star Cottage Garden Guest House, naked. It was 5am and there was a burning promise on the horizon. It would be easy to mistake the feathers for some 1920's couture evening dress, she thought. She raised her arms to unveil her fully formed wings. She imagined her feathers as an oil slick of iridescence against the Pembrokeshire skyline.

Her mum had brought her to the Southern Welsh coast a couple of times as a child during the summer holidays. Summer of 1988, their ageing Ford Sierra had died, not even a cough on ignition. Fei remembers the bonnet smoking and being quite comfortable with the idea of being stranded here. They'd spent the extra day exploring Marloes Sands. Fei remembers learning how to spell the word 'peninsula', the excitement of being surrounded by an unruly sea, the prospect of only a thin neck of land connecting them to their ordinary lives. The car Fei hired had got her here without any complications and was perfectly capable of the journey back.

Maureen, the guesthouse owner, a spritely old lady with a cauliflower head, was surprised at a guest so early in the season; more so on discovering Fei's lack of luggage. She had her bike, which Maureen suggested she keep next to a cherry tree in the back garden. The Cottage Garden was just that, a quaint little cottage garden encircling a house that accepted guests, its unique selling point that each of the three bathrooms had a shower.

Fei concealed her feathers with an extra-large, olive green hoodie and grey harem jogging bottoms. Her unchained bike leaned against the blooming cherry tree, waiting.

It was a 50-minute cycle – past the crumbling castle, sinking into the terrain, past the Fisherman's Church, past the creeping heather, the yellow wagtails mingling between cows – before Fei reached Saint Anne's Head, stretching out into the Atlantic, the horizon's promise quickly unravelling. The red sandstone cliffs stand like a diary recording the earth's faults. The patroness saint of unmarried child-less women and sailors keeps watch over them, assisted by mating pairs of razorbills, the kind of birds that encourage their young to abandon the nest and launch off the cliff-edge before they can fly.

Fei strips: there are no human eyes to judge. She speeds toward the horizon. Muscles in her thighs blaze. She peddles, releasing her grip on the handlebars until her wings lift her and for a moment, she does fly.

The razorbills accompany her out to sea.

SECTION THREE

GLIMMER

DIGITAL

Patience Agbabi

Minutes after she gave birth in The White Room, the texts beeped and buzzed on the looma, bright pink neon on grey. *Well done! Do they look like you? Welcome2theWorldBabyK.* But not a word from J-Myer.

I-Cara cradles the looma in her left hand as she scrolls. Messages from folks she's never met, from all coordinates. The baby's asleep but its eyes are open, on standby. It stopped crying when the birth-bots swaddled it.

It? Baby's a girl-child. I-Cara will choose a name to replace the number when her child reveals who she is. As soon as baby drew breath, they tagged her ankles: K-23. 23rd citizen, Generation K.

K-23 is bronze like her mother with eyes so dark blue you can't see the pupils. All arms and legs till they bound her in cotton like a mummy. When she cries, I-Cara's reminded of her late mother, dying but fighting.

The baby has fists like a boxer, like she wants to beat the crap out of the world. Like she didn't choose to be born. Birth-Bot-12 is a talker, says K's hands will straighten out with time. That it's nothing to fret on.

But I-Cara longs to cover her daughter's hands with scratch mitts like they did in the old days to stop them clawing their faces. She

imagines the tiny white gloves hiding her baby's clenched imper-
fection and her dead mother sat at the bedside, eyes narrowed,
She's perfect. Remove the gloves!

I-Cara presses the yellow *I want the toilet* button. Scared to stand
up on her own in case her insides spill out onto the bright white
floor. She feels like she's been run over by a plane-train, tramlines
etched in her back.

Birth-Bot-12 emotes, *You're doing well, I-Cara,* waits outside
while she pees pink champagne into the bowl, leaving the door
ajar as instructed. The bot supports her back to the bed. *You can
bathe later.*

They haven't cleaned the baby yet. Her mop of black hair is gelled
with blood. She smells of salted meat. But there's something else,
freshly laundered sheets. I-Cara inhales her. Pure joy.

The clock on the wall says: 06.02. 28°. It's getting light but I-
Cara's energy is dipping like dusk from the labour. When I-Cara
was born, her temperature flew so high they plunged her into an
ice bath. She was named for Icarus.

This baby's a miracle. The love-in with J-Myer was brief, more
a meeting of minds than of bodies. J's rarely spoke to each other,
they texted, and never to I's. Thought their subcutaneous implant
made them superior.

J-Myer was different. She loved his blue-black skin scattered
with freckles like stars in the night sky and the quaver in his voice
when he spoke of the planet, wishing there were no people on it.

The earth created us, he'd say. *Earth is the centre of the universe, not us.*
He hated humans. *For breeding technology without the skills to raise it.*
Hated

his implant, how it kept track of his life, his heartbeat; how the system kept track of him from birth to death. *J's are bots, I-Cara, machines. Bots can't make babies.*

When they coupled, bronze on blue-black, he cried for the human contact and she knew, even then, something had happened inside her she couldn't yet name, something different.

They split when he caught her texting. Never knew she had a phone, that she slept with it nightly, called it the looma, the family heirloom stretching back to the great great great Z-Gemina.

Texting a friend in Peru about chocolate. She told him they'd never met but the friend knew about chocolate from the old days. *I don't give a damn about chocolate*, he said. *I thought you were different.*

By the time she confirmed the with-child, he'd switched himself off. She doesn't know where he is in the world, how long he'll survive in that state, mentally, physically. I's are tougher than J's.

Who's the father? Birth-Bot-12 had asked. I-Cara clammed up, *I don't know*. The room was a white box apart from the tempo-temperature clock. The birth-bot laughed, *That's what Mary said. Immaculate conception!*

J-Myer. She refuses to speak his name aloud, tell the world that she crossed the divide, now he's gone. Doesn't want to hear them say, *I told you so. Generations don't mix.*

Her heart is a big, echoey room with someone beating a drum in it. She wishes the baby could talk. She knows it takes six weeks for a baby to smile. She doesn't know how she's going to last six weeks.

The looma is fuchsia pink, studded with fake diamonds. It's cradled in I-Cara's left hand, still beeping and buzzing, refusing to settle. *ase; jadfjl; kjl;.* Text from an unknown number. Someone's child grabbed their phone. Baby

K-23 starts screaming. I-Cara freezes at the sound. She tries to sit up in bed but feels a gush of blood on her pad. The baby is punching the air in its glass cradle but the screams might shatter it.

It takes Birth-Bot-12 a minute to arrive. Already, the baby's calmed down. Only the legs are thrashing. The birth-bot hands the baby to I-Cara. She smells like grilled marshmallow. I-Cara feels an avalanche of love.

I-Cara wants to hold the baby's hand. *Her* baby's hand. She wants to feel the tiny fist lock around her forefinger. But her baby's hand is a clenched fist. When she touches it, K-23 screams.

I-Cara wants to go home because this room is a bright white box with a digital clock whereas home is soft and sparkly and subterranean. She made spinach and pumpkin soup in cartons and put them in the freezer.

Nothing wrong with her baby's hands. It's quite usual for newborns to surface bunched up. They spend nine months squashed inside the womb. When they come out, it takes time to open up to the world; she learnt this from the looma.

The looma needs charging. I-Cara presses the green button and the birth-bot appears by her side. *Ready for that bath, are we?* I-Cara feels tearful about her phone being charged in the office. She wants to feel connected.

The bath is a baptism. They've added pink birth salts and though there's no smell, I-Cara imagines roses. Her belly skin is a punctured balloon. The water cools down too quickly and the birth-bot helps her get out.

Your phone's a bit of a handful, they say as they towel her down. There are streaks of pink on the white towel. I-Cara puts on her knickers with a fresh pad. She is clean but emptied, bereft.

The looma has moved half-way across the office table like an overactive washing-machine. Already, it's landed twice on the floor. Nothing is broken, nothing the eye can see.

When will her hands open up? I-Cara asks. The birth-bot emotes, programmed with the right answer. *In time*, they say. The clock is flashing on the wall. It is 08.22. 29°.

The toast is delicious, the everydayness of cold butter on hot, crispy bread that I-Cara needs. The pleasure and comfort of chewing. She stretches, a flower that's just been watered.

K-23 is asleep but her dark blue eyes are still open, doll-like. Her tiny chest is rising and falling; it begins to vibrate. She snuffles, whimpers then screams. I-Cara presses the red emergency button.

We need to keep her under observation, the birth-bot says. K-23 is transferred to a different glass case. I-Cara begins to cry. But Neo-Doc-7, a bald person with horn-rimmed glasses, assures her all will be well.

The baby is wilting. The baby's connected to multicoloured tubes and her eyes are closing. She doesn't even cry when I-Cara strokes her clenched fists. I-Cara wants the toilet but can't leave her baby. She won't leave her baby.

The birth-bot gives her phone back. *asdfajlk;jl. asdfasd.; lkjljml. asdafda.k; ljkljkljkjljkjlkj. asdfasfd.* No other messages. I-Cara cradles the looma in her left hand and taps out a message *Who are you?*

She strokes the baby's head with her free hand. The monitor shows regular spikes. There are too many tubes. K's eyelids flicker and stare up at her. The neo-doc checks the monitor.

K-23's hands are opening like someone smiling for the first time. The movement is in slow motion but I-Cara can feel the loosening, the miracle of flesh exposing itself to the light. The smell of roses.

She looks at her baby's tiny hands as if looking at hands for the first time. The fingers are short, bent and stumpy, palms the size of a mobile screen, covered with a thick crust of mucus. I-Cara weeps.

The neo-doc is explaining they'll keep her and the baby in hospital overnight for observation but they should be able to go home tomorrow. I-Cara's not listening. She's looking at her baby's hands.

She lowers her forefinger into the tiny glass cot, to the middle of K-23's right palm. Her baby's fingers fold into a tight grip. I-Cara's heart is thumping in her chest.

Her baby's palm is an old woman's palm. It's hard and bumpy, as if embedded with fingernails. But I-Cara's baby has fingernails, four fingers and two thumbs. Everything's where it should be.

She needs to pee. But when she tries to leave, the baby screams. The neo-doc is surprised. *They don't form attachments this early*, they say, adjusting their glasses. I-Cara leaves but can't wait to get back.

So this is what it feels like to fall in love. To crave the return. And now she could stand here forever, in this tiny room with its beeping, buzzing machines, K-23 holding onto her forefinger like a clam.

Her other hand cradles the fuchsia, diamond-studded looma that has been quiet for the last half hour, the virtual friends returning to their virtual lives.

When you go, the birth-bot emotes, *it's like she's having a boxing match with thin air*. I-Cara feels guilty for having to pee on the hour. But K-23 is going to pull through.

Only now does she allow the façade to slip. Her baby's not going to die. She can ditch the capable-I's-are-invincible act. They give her some tablets that will wear off before the milk kicks in.

She's stroking her baby's damp curls. The baby bends her own forefinger and taps her tiny opposite palm. Tap-tap-tap. Tap tap tap tap tap. Like an SOS in the olden days.

I-Cara feels the looma buzz in her hand. A message pops up on the screen. *hhh. nnnnn*. As if to acknowledge, *This is who I am*. I-Cara looks into K-23's dark blue pebble eyes, her daughter, the future.

CHILDREN'S STORY

Koye Oyedeji

1

It starts with Kim. Even though Emeka is expecting her, he is still startled by her presence in his bedroom; the way she steps around the strewn clothes like a guest, but then sits on his bed as if she's done it a hundred times before, parking her jacksie on the Thundercats quilt cover that was, up until this moment, his pride and joy. Now he's just embarrassed by it. 'You alright?' she says, but he doesn't reply. He's eyeing the straight hair, pulled into a bun, the hooped earrings, the loose Coca-Cola rugby shirt that hangs off her body, the snatch of a bra-strap, the tight pull of the laces on her Hi-Tec Squash. He's thinking about her outside of these things, or maybe in just some of these things: in the shirt, but without the jeans, in the jeans but without the shirt. He's thinking about all the things he's seen in the crumpled and tattered magazines he has pulled from beneath his brother's mattress, all the theatrical squeals and thrills on VHS cassettes.

We're doing it here, his older brother had announced, just half an hour ago. But Emeka hadn't let that actually sink in. Until now. His brother Junior had been errant even before their father left, but now Junior was just setting records and popularising clichés. Making history. Taking prisoners. Raising hell. Emeka never hears any of it first-hand, but there are stories – hand-me-downs from the older boys in the area, mostly delivered with disbelief and wonder. *I heard your brother took Patience up to Gilbert's flat, while Gilbert's mum was in hospital overnight for knee surgery. Is it true Junior jooked Aida on the roof of the Wendover building?* Emeka doesn't know.

He's only ever witnessed the epilogues – fights between Junior and other boys, boys recently jilted; boys with bruised egos who'd done the jilting and regretted it in Junior's wake.

Today is about as involved as Emeka has ever been in his brother's affairs. He has done as instructed, as *ordered* – brought the VCR into his bedroom, which doubles as a guest room ever since their mother had them move the old bed in from her room. Junior said he was going to need it, Emeka's bed, the bed their parents once slept on. 'A *double* bed,' said Junior, to be clear and cruel. He was coming back, first with Kim and then with Gilbert and when he returned the second time, he wanted Emeka to disappear – from the bedroom, from the flat and maybe, if Emeka was feeling generous, from his life altogether. 'Make like a ghost,' Junior said. And though it isn't yet ghost time, Emeka is startled nonetheless at Kim turning up. The first girl to ever set foot in his bedroom, and it shows.

She crosses her legs, smoothens out the creases to either side of her, and high-arches an eyebrow at the single-sized quilt on a double bed. Then she gives him a look, as if to say *wot are you starin' at me for?* To be certain he understands, she says: 'Wot you starin' at me for?'

He quails, words escape him. Movement too. You'd think she was holding a shotgun to him. But if he cannot be confident, then perhaps he can be kind: a superhero in waiting. He considers what's at stake. Junior will return with Gilbert. That's the plan. And though he will be kicked out of his own bedroom, and will not witness these things, he knows what they are. They will try to convince Kim to *do it* with the both of them. He knows what *doing it* means. He's twelve, not two. Old enough to use the word 'convince'; to know that Kim is unaware of Junior's designs, that it's likely she wouldn't be there if she was. Patience has since moved off the estate – sent home to live with her dad in Ghana. He wouldn't want Kim to feel as if she needed to leave the area. She doesn't have to. He can bring the Superman vibrations. Save her from a disaster. Drag her from the rails. Avoid the oncoming train.

As simple as. Open your mouth. Tell her it's a lie. Tell her that there is no pirate copy of *Teenage Mutant Ninja Turtles*. Tell her that Junior is on his way back with Gilbert. Tell her: Kim, you need to leave, to get out while you can and go quickly. Now.

'Do you have a girlfriend?' she asks, jolting him from his thoughts. If Junior were there, he would answer for Emeka. He'd say 'Him? Of course not.' And it would be even worse if Gilbert were there too because Junior sometimes punches Emeka on the arm, sometimes in the back, just for Gilbert's pleasure. His brother often tells Gilbert – tells whoever will listen – that Emeka is gay or going to be a virgin for life. His laughter is just a little too loud, a little too hearty.

'I reckoned not,' Kim says. 'The way you gaping.' She crosses her legs and shakes her head. Emeka looks away and busies himself, swiping at the dust on the VCR. It's a prop, and those are his fingerprints in the dust, and that makes him some kind of co-conspirator. But Kim is a big girl, and she is being rude. Blunt. Too blunt, so he'll say nothing. She doesn't deserve his help. Besides, she's only into Junior because of all the gear he has – the Wallabies, the Chippie chinos, a Walkman. But acting flash shouldn't matter. So there you go. He will mind his own business, thank you.

She points to his stack of comics wrapped in protective plastic and white backboards. 'What's this?' she says. He sighs because the quilt cover is enough to feel embarrassed about, and now there's this too. 'My comic book collection,' he mutters, when she asks again. She tells him her brother also collects them. 'Yeah?' he says, because Justin is a good friend, because he knows this already, but doesn't know what else to say. 'Yeah,' she replies. 'Yeah,' he says and nods. 'Yeah,' she says, and smiles, her thin lips pressed together. Thin lips, he thinks, are no kind of lips for a Black girl, but it is a great smile, and he decides that he would love her lips, if he was given permission to. 'You remind me of my younger brother,' she says. 'Yeah?' he says. 'Yeah,' she says, 'But it's not as though…'. She trails off. 'What?' he says, he wants her to finish the sentence. 'Don't worry about it,' she says, shaking her head. He nods, and he's still nodding even though the moment has long since passed. She makes a face at him, crossing her eyes and tucking her tongue into the pocket of skin beneath her bottom lip. They laugh and the laughter lingers long after they've both grown quiet.

He should tell her, he thinks.

He can feel her eyes on him, but he keeps his head down and his fingers clasped together, and he is silent. He doesn't know how long he remains this way, but it feels like years pass before he hears the sound of the front door open. He gets up and leaves the room.

2

He was not in the room when whatever happened, happened. This is why, in the beginning, when he first feels the symptoms of Yen-possession, Emeka is convinced that it's a case of mistaken identity, that even a Yen can make mistakes. He cannot get over the overwhelming feeling that he is being watched. He cannot put a finger on the source of guilt he is experiencing nor shake the sense that the guilt has a pair of legs and is following him. Classic textbook symptoms of Yen-possession. He puts aside tube TV, his annuals and his Texas Instruments. He spends the hours after school in the local library, trying to find out whatever he can about the Yen.

From what he looks up, reads, and hears, no one can agree on what the Yen is. He finds books in the adult section, on the science shelves with text that he finds confusing and beyond him. His science teacher isn't much help either, turning his question into a five-minute lecture on psychic phenomena, quantum mechanics and how so much of the world around us can only be explained through hypothesis. He already knows what a lot of other pupils at school think, from those who believe it's just hallucinations to those who reckon it's something that happens when you smoke too much puff. Most of the girls just call it Boy Crazy; they expect every boy at some point to lose their minds.

He turns to the men who are left in his life. He starts with

Uncle Festus, since he's the only person who still visits now that their dad has left. Festus is an a friend of their father's and not an uncle in the true avuncular sense, but who, like every Nigerian man old enough to be their uncle, is called that out of deference. When Emeka asks him to explain the Yen to him, Uncle Festus says that he is too young to talk about such things. So Emeka asks his Sunday School teacher, Uncle Lawal, who lowers his voice to whisper that the Yen is the living embodiment of sin. Mr Zagadou, his Saturday school leader, tells him that Yen is Yin, and leaves it at that, as if he's meant to know what that means.

There are things that he has always known about the Yen, the noise that's been around for as long as he can remember: movies and TV shows that portray the Yen as everything from angels to affirmation of our darkest urges. Pop songs that describe what it's like to fall in love with a Yen. Stand-up comedians claiming that the Yen is mostly found in females. Classified ads and flyers from Diviners promising exorcism at a small, reasonable fee. Newspaper reports of women who retaliated against abusive husbands, quotes from court testimony, women who report the feeling they've "lost something", others using the word "taken". Graffiti slogans on the walls, anarchists pronouncements. EMBRACE THE YEN. THE YEN LIVES IN US ALL. Cult leaders proclaiming that their congregation has freely given their Yen to men, an offering of sorts. Survivalists arguing how hard it is to imagine a man freely accepting the presence of a Yen. The end is nigh, they say. Every year is the final year. There'll be one Yen to rule over all the others.

Still, Emeka is a believer, despite all the conflicting things he hears and reads. He feels what he feels. The presence of a Yen. He is convinced that it is Kim's. That it will follow him until it gets what it wants. He doesn't know what it wants. And this is what scares him most of all. This and the question as to whether he is being punished, that he might have done something that deserves punishment.

He runs to the market on the weekend, where he knows he'll find Yungman – a firm fixture in and around the area, part tramp, part mad man, part soothsayer. The word on the street is that he has been Yen-possessed for years. He finds him near the mouth of the market, standing on the street corner in stained jeans and a well-worn duffel coat. His hair is as picky as hell, and his teeth are a highlighter yellow that flash in the daylight. Emeka draws close to him. Close enough to hear him and hearing enough to want to step closer and hear it all. Yungman is warning the world that it will continue to suffer as long as men take from women what they are supposed to keep for themselves. He says the neighbourhood has gone to rot. How there are too many Yen running about, too many lady souls smashed to pieces.

Yungman locks eyes with Emeka and stops. They're close enough for Emeka to reach out and touch, and he feels the urge to do so, but is put off by the stench. Yungman smiles and scurries off into the market.

3

Emeka's friend, Darren, is full of fatherly instruction. 'Haunt,' he says. 'Never use that word again. The Yen aren't ghosts. You won't lay eyes on them; there aren't see-through versions running about the place. They don't tip shit over. Bad man,' he says, 'I don't have to tell you: it's dangerous having them around like this. They'll make you wanna kill yourself. Why you think all those pop stars are losing their minds and overdosing?' Emeka shakes his head. He wants help understanding what he feels. The guilt that kinda-sorta comes into your bedroom and stares at you. 'Raah, wicked man,' Darren says and flicks his wrist. He springs off his sofa. 'That's deep. Wouldn't you have had to snog Kim or something?' Emeka nods. 'Let's be honest, bad man, there's no chance of that,' says Darren.

Darren pulls a copy of *A Beginner's Guide to Communicating With Spirits*, 4th Edition from his mother's bookcase. They try a few things. The Ouija board is useless; there's no one on the other end – a proper waste of time. They try a pendulum with some string and one of Darren's mother's costume rings. They conduct a séance, even though Junior once told Emeka that Black people don't have any good reason to be conducting séances. They place a candle and a saucer on top of a plastic step stool and sit on either side of it. They hold each other's hands. Because the book says to do so. And the book says they should chant what cannot be written. 'You wot?' says Emeka. 'What cannot be written,' Darren repeats. 'Look,' he says, 'it's written right here.'

When this doesn't work, they turn to more traditional methods of investigation. They invite Justin to hang out with them and wait for him to bring up his sister: news of her going steady with Junior, or any mention of her wanting to kill him. But Justin doesn't say anything about that, and not saying anything doesn't mean anything. Darren believes Emeka should *ask* Justin if his sister is in anything with Junior, or ask Justin to ask Kim, but Emeka can't do that. You just don't ask a friend about these things. That's a no-no. That's disrespect.

He tries to hold a mental picture of what Kim looked like that evening in his bedroom. What he calls 'Kim That Day.' In a Coca-Cola rugby shirt, a pair of bleached jeans, her Hi Tec Squash trainers. He'd spent those hours knocking on friend's doors, found none of them home, and wound up just walking around the area, trying not to think. In the end, he went up the roof of Wendover, the nearby high-rise building. He'd heard Junior took lots of his girls there.

The roof had been living in Emeka's head as a kind of addendum to the bedroom, the place where Junior brought Jamie and Adelaide and whispered promises into their ears; where he brought Coraline and told her what she wanted to hear, that yes, he was officially going out with her; where, three sexual encounters later, he brought her back to break up with her. It is the place for all of this and more, whatever Junior wants it to be, the place where Emeka sat that night and imagined telling his brother to shut the fuck up, shut the fuck up Junior; just shut, the fuck, up.

Just this one time.

4

So now the Yen follows him to school. It meets him in his Period 2 science class as he's hard at work, using a scalpel to carve a hairy penis, with warts on the balls, into the countertop. There's that warm sensation again and the thought that someone is watching him, something is judging his work, his behaviour. He is not altogether scared, because by now he has gone weeks with this sensation, this felt presence, coming and going. If anything, it surprises him that it is here at school. He has only ever previously felt it in his bedroom. He raises his hand and asks to use the toilet. He tells a classmate to bring his rucksack along to their next period.

Days later, while passing through the market, he sees Yungman again and decides to follow, watching the man's red Liverpool top flare through the market bustle. Emeka keeps his distance, stopping whenever Yungman stops, tottering on the edges of the crowd where it's at its thickest, as though reluctant to submerge himself. He thinks about the man's eyes, how wild and unfocused they are.

Then Yungman is off again, squeezing by an elderly woman, heading further into the market's belly. Past the Halal butcher shop where the bruised boiler chickens hang from hooks, a wise squint in their dead eyes. Past the fruit and veg stall, and the middle-aged veteran who bellows 'TWO FOR ONE-FIFTY THE 'EDS', like the rest of us are supposed to know what that means.

Yungman hurries on through the throng. Emeka follows, pushing through the openings between the cramped bodies and the dreaded pushchairs. He stops at Portland Street, which is a halfway point in the market, a spot where you can stop for air on busy Saturdays. There's the shout, 'Cross that road and I will slap the hell out of you!' and he watches a woman rush toward her halted child. She snatches her up and clips the little girl behind the ear, despite her obedience. Emeka looks ahead again, at the second half of the market. He thinks he sees a snatch of red, but then Yungman is gone.

Normally he would head in this direction anyway, to Walworth Road, and then on a bus to Camberwell, where he'd spend four hours in the rec. centre. But the thought of having to sit through Saturday school today is jarring. He turns around and heads back the way he came. Mr Zagadou can mark him absent twice, three times over; he couldn't care less.

When he gets home, he kicks his shoes off in the passageway and enters the living room. There's a blazer on the sofa, and Uncle Festus' distinctive moccasins on the carpet. So early in the day and soon after he had left them there, the boy thinks, his hands on his head as he lowers himself on the sofa, his feet between said moccasins. The carpet underfoot – balding faster than a Cybill-Shepherd-chasing Bruce Willis – is a sign of the times; everything feels like it is rotting away, that the young are withering inside, the old withering with age; and for God sakes, the melodrama.

He hears the bedroom door open, and someone thundering down the passageway towards him. It's Uncle Festus, thankfully dressed, in shirt and trousers. 'Will you not say hello?' he says, with more production than offence. The boy says nothing. And then his mother is at the living room doorway, her buba hastily thrown on. She sneers when he looks up at her, when he looks up at her like *that*. 'What are you doing here?' she says. 'Why are you not at the school?

5

Emeka sits on one end of the sofa, picking at where the plastic covering has come away from the armrest. His mother is standing over him, giving him the what-for. Junior sits at the other end of the sofa, revelling in what he is witnessing. Emeka has decided he is not going to church; his prayers have failed in recent weeks. But he cannot tell his mother that, so he mutes her instead, and concentrates on his destruction. The plastic is on the sofa because, once upon a time, they were going to ship it back to Nigeria. 'Back,' his dad had said, as though it had originated there. Everything was going to go *back* once things had settled in Nigeria. 'Once we are ready to return,' his parents had said again and again, and again – as though their two boys had been there before. Again and again, until his parents were no longer in chorus. Today, Emeka picks at the plastic as though it was part of his dad's plans.

Junior gets up to open the door for Uncle Festus, who collects them each Sunday, after dropping his wife at church early. When Festus enters the room, Emeka's mother greets him, prostrates, and then turns back to Emeka, her voice a little louder. 'Do not upset me with this nonsense,' she says, placing an emphasis on the first syllable in nonsense. 'What is it?' Festus asks. 'He says he can't go to church,' Junior replies, 'he says he's sick.'

And he is sick. He's rubbed Vicks under his eyes, and now they are red and tearful. He's placed dice in his sock, so he walks with a limp. But the combination of two very different ailments is too much for his mother. 'Leave him,' Festus says, 'can't you see the boy is not well?' And his mother replies, in English, for the boy's sake: 'Is church not the place for the sick to be made well?'

No, no it is not. Not that church. Not with the rumours that swirl amongst the congregation. His dad has committed the sin of adultery. He has run off with an oyibo, a woman who is having his half-caste child. Some say his father ran away from a Yen, even though you're not supposed to believe, or at least talk about, such things in the church. It wouldn't have mattered if they could. He and Junior are just children. No one has told them anything in the last year, much less the truth. They are left to decide what they believe. Who they believe. What it is they believe in.

'This is not such a bad thing,' Festus says, but the boy's mother does not budge. She is wearing a long dress, one of three Western dresses she ever wears to church. It has a bold flower pattern, shoulder-pads. It is a holdover from when his mother might've fancied herself as a Black Krystal Carrington, given the *Dynasty* fan that she once was. Not anymore. Everything is different now. Their mother is no longer interested in shows like *Dallas, Moonlighting* or *Knots Landing*. She doesn't appear to have any interest in entertainment, or leisure, or even them — at least not Monday to Saturday.

His mother relents. She snatches up her purse and overcoat. 'Oya,' she says and the three of them leave the living room. He listens for the closing of the door but, before that, for what Junior will say. But Junior doesn't say anything. It's like attending church is the one thing that their mum is still able to get Junior to do without complaint.

Emeka waits. Ten minutes of just his breathing and the miniature grandfather clock on the mantel above the gas heater.

He leaves the flat, skipping in the rain, across the footbridge that links his building to the adjacent high rise. He turns, briefly, hearing that empty patter, feeling that sense of someone splashing in the puddles behind him. He heads down the stairs that lead from the high rise's mezzanine to the ground, and then he walks behind the rear of the building, past the concrete football pitch to another maisonette building on the estate. He knocks on flat 52 and, to his disappointment, Justin opens the door – he was hoping he wouldn't have to explain himself. They exchange the typical pre-teen pleasantries and when these wilt and the unsaid question, *Why are you here?* begins to linger, the boy finally breathes in and brings himself to ask if he can speak to Kim.

Justin frowns and asks why. Not knowing how to put it, Emeka says what he thinks might sound half-passable: that he has a message to pass on from Junior.

Justin heads in and minutes later Kim emerges, brittle and impatient, a protruding vein dividing her forehead, like a shivering worm trapped under skin. She barely opens the door for him, exposing only one shoulder and half a face. 'What do you want?' she says and raises her eyebrows as he begins to stutter his way through his words. 'I-I-I don't know how to ask this,' he says. She breathes in sharply. 'Ask what?' And when he doesn't immediately answer, she jumps back in. 'Your brother's got something he wants to say to me? Tell him I said up yours, and he can get lost.' 'No, no, no,' Emeka says, realising his lie has undone him. 'Yeah, yeah, yeah,' she replies, and then starts shouting for him to get lost, for him to get lost before she does his head in. The door is slammed. Emeka decides he better get gone before Justin opens it again to see if he is still there.

6

It takes a couple of days for Junior to learn about Emeka's visit, but Emeka has been waiting the entire time. He's on his bed, wrapped in his Thundercats quilt cover, hiding himself from the Yen that lingers in the room, when Junior rushes in. His brother starts pounding him with trained force, hard enough to hurt, but not hard enough to cause a commotion or give the boy enough of an excuse to holler and alert their mother. Emeka assumes a defensive position until the storm has passed. 'What's wrong with you?' Junior asks. 'Don't you know I will buss you up? Why you tryin' to distress me? Why you tellin' her I want to speak to her? I never told you that.' 'I'm sorry,' Emeka replies, and resumes the defensive position when his brother fakes punching him again. 'So fucking weird,' Junior says. 'You're a fucking perv. It's all that wanking. Going to your head. Don't think I ain't found all those magazines under your mattress.' It's a lie. The dirty magazines are Junior's. And Emeka realises that if his brother can lie about this, can lie so ridiculously, he can lie about anything.

'Why is Kim's Yen following me?' Emeka blurts. 'What?' Junior replies, and for a moment his face is a picture of intense scrutiny before he erupts with laughter. 'Kim? You wish,' he says, still cackling. 'Your problem ain't that a Yen is following you; problem is you ain't got one to *follow*.'

Emeka feels his blood run hot; Kim is just another throwaway thing for Junior. He has no fear of the Yen. Emeka recalls when a dad of one of Junior's girls turned up on their doorstep screaming and cussing, wanting to do Junior harm. He had a thug's hallmarks this dad, triceps the size of a Teenage Mutant Ninja Turtle, a flattened nose, knuckles that could file balsa wood, fists like old school mallets. There was terror, but also joy, a faint pleasure that Emeka will never admit to, the sick but satisfying thought that his brother might finally get what he deserved. He didn't. The man – Jamie's father, he believes – did not thunder his way past the boy's mother; he did not make his way to the bedroom where Junior hid until it was safe to emerge. Instead, the man's vitriol, short and bitter, was thrown at their mother. They were a family of bloody Black savages. When they weren't preying on welfare, they were preying on children. 'I'd have more than a word with your husband,' the dad had said. 'But I'm guessing he ain't around, is he?'

Then there was the aftermath. They sat around for hours. He recalls his mother's threat – the last strike she gave Junior, the last strike she gave him six strikes ago. Uncle-not-uncle Festus had turned up. Just as he used to on Sunday evenings, to drink beer and eat rice with the boy's dad, and Festus's wife would ooze to the kitchen to offer the boys' mother a limp hand. Otherwise, Emeka would see the pair in church, scolding children, holding a hand aloft in prayer, switching out the numbers on the hymn board. But that night Uncle Festus had turned up alone, and had sat beside his mother and placed his hand over hers as he scolded Junior for bringing shame to the family's name.

'Get out,' Emeka says to Junior. 'Get out.' He repeats the words over, until there are tears welling in his eyes and his voice is louder than the laughter. Junior shakes his head, a message Emeka has received for what feels like forever: *how can this boy in front of me be my brother?* Emeka is sick of it. He climbs off the bed. 'Out,' he says, and clenches his fists, knowing he will not lose today if it comes down to this, that today is not a day to take a beating, that at the very worse he's walking away from this a bruised Superman, but a fucking Superman nonetheless. 'Do it,' Junior says, and he does, he cracks a fist across his older brother's mouth.

Emeka steps back, fists unclenched, and waits for Junior to come at him. But Junior doesn't retaliate. He wipes the speck of blood off his lip and considers what has just happened. The punch is near painless, tepid; but the act, the swing of the fist is strange, new and outrageous. Not Emeka at all. And now he understands. 'Shit,' Junior says. 'Oh shit, oh shit, oh shit.' He turns, opens the door and leaves the room.

7

Emeka is on the roof of the high-rise building. He can see the expanse of Walworth from here. The Michael Faraday school, the mock Tudor houses, the other maisonettes and high-rises that belong to the estate. And, beyond all this, an urban vista that seems to scream opportunity, when really there isn't much of any, there isn't anything.

He sits in a complimentary rush of breeze and altitude. He feels the Yen here too, on the roof. Beside him. He stands up. Blood rushing at his temples. He nears the roof edge. Even its words, the way it speaks to him, is through the senses, the dread sense that he should jump, that he should go ahead and do it. He peers over the edge, watches the cars roll up and down the roads, oblivious to what's above them. The wind picks up a little. He steps back and heads towards the access door.

The Wendover building is on Portland Street, a ten-minute walk and he is at the market. He pushes past bodies, ignoring their complaints. He submerges himself in the tight crowd, as though he might hide among them, feeling there might be safety in numbers. He is alone amongst all these people, as alone as he was up on the roof. But now the solitude is loud; it is resounding. He is by a stall where a dread sells incense alongside laminated pictures of Haile Selassie and red, black and green leather bracelets. There is a tall woman at the stall, and even though she is wearing a deep purple cloche hat, he can still see her ears, and big earlobes weighed down by these large-hooped earrings. She wears a beige blazer over a tight white top that has laces tied all up the front of it, like a girdle. She wears a white skirt, black fishnet stockings, black boots. Emeka's eyes linger on her black bra, pushing through the top. She turns and looks at him. She has strong eyebrows or, better put, she has strong eyebrows for him.

And this is when he feels it again, here in the market.

It is there, over there, to the left of him; it has just passed the space between the stall selling beauty products, the stall selling socks and underwear. When he looks up again, Yungman is there. Babbling to himself. Emeka walks over towards Yungman, and thinks about what they might say about him in the weeks to come.

You might've heard about this boy. How he was desperate, even before he was a teenager, to wrestle free from his virginity. How his brother once kicked the living daylights out of him for walking in on him with a girl. How the boy had made the mistake of walking into his own bedroom without knocking. *I heard he never quite got over them tears. Or Daddy's absence. Maybe his brother's bullying too. His friends avoid him. They ain't talk to him anymore.* Talking. He's always talking. Every Saturday, out by Portland Street. He comes out and joins that tramp. The two of them just standing on the corner talking. *You cannot see who they's talking to. They talking to a Yen.* Some say he lost his Yen. Some say that's impossible, he's a boy, a male. Then some say his brother took it. Others say that's disgusting. *That's like incest.* Then those who say his brother took it come back and say no, not like that.

Emeka is in front of Yungman now, closer than he has ever been. Close enough to see that he's been crying. The man lowers his voice, he is talking under his breath.

Emeka leans in a little closer to learn the words. He tries to hold a picture of Kim in his head. Kim That Day. But no, there's nothing.

THE FALL OF THE HOUSE OF PENRHYN

Peter Kalu

Morning, London, 1950

A grey mouse was wriggling in a wire noose on the hallway floor. I stepped over it, tapped the frosted glass of the office doors and entered. Albert glanced up at me from between two piles of papers. He picked up his fountain pen and began signing off letters, signing and blotting, signing and blotting; all the while sucking on a pear drop that hung pink on his tongue like an extra nipple. Behind him, the windowpanes shook. Twin jack hammers were breaking rubble on the bombed-out plot adjacent to us. It was a frantic, anxious time in London, good for insurance companies. Albert's shirt was blotchy with sweat, an effect of the building's addled central heating.

I sat waiting expectantly. He shuffled his mouth nipple to one side.

'Choice: mortuary assistant, died accidentally locked into a mortuary. Some anomalies on the claim form. Newcastle.'

I knew it as the city of falling window cleaners and exploding televisions.

'What else?'

'Penrhyn Castle. Clapped-out baronial home. Old money pile, with paintings. Had a garbled conversation from someone calling themselves Ham. On behalf of the owner. That's his name, Ham, not his lunch.' Albert had long ago abandoned full sentences. He handed me the Penrhyn file. 'Take a look.'

I didn't. Unperturbed, he tapped his left-hand column of

papers. 'One of the Statelies. Being reappraised. Policy decision. Dilapidation. War Office Requisition damage. Risks escalating. Desperate owners. Not unknown for them to light a match, release the money. Death duties. Taxes. The genius founder often followed by a succession of fools who fritter the money away. Becomes one big shackle on the family. And they want rid. Whoosh.'

'So, an inspection?'

'Correct. Assess security and risks, anything unexplained. Anomalies. We sent a fellow last month. Took early retirement directly after. Didn't file but mumbled something about not to stare at the paintings. Never made sense. Drink involved. Possibly.'

I wondered about Albert. He saw drink in everything. Perhaps because drink was everything to him. The agent's disappearance was unusual though, a red flag to insurers. I was intrigued.

'OK. Don't stare at the paintings. Anything else?'

'Long scenic drive, North Wales. I heard you hit some hard times, Tracey. Your erm, close friend. The hospital. My condolences. I kept this one for you. It's an easy visit.'

'OK, I'll take it.'

'Erm.'

'Something else?'

'You don't look well. Steady hands on the wheel, eh?'

I went back out into the fog of a bleak November London. My Ford Zephyr Zodiac chuntered through traffic. The trunk road cruise out of London felt good. After Elspeth's death, what Albert had alluded to, and the awkward funeral and all of that, the pall had become an internal smoke that numbed everything.

Me and Elspeth. We never lived fully. We'd wanted to be splendid in silks, attend the grandest society balls in our finery, and bop and jive. Yet her father was set against me. 'Tracey's dark, dark, dark,' he whispered to Elspeth once, and 'Is he a man or a horse?'

My Zephyr breezed its way through landscapes that J.M.W. Turner wouldn't have minded flicking his brushes at. I felt another pang. St Martins School of Art had been super. Then war sucked all the frivolity out of London and the art commissions with it. Shortly after armistice, I'd taken a little job in insurance, a tide-me-by as a door-to-door collector. Unexpectedly, I enjoyed it. Visiting the homes of the East End working classes and exchanging their shiny pennies for funeral policies. I was good at my job. Promotion came, bigger risks, inspecting high value buildings. Yet my fingertips still tingled, imagining paint brushes.

I drove on through the cloying grey as the ribbon of road and blurs of fields spooled before me. Then came a glorious thud of rain on the roof, as reassuring as the metronomic sweep of the Zephyr's wipers. Ahead, as I was overtaking, the high cab of a forest-green van hit something and there was a splatter of black feathers onto my windscreen that scared me. I swerved but held on. The wipers and the rain cleared the feathers and blood. I passed three hay wagons; the sky began pinking and my mind turned to Penrhyn and Albert's phone call with Ham. It was a curious name. Ham, the cursed son of Noah. Ham, the character in *Prince Zaleski,* the baroque short story by the Victorian writer, M.P. Shiel that I'd read three nights ago: the dutiful Negro footservant of a slightly mad, Abbey-dwelling white master. The story had stuck in my mind for three days solid and showed no signs of working itself loose.

Fields flashed by. Telegraph poles were twigs, fields lakes of molten straw, rain streaking the windshield. I began to see watery images of Elspeth and I. Huddled in fogged doorways, French-kissing. Running, shrieking through the St Giles nights. Wrapped in glee by Westminster Bridge. Swapping limbs in linen beds, rubbing joy into damask wallpapers. At Frensham Beach, we'd buried ourselves in sand up to our necks. Elspeth. *As you were.* Then polio locked you in a half-Nelson. You cried and I caught your tears. You grew extra knees and elbows. Gargoyles sat on your chest. Clouds seeped in through the windows, and I desperately licked the salt from your blistering armpits. You became a Hellenic marble figure draped in hospital sheets. The dark hunkered down on us that night; you trembled, whispered for me to come closer because you were dying. You wanted me to remember you only as you were. Your last words, 'Come now and kiss me.' I leant to kiss you, Elspeth, and you died before our lips touched. I fell into you, kissed you, willing you back alive. *As you were.* They hauled me off, warning how polio can vault, wrapped you in winding sheets. I turned my back, looked through antiseptic glass.

An alert. I was driving too fast, the oil light blinking red on the Zephyr's dashboard. I pulled over, let the engine tick down, watched the sky become ruby then fed the radiator some water, took some deep breaths. We limped on.

Approaching Penryn in twilight, there was only the Zephyr's sweeping headlights pulling blotches of green out from blackness, and the moon above, being slowly throttled by massing clouds. I saw the looming hulk of Penrhyn Castle before I found the road, and coasted slowly along the tree-lined drive, the car's tyres mushy underneath, the engine panting again. By a ruined stable, in a snort of exhaust, I pulled up. The night air held an earthy sweetness, moonlight broken by branches. A vague foreboding welled in me. I followed a screen of tree silhouettes: poplars, skeletal aspens, a slew of oaks. Ochre faded to umber as shadows bunched. Leaf debris squelched, its early bloom of rot mingling with the tang of Welsh coastal salt, the sulphur of burning coal and some sickly, late-flowering shrub.

I came to a clearing. There it was in its full glory. Penrhyn Castle. Its leaden hue magnificent, clouds wreathing its heady castellations. The castle looked febrile to me, the huge mass of it unstable, swaying in the wind, aspens blustering at its sides. I took the stone steps and heaved at the huge, bolt-studded oak door. It opened with barely a whisper. I stepped in. I had my torchlight from the car but held off and let my eyes slowly adjust and my nerves settle.

I was inside a vast atrium. Fluted pillars soared into a vault where eaves and murder holes looked down vertiginously. A burst of lightning came, throwing up a facing wall of stained-glass that ran as high as the eye could see in signs of the zodiac, the ecclesiastical by degrees replaced by the sepulchral, reds shifting to vermillion then sienna, the whole of it pulsing in the electric storm. The storm abated. Then only the November moon seeped through skylights.

My eyes hurt. I looked away from the glass into the void.

'Hello! Hello?' I called but there was no answer.

The Hall held no furniture. Using the torch as guide, I crossed the floor and worked my way through cavernous, musty downstairs chambers. A spiralling stone staircase took me on a sharp climb to the next level, and I made my way across a bewildering series of rooms where ceilings were decorated in stuccoed medieval faces, knots, and charms. Inside some of these rooms, against damask-papered walls, there hung framed paintings. I allowed myself a quick glance. Haughty, long-dead faces in fine clothes looked down at me impassively. I swung my torch onwards. Finally, at a doorway lintel, up high in the castle, I saw a slit of artificial light. I called out another lusty hello and pushed in.

A filament light bulb shed a flickering yellow glow over a small yet tall room, crammed with objects. My eyes swept across an antique globe held by a brass half-bezel to its gleaming wooden base, at an axis that seemed awry. An upright piano of faded flame mahogany. A dusty, glass-dome aviary of stuffed birds including at its centre one resembling a blue-winged tit, posed in swooping flight. A jewel-encrusted greenstone pomegranate. Another model ship, a galleon made of glued matchsticks, the glue still detectable in the ammoniac tang in the air. A clay tablet of Babylonian hieroglyphics, over which fresh pictorial markings had been etched. A floor lamp candelabra of a Venetian blackamoor, with fittings for six bulbs, unlit. A folded, veneered centre table in marquetry.

In the air I heard the delicate peal of a thumb kalimba. Perhaps a mechanical device, its plaintive notes slowed. I turned to the source of the sound. By a cold fireplace, in a high-backed chair, I could see a male lap. The owner of the lap was browsing through a book of Negro hair patterns, in lithograph. He turned to look at me. His hair resembled a straggle of wild, black roses, matted

petals falling across his forehead and around his deep brown neck.
He placed the kalimba down on his book. There seemed a lividity
in his cold hands as he shook mine. He bowed. 'You are an
emissary of the new Queen, Elizabeth?' he asked.

I was baffled. I shook my head. 'Insurance agent.'

He brushed dust off a Chesterfield with a black-feathered fly
whisk and asked me to sit. 'Pity. I have written to her. She needs
must pay me a visit. Queen Victoria scratched her initials into the
windowpane here once. We are ready now for Elizabeth!'

Bonny Prince Charlie probably visited here, too, I decided. I
asked him his name and his reply confirmed my suspicions.

'I am Ham, born in summer of 1830, in Denbigh Estate,
Clarendon, Jamaica.'

'It is now 1950. That makes you over one hundred years old,'
I said gently, unable to deny the stench that came from him.

He dismissed this. 'The passage of time holds no relevance for
me.'

I sat and explained my visit. 'I have been sent by the insurance
company. You received our letter?'

'Of course.' He was back in his chair now and began toying
with the black arm of an aquamarine-coloured record player. I
decided he was a squatter, perhaps a shipwrecked refugee off the
Empire Windrush, blown by fate across the English hills to this
damp coastal Welsh forest. If not, then some poor colonial soldier
who'd lost his bearings. I was overwhelmed, not with abhor-
rence, but with pity, and decided to let his fantasies run free while
I quietly assessed the building's condition. Eviction and injunc-
tion could be executed later.

'What news?' he asked me. 'I have not stepped foot outside
since arrival. I was sent by Edward Pennant, the grandfather of
Richard, whose Denbigh estate I once oversaw.'

I shrugged, unsure how to reply.

'London smog and polio is the news,' I said finally.

He paid my answer little heed. 'Did you hear footsteps outside
just then?'

'No.'

'If Baron Pennant appears,' he continued, 'turn your face to the wall. I can see from your colouring you are of Negro blood yourself so you must understand service.'

I was shocked. His words bruised me, and I felt intimidated by his brazenness. 'It's merely a suntan,' I said; I felt myself flushing, nonetheless.

'So say all mulattoes. Mulattoes are the worst. With all their posing and minstrelling. Worse than we house Negroes.'

He continued to weigh me. 'It does not take great ratiocination to perceive your plan here.'

'It is a routine visit. The insured sum was doubled recently. Why the change?'

'The end is coming, is why. Must we persist with this dry conversation? What is new in the world? What fresh feats of wonder achieved? The year again?'

'1950.'

I saw him absorb this.

'Perhaps that explains it,' he said at last. 'The reckoning is nigh. There is a man came before you, left his card. Joseph Johnson, a fellow of ill-repute, horseback rider, he wears a ship upon his head. He came from the underlands and claimed that he owns the castle in lieu of death duties and has brought a legion with him. He demands his legions be allowed to sit in the chairs, eat at the table. On behalf of the Baron – First Baron Richard Pennant – I relayed to him a firm *no*. Yet he persists. Mustering forces. You will hear his horse's hooves tonight. Everyone is in uproar.'

This Ham was mad as a hatter. 'There is no-one but ourselves here?' I gently suggested.

He shook his head vigorously and shot me a look of disdain. Then, gradually, his bodily tension dissipated, and he became solicitous.

'Forgive my manners. You must be hungry and need facilities?'

'That much is true. May I make a short phone call?'

'The line is disconnected. But food is ready, I had expected you.'

He lifted a domed lace net that covered a serving tray to reveal a plate of cold meats and sliced, boiled potatoes; he unfolded the marquette table and slid plates and cutlery from its concealed base.

'Pull your chair closer, and let us tuck in.'

Despite my misgivings about eating anything this man provided, I was hungry and decided as long as we ate the same food, the risk was negligible. I watched him closely out of the corner of my eye as we ate.

After our meal, Ham lit a fire, settled back and puffed away at a chibouque pipe. The smoke filled the air with the sweet smell of cannabis sativa. He became reflective.

'These walls. You see how thick they are? Their purpose is to keep out invaders.'

'And do they succeed?'

He was unaware of, or indifferent to my gently mocking tone and continued reflectively. 'Intermittently. If I sleep, they take over. It's mayhem. Blue devils with slate-black eyes, marshalled by that Johnson. Others tunnelling up from the quarries. They are determined. Slit their eyeballs and they'd still breach the ramparts, find their way through, you understand? Only eternal vigilance holds them back.'

I had experience of madness, when visiting Elspeth at the hospital. This sounded like post-concussional syndrome: the hospital corridors had been full of such poor souls, and I had become familiar with the look. I indulged him.

'Does the Baron Richard Pennant mind these visitors? Perhaps he doesn't.' It was the wrong thing to say.

'The Baron is adamant! Repel them by all means!'

I waited until he had calmed, then tried again, hoping by logic to persuade him to face his fears, as I understood psychiatrists recommended in cases such as his, where suppressed mental images might be distorting reality. 'But you yourself say the end is coming and they can't be stopped? If so, why do Baron Richard's bidding? Why hold back the tide?'

He remained calm this time and puffed away, thinking. Finally, he found a conclusion and spoke it to me with certainty. 'Gradualism is the key here. I've been talking with the Baron for years about manumission and its repercussions. Yet he is an obstinate man. You recall the quarry strike? Many died waiting for him to change his mind. Nonetheless, I am making headway, he is shifting. Perhaps it is imperceptible to most, but he is coming round.'

'Why not expedite matters and simply let these marauders in? See what happens?'

'The marauders?'

'Yes.'

'I can't do that. The master has not willed it.'

I raised my eyebrows to this phrase, and he shrugged. 'Yes, I follow your thoughts. I am a traitor, a house Negro.' He gestured around vaguely. 'But what a house to be the Negro *of,* you must admit. If any abode were worthy of devotion, this is it.' He took another puff then continued. 'Nothing is ready. This stone, which in your eyes seems grey, is still pink to Richard. As is the globe, whichever way you spin it. It is an irony. Richard's grandfather, Edward, has offspring among the Negro population of Denbigh. The two sides are not so far apart as they imagine.' He spoke softly, almost in apology. His ramblings seemed to have exhausted him. 'Do you need a chamber pot? There is no plumbing, and the latrines are quite far away.'

I declined. He shrugged. 'You can piss in the corridor if you must.' He moved a hand towards the record player again.

'Does it work?'

'Yes. I will play you something.'

He found a disc, unsleeved it, placed it on the turntable and lowered the needle.

A bop. Oh, God. Not that. Elspeth's favourite tune.

Elspeth's black turntable came to mind. How we'd loved that box and its exotic sounds. To dance in her arms again.

'You like it? Your eyes are wet. I can tell you like it.'

Elspeth's sick-bed crying.

'Smoke this. Piss in the corridor if you have need.'

With this last strange yet kind counsel, Ham fell into a narcotic slumber, the pipe slipping from his hand and his eyelids falling.

I settled in my chair. If ever there were a place for gloom and despondency, this sad hermitage was it; the Newcastle mortuary would have been merrier. After a while, I stepped into the corridor and relieved my bladder, then re-entered the room and made my way to the solitary window. The view was of a chiaroscuro: charcoal trees heaving in high wind. I sensed again the castle's own restlessness. Calmed perhaps at the sight and sound of Ham sleeping, I spread myself out on a chaise longue.

I found myself sliding back to Elspeth.

She is pulling me to the beach, her gamine face lit with joy. We run a three-legged race through dunes, tumble, make love in a rivulet, become fish, swim out to sea. We join a circus, tightrope across the Niagara Falls, call ourselves the Blondin Sisters, and are a sensation; we stroll London's Kodak streets together, naked but for goose bumps and elkskin shoes. I remember the night she returned my love letters, saying it was all too much, I was too much, those letters scented, strewn with burgundy kisses, thrown on my floorboards, and I ignored her laments, smuggled her in and we lit the paraffin heater in my bombed room, and she was voluptuous, glistening in my arms, and her beauty shone in the peeling walls as we burned.

Sprawled on the chaise longue, I could hear the hooves of a horse at canter, outside. A piano was playing a refrain, *andante*, in the Great Hall, its keys tinkling high. A flutter of wings, a bird, hovering somewhere close. The blue tit was before me, escaped from its glass aviary and in my face. By dips of its short red beak, it bid me follow. We went down spiralling stone steps by some swifter route than I had used for my ascent, and I soon found myself in the Great Hall once more.

Now it was fully lit and furnished in regal splendour. Four pendant chandeliers threw a shimmering crystal light on plush, high regency gold furniture. The walls were glittering Italian

marble. Heavy, gilt-framed paintings hung at every turn. Rococo
clocks tocked on ebonied tables. A gleaming black grand piano
had its lid up. I stared at a bucolic eighteenth-century Jamaican
rural landscape painting. The piano began playing. A sack-clothed
figure in the landscape painting bid me turn around and when I
did, it was to a scene of sublime anarchy. Gargoyles slithering
down pillars, a host of stone angels hovering high, a flock of
bluebirds tweeting joyously as they flew up to balustrades
where robed saints resplendent in Tyrian purple, were chanting.
Machinery in a painting of a quarry began turning. Four Magi
wrapped in robes of cobalt blue conferred by a row of flourish-
ing palm fronds. Cries. Shouts of glee. A limestone fireplace
blazed too hot for panpipe-playing putti who jumped down and
rushed, giggling, to chase in and out of crimson atrium curtains.
Cockerels spread their feathers. Flamingos strutted across the
burnished floor.

The clip clop of horses' hooves. A woman on horseback was
right in the middle of the Great Hall. She wore a hat that carried
upon it the shape of a galleon ship; her gleaming black stallion
stood proudly to attention. Around her, clutching tridents and
dripping blue water, legions of Africans in rag clothes. One used
a trident to tap a golden grate. The grate slid back and a succession
of slate-grey families – women, men and waifs, with broken nails,
straggly hair, and vacant expressions – clambered out.

I wept. These people were my people. Banished forever from
this Hall, burdened by the loads that brought its wealth, by some
strange wonder they had arrived.

The horse neighed. Its rider gave an order and a cohort of the legion
rushed off to another chamber, returning swiftly with a huge
banquet table that they carried to the centre of the Hall. The legions
began to dress it for a meal.

All the paintings were coming alive now. I struggled to believe
what I was seeing. My heart leapt with fear as a roe deer bounded
across marble and out into an anteroom. Crones. Young washer-
women. Dozing bathers. All eased themselves out of frames and

onto the marble floor. Swaddled babies bawled, hurled off their wrappings and ran along the Axminster carpets.

There was a pained cry of 'Never!' I looked over. Inside the grandest painting of all, Ham's master, Baron Richard Pennant had stirred. The baron hoiked up his black trousers and stepped out of his frame, looked around then raised an accusing hand to the hatted rider.

'This is outrageous!'

The horse whinnied. The rider steadied the stallion. 'Bite your tongue or we'll send you back into your painting. Baron Penrhyn, I believe? I am Josephe Johnson.'

'Get this dark rabble out. And these Welsh quarry oinks too!'

A curse in Welsh rang out.

'Get out, all of you! Who the devil are you and what are you doing here?'

'We are the ones thrown overboard from your ships,' Josephe Johnson said. '*The Zong. The Henrietta. The Hope. The Trouvador. The Esmerelda. The Hannibal. The Madre de Deus.* We are the insurance losses you claimed. Down there on the ocean floors, we did not rest. We linked up and, arm in arm, walked along the bottom of the oceans all the way to… where is this foul place?'

'Penrhyn,' someone shouted, then spat.

'Penrhyn. A toast to this hellhole Penrhyn!' Josephe Johnson called out to the myriads, 'before we burn it down!'

'To Penrhyn!' the crowd clamoured. Goblets sprang up in everyone's hands, even the panicked baron's. Manic cheers ran round.

I was both elated and afraid. A wild, liberating energy ran through me, inspired by the awesome Josephe and her legions.

'We have come to claim what is ours, Baron Pennant. Death duties, you understand? You, the insurer, approach. We summoned you here for a purpose.'

The rider was pointing directly at me. I had not realised I was part of this wild narrative. I stumbled forwards. Above us, the flock of bluebirds fluttered.

'See the grand piano, Tracey. I know you play. How about a

shanty or two? Baron, are you going to minstrel for us? You sport the attire already, the fancy shoes, cane and hat. Let's have a jig, Baron Richard!'

I was dumbfounded and frozen.

Josephe Johnson vaulted off the horse and strode to the piano. She lifted back the keyboard cover. Acid mockery filled her voice.

'On the spirit of Haiti, a royal jig for this hellhole, Penrhyn and its slave-master! Find the Baron a crown!'

Someone cut loose a side-chandelier and jammed it on the Baron's head.

He snivelled and pleaded. They hauled him up and by squeezing parts of him, had him ramrod straight.

'Excellent,' Josephe Johnson called. 'Now Baron, Insurer, dance! Dance, you two!'

The band closed in on us. Was this some bizarre pirate tradition, to have their captives dance before they killed us and burned the Hall down?

The baron's hand, wet with fear, slid into mine.

'It is best to obey,' he murmured. We made a few hesitant steps. The riotous assembly swung on. The African legions and the quarry workers danced away, along with goat face, owl face and the gargoyles, across the marble floor of the great Hall.

Then Josephe was between us. She swung Richard round by the shoulder. 'With me, now. And let us swap crowns, Baron. You wear the ship, I the chandelier.'

And so it was done. Josephe sashayed up and down with the terrified Baron Pennant to claps and cries and drunken drumming of the banquet table.

A gong went. 'Feast!' Josephe cried. 'It's been a long time coming! We dead have built up an appetite!'

The dance was abandoned in a general rush.

I felt trapped in this lunacy and yet strangely alive.

The three Magi swooped down from the eaves and took seats. Quarry families sat among plantation workers. The oil painting aristocracy draped themselves willy-nilly. I passed Baron Pennant a filled, steaming plate which, grudgingly, he took.

'It's the nadir,' he mumbled.

How the mighty are humbled. I laughed at the absurd justice of it.
All my fear floated away. The Baron continued his mutterings.

'You think I want these slaves and plebians lounging in my
saloon? Fucking in my bed? Smoking my cigars?'

'I find the sight amusing,' I said. I felt light-headed. Josephe
and her legions and the quarry workers were the Baron's – and in
times past no doubt the insurer's – enemies. But they were
cousins to me, kith and kin.

'It is filth. Next the plantation cattle will arrive and stake their
claim. Now what fresh hell is that?'

A drayman was passing with a barrel on his shoulder. 'A
powder keg. We're going to blow you up!' he proclaimed.

I watched as fornication of all varieties took hold among the
curtains, along the balustrades, on the banquet table itself.

I smelt smoke. I turned, saw a lick of flames under the golden
grate in the Great Hall's flooring, and I knew then it would all
burn.

Elspeth came and sat with me. She circled my neck with her
arm, and we kissed. My joy was complete. We were as we were.

I woke in Ham's chamber to morning vestiges of dreams. The
blue bird was in its aviary. The model ships at rest. The castle
quiet.

I looked out of the small window; the castle grounds were
deserted. I ventured down to the Great Hall. It was empty, the
gargoyles on their stone pillars, the monk heads in the stucco.
Disconcerted, yet relieved, I climbed back to Ham's chambers.
He had woken, and challenged me at the door: 'You let them in
last night? I can see it in your eyes. Joseph Johnson and his hordes,
you let them in. You let them run wild!'

I brushed past him, but he kept on. 'You fool. Utter and
complete fool of a man. The die is now cast. Ruination approaches. This place will burn. I must away. I will report this to
the Baron, but you will see me no more, I am away.'

He packed a saddlebag and stormed out. I reflected that his

withdrawal was convenient. I would otherwise have had to evict him; now that deed was done.

Faint images from last night still played in my mind's eye. The horse and rider. The Magi. The flock of bluebirds. I tried to rationalise. My tiredness. The effects of grief, the fug of cannabis smoke. Even, perhaps, the beginnings of a polio infection. But there was something more, and although I could not articulate the cause and effect of what I'd experienced last night, I felt some channel opening within me.

I turned, my eye caught by something. Amid the disarray of the room, low down, there was a miniature of the grand portrait of Richard Pennant, First Baron Penrhyn that hung in the Great Hall. The dog in the miniature stepped out and brushed against my legs.

I patted it, felt its soft fur between my fingers; then left.

DEVOTED

Claudia Monteith

Ilona has only the one name. It is an old name that has travelled far and when she calls her name out loud, she can feel the distance it has come, and it thrills her. There is no trace of the family name that once accompanied it. No trace of the family, split and scattered in all directions, further back than she can remember.

She loves the Woods but one of the many benefits of the Big City is that it swallows up all kinds, accepts all inconsistencies without judgement or comment. The Big City cares about no one and everyone in the same way. Ilona can leave the shadow of the Woods if she wants and sit on the wide-open lawn of a park and enjoy the sun without comment or intrusion.

She is alone. She doesn't mind. She doesn't mind the cold. She doesn't mind the heat. She doesn't mind the rain or the sun. She loves the wind.

She doesn't expect anyone to notice her, certainly not to approach her. She is used to people keeping their distance. So when the man greets her with a smile, she is startled, her yellow eyes wide. He speaks in a gentle tone. He is polite, asks if he can sit beside her, there on the grass on the hill in the park on a summer's day that is light and warm and the breeze gentle on her skin. She nods, curious. And he smiles again, asks for her name.

He says his name is Douglas, Douglas Bond. 'No relation to James,' he adds. He gives a little laugh, but when she stares at him blankly, he coughs and blinks rapidly. Then he tells her he is on his lunch break and that he works at the local bank. He says he hopes to manage his own branch one day. He leaves a pause for her to respond to this and when she doesn't, he asks if she is also on her lunch break. She says she isn't hungry. He remarks that she doesn't look local and asks where she's from. She says Far-away and he says he is from far away too. She shakes her head to say that they are not from the same Far-away but he doesn't notice. He talks about the challenges of life in a new country. He talks about how much he misses home and about how important home is to him. He asks her if she misses home too.

This is a lot more conversation than Ilona is used to or cares for, so she doesn't answer but simply turns away and looks at the clouds rolling by. Then she hears another question in her own mind, inspired by the man sitting at her side although by now she has almost forgotten he's there. She asks it aloud, talking directly to the wind.

'Could there ever be a home for one like me?'

Douglas is a kind man who wants things a certain way and only sees what he wants to see. When he was a boy back home, he came across a page torn from an English *Homes & Gardens* magazine. For many years he kept the page carefully folded and flat in the bottom of his drawer. He looked at it often, absorbing every element of the empty living room scene. The candles on the carved mantelpiece, the vase of rhododendrons displayed in the hearth, the leather sofa layered with plump cushions and, on the coffee table, a bowl of green apples. He cherished every detail. The books on the shelves, the rug on the floor, the standard lamp, the footstool. This image was the epitome of a good life. Douglas believes that with hard work and dedication he can manifest such a life for himself in this new country.

And when he saw Ilona sitting on the hill, he thought he saw a woman who was lonely. When he saw her matted hair and ill-fitting clothes, he thought he saw a woman who was lost and needed guidance. When he talked to her and she said so little back, he thought that she was shy. And when he hears what he thinks is the answer to his question, he thinks that she is in need of a home and that he can provide one for her. He decides that a shy and grateful wife is just what he wants.

'When can I see you again?' he asks.

'Soon,' she says. 'Just walk away, down to the bottom of the hill and then turn around and look up. I will still be here.' Then she adds, 'probably.' Because you never know.

He laughs. 'You're adorable,' he says.

There and then he decides to court her. She gives him no home address or phone number, no surname to look up, but he is determined. He goes to the park every lunch hour and sometimes she is there and in this way a relationship of a sort develops. He tells her that he is planning to buy a house and asks her if she will come with him to see it. She is curious and agrees to do so.

It is a newly built, compact, two-bedroomed terraced house with a neat little garden that backs on to the far end of the park. Ilona follows Douglas from one empty room to the next, wondering why one person would want so many rooms. One to eat in, one to wash in, one to sleep in. When they enter the main bedroom, Douglas suddenly turns to her and goes down on one knee. He holds out a small box and opens it to reveal a ring. She laughs out loud at how funny people are and his face crumbles. He quickly stands up and apologises. She leaves the room to continue her tour of the house and wanders into the smaller bedroom next door. She likes how enclosed, quiet, and empty it is, like a little cave. She likes how the window looks over trees that are moving in the wind. And she wonders how it would be to live in a house.

When Douglas joins her to apologise again for his misguided intentions, she says, 'Maybe I could live here in this room, for a while.'

Douglas understands this as a yes to his proposal and takes her in his arms. Alarmed, Ilona shoves him away and growls. Douglas steps backs, apologises again. He tells her that he respects her modesty and promises that he can be patient in matters of physical intimacy.

'You will live here with me,' he says.

'It might be nice to be out of the rain over winter,' she says. And he laughs.

She seems content to let him manage the wedding prepara-
tions and he's happy to do so. He keeps it simple. He wants it
soon. His own family live too far away to come and so he makes
little of the fact that she invites none of her own. He asks if she
would prefer to meet at the registry office or if she would like him
to collect her. She says she will be in the park. He thinks it
romantic that she wants to be collected from the place where they
first met.

On the morning of the wedding, Douglas walks back and forth
through the park in his suit and pocket carnation, searching for
Ilona. Finally, he finds her sitting by the pond, watching the ducks
and licking her lips, her feet in the water. He runs to her. She is
dressed the same as she always is, and her hair is the same matted
tangle.

He frowns. 'Ilona,' he says. 'We're meant to be married today.'

'Oh,' she says. 'Okay.'

At the registry office, he looks around at the few friends he's
invited. They smile back, embarrassed for him. But what does
this matter? Douglas thinks to himself. We have our whole lives
ahead of us.

They make their vows.

He promises to love and honour her, forsaking all others.

She promises not to eat him. He laughs.

Because of the mortgage payments, there isn't much money
for a honeymoon. Douglas takes Ilona to the seaside for the
weekend to stay at a modest bed and breakfast. Ilona enjoys the
speed of the car ride down the motorway and opens the window
to feel the wind in her face. And when she sees the sea, she runs
straight in with her clothes on. 'Ilona!' Douglas cries. 'It's the
middle of November!' but the wind carries his voice away in the
opposite direction. He looks on helplessly. He smiles and nods at
the quizzical looks of passers-by. He wracks his brain for an
explanation of this behaviour that will fit in with his desired
version of how things need to be. While he sits on the pebbled
beach, watching her dark head bobbing about on the waves, he
begins to wonder if he's made a mistake. But when she finally

returns, she is shaking with the cold and smiling in a way that he has never seen before. Her teeth glisten and she's so happy that he doesn't have the heart to be cross with her. He wraps her in his coat.

They have a nice room that looks over the stony beach and the sea. Douglas lies on the bed and waits for his wife to join him. She is in the bathroom a long time. He knocks to check if she is alright, but there's no answer. He manages to open the door with his library card but she's not there. The small bathroom window is wide open. Outside the window is a three-storey drop to the backyard below. He rushes down the stairs. There's no sign of her.

Heartbroken, Douglas returns home to his new house and finds Ilona curled up and asleep on the floor in the upstairs room that looks over the garden. She looks so peaceful, and he is so relieved that he breaks down in tears. She wakes and sees him there, crying at her feet. She licks the tears from his face, enjoying their saltiness.

With an up-to-date collection of *Homes & Gardens* for reference, Douglas begins to furnish the house to fit the vision he's carried in his mind for so long. Ilona ignores the regular arrival of furniture and household appliances, but she likes to scratch her nails on the wall-to-wall carpet. Douglas tells her it is fifty-eight percent wool. Ilona presses her nose deep into the pile, but she cannot smell the sheep.

He buys a king-sized bed with ample drawer space underneath for storage. He buys bedside tables and bedside table lamps. He buys a duck down duvet and pillows and Egyptian cotton bedding to match the curtains. He makes up the bed, and then brings her into the large front-facing bedroom to show her. She tells him she prefers to sleep in the back room with the view of the trees. He says that room is too small, it's for the baby when it comes along. Then he sighs and says that he will move the bedroom suite if that is her preference. But she says no. He can keep his big bed and his little tables and lights. She prefers not to have a pile of furniture to climb over; it would only get in the way.

Douglas's jaw tightens. 'You're my wife,' he says. 'I have been patient up until now.'

'Hmm,' she says, and pats him gently on the head.

Douglas takes this small piece of physical contact as a promising sign.

'When you're ready,' he says. 'I'll be waiting.'

Douglas waits. And while he waits, he works hard. He gets his promotion, becomes a bank manager of his own branch and can afford the finishing touches to make his home complete. He buys a glass coffee table. He buys books for the shelves, a rug for the floor, a standard lamp, a footstool, and a beautiful china bowl for the apples. He buys Ilona dresses that she doesn't wear and household appliances that she doesn't touch. He believes that in time he will win her heart, and that with patience and devotion, he will heal the trauma that he imagines has made her so distant.

His persistence has some effect. Ilona comes to enjoy sleeping indoors. It makes a nice change. She likes the roast meat that the man cooks on Sundays. And she has grown fond of his funny little face and the way he tries to contain the emotions that ripple across it. She likes the sound of his crying late at night and his cheerful hum when he makes breakfast in the mornings. And sometimes she lets him accompany her on her long walks. It is because of her fondness for him and his ways that she stays so long, much longer than she thought she would. And when it is that time of the month, she keeps her promise. She doesn't eat him.

Sometimes he shouts about the dirt that accumulates in this house of his. It makes her laugh to see him so excited. What does he expect, so shut away from the elements? What else can the dirt of life do without the wind or rain to clear it? He shouts about the vacuum cleaner and the washing machine. He tells her that she should use them. She tells him that she doesn't enjoy his noisy machines. His shouting stops being funny after a while, so she gives him a clip around the head. Nothing severe, just enough to bring him to his senses. It seems to work. He stops shouting and makes no further fuss. He plays alone with his appliances at the weekend, moving the dirt of the house around in the ways that seem to satisfy him.

Years pass. Ilona decides it's time to move on. She has been too long in this place. She has learned all she can from living in a house and from married life. She has forgotten who she used to be. Central heating makes her itch. Looking at trees through a window is stupid. She has become lazy and misses the rain and the sun. She longs for the wind. She tells Douglas that she's leaving. She thanks him for his time.

He doesn't seem to understand. He can't seem to comprehend her words. She patiently explains what leaving means. Then he asks why? Is it something he's done? Is there someone else? He says he thought they were happy, maybe not like other couples, but in their own way.

He says, 'We laugh a lot, don't we?'

She says, 'Yes. But never at the same times.'

He says, 'If there's something I can do to make you happy, I'll do it. All I've ever wanted was to make you happy.'

She says, 'That was never what I wanted.'

Then he pleads with her not to leave. He tells her that he's given her the best years of his life. They've been through thick and thin together. How can she just throw it all away? He has put up with her unusual ways, grown to love them, in fact. He's been faithful and devoted. He doesn't think he could bear it if she left him now, after so long. He asks her to consider him and his feelings.

She considers. It is true. It has been a long time and he has been devoted. She doesn't want him to suffer unnecessarily.

She eats him after all.

DAISHUKU

Irenosen Okojie

There'd been four occurrences of his body bending time backwards. Nobody would believe it but it had. Here. In this instance,
he was fifty, fallen through the speckled void into London,
languishing in one strip of intersecting subways pulsing like the
city's varicose veins. Here. Elephant and Castle. Night time.
Homeless. A howl in competition with the roundabout's traffic
lights, the screeching of tyres, impatient bodies milling about.
Daishuku prised his cold lids open as if to counter the ache in
numbed fingers clutching a Styrofoam cup of tea he didn't
remember, of course he didn't. He'd inherited the tea, the frost,
the oil spillage on the steps leading in, the smell of chips in hastily
coned paper, the patter of footsteps streaming to and fro, the
looks of contempt, the swirl of coats hiding invisible pregnancies
in thin linings, the occasional drop of coins threatening to scatter
the murmurings of his head, like mosquito legs in the cold. He
took a sip of the tea, shoulder-length stringy hair streaked with
grey dipping forward. Mouth warmed, he gulped some more, a
dark trail running into his beard. He set the cup down with a
shaky hand, his knuckles red, the skin around it pale and thin, a
cluster of tiny brown spots edging towards his fingers. He patted
himself down slowly. He was clothed in rags; the scent of sweat
mixed with beer lingered. He tasted beer in his throat, beneath
the bland warmth of tea. Worn plimsolls on his feet were
wrapped in white plastic bags. He considered the sum of his new
beginning. Its parts separated in the dank subway. He considered
the bleakness of it, crawling gently towards stained chip paper

refashioned into greasy blueprints. He began to chant, 'Daishuku.' A name. A memory on his tongue. He poked coins in the silver bowl before him. A fleeting image appeared: the grotesque shopping mall's pink elephant drinking oil from the subway steps before skidding on the ice, breaking its neck to interrupt the overwhelming feeling of loneliness.

After a few hours, the influx of commuters waned to occasional figures dribbling in different directions, bearing cracked mouths from mopping spillage at the edges. Daishuku inhaled deeply, a weightless passage of air twisting within him, uprooting organs. He pictured those organs growing on trees, as fruit lining the pavements, lungs weighing down branches, kidneys protruding from the base, heart growing out of the trunk: a decorative gift, a bloody, plump, garish Christmas bauble, a world in disguise. The underpass swam. He felt light-headed. He was used to this. *Why are you always ungrateful for your inheritance?* he asked himself silently. *Not through what you say but by your body's reactions*.

He tipped the silver bowl, stashed the coins in his trouser pockets. Above, the voices of teenagers gleefully arguing filtered through. He flexed his fingers, placed his hands on the bowl. He raised his head up, opened his mouth. The tear on the inside of his left cheek happened in split seconds. He ran the tip of his tongue over it, giving it a permission of sorts. It oozed a multicoloured concoction that flooded his mouth, lined his tongue like an ambrosia. He spat into the bowl. A quiet conduit that could upend the items from wreckages, pin them into a labyrinth of doorways in the dark. He rummaged inside his black jacket, which had the word *Awake* printed on the back in blue lettering. He pulled out a scruffy white handkerchief with a spider's diagram of the surrounding area, the words *Station, London College of Communications, Bus Stop, Shopping Mall and Pink Elephant* circled. He stood up awkwardly, leaned against the wall listening, gathering himself. He pushed off into his stride, like a swimmer into a stroke. These were his alarm bells, indications the timer had started: an injury producing a small rainbow, a rumbling from an internal opening, which meant he needed to move. The bright-coloured mucus in the bowl shimmered, thinning, lique-fying. Daishuku headed into the night, coins jangling in his pockets becoming moonshine against his fingers, the heads and tails of fortune wrestling on zebra crossings while traffic lights sang.

He shuffled along in the cold, noting the swirl of night activity with the eye of an outsider: handfuls of people at each bus stop spilling in and out of large red buses pulling to a stop by seated shelters, the glow from the one remaining stall shuddering, the man inside selling confectionary, lighters, cigarette cases, blow-ing on his hands intermittently. The odd lampposts springing from pavements were tall, steadfast, unacknowledged guardians of the city. He coughed on the handkerchief; tiny bright spots appeared over the diagram. He shoved it back into his pocket. The plastic bags on his feet kept getting caught along the pavement so he untied them, dumping them in an overflowing bin. A rush of frosty air crept through the holes in his plimsolls, a wind through his soles. He walked to the pink elephant, placed the handker-chief beneath it, moonshine on top. He knew in the wake of his departure, when the timer stopped between the slowly eroding bodies on concrete pathways, some would become smudged in the fog, unaware when men like him borrowed their costumes, leaving fingerprints fading along the edges of their lives, building waning refuges on cold shoulders that could be toppled by a breath. He felt small in the fortress of the city, a broken atom in a big tattered coat, the big coat flying above roaring, a robust, darkened cloud jacket spilling corn grains from its pockets, below, at the roundabout, the car tyres skidding on grains, on soft points of earth that had travelled through pockets. A raucous group of men from a stag do passed him; one spilled beer on him, patting him on the back, handing him a Monopoly note. His friends laughed.

Another harassed-looking man wielding a briefcase spat, barely missing him. A woman pushing a pram filled with shopping but no baby forced him into the road. The ache in his chest deepened. This was what it was like to lose everything. He knew this feeling.

It never stopped hurting. He spotted a baguette in a Sainsbury's bag poking from another bin. He picked up the pace, noting people didn't acknowledge him except to express their silent disdain, their superiority, their relief that these weren't their circumstances.

They weren't responsible for any of it.

He spoke broken Japanese mixed with English to the tube-station attendant, who wore what looked like a large orange bib over his uniform. *Have you seen my Mae?* He asked. *Mae keep Alzheimer's in suitcase.* Daishuku shifted his weight from one foot to the other. The attendant pressed a button on his walkie-talkie. A static sound emanated briefly, like a television channel that hadn't been tuned in. He motioned to the opposite side, pinched features more pronounced as he spoke. *Follow that road round, then all the way down, about twenty minutes' walk. There's a shelter and soup kitchen. You want to get there as soon as possible. It gets pretty full up by now but they will HELP you, okay, hmm?*

Daishuku pointed in the same direction repeatedly. *I go down, go down!* he announced, as if it were a revelation. The attendant nodded patiently, smiling stiffly, already turning away to indicate the conversation was over. Daishuku left the station entrance, his feet frozen, plimsolls damp from light rain. He pressed his hand against his rib as a sharp pain shot through it, the collapse of a small bone growing in the wrong direction. He heard the shattering in his peripheral vision, like autumn from a black smoked bottle. He saw small nails falling from the sky. Though attuned to these occurrences, these unexplained growths on the margins, they left him disoriented. Bright spots from his mouth were now on his coat, becoming patches. The patches became claws; the claws changed to bright, blind gulls. The blind gulls lost their heads to the city's rooftops bejewelled with raindrops, left their bodies to hatch memories in subways and underpasses, their feathers runny in bowls exposed to the elements, the distant chime of coins serenading the bowls' rims, the nails from the sky piercing their heartbeats. Their margins were thumbed, lifted edges where they were runny claws in ribs, while Daishuku's bone breathed in a damp plimsoll.

The periphery loomed. Wet tendrils of hair stuck to his neck. He hurried on. He followed the station attendant's instructions, pressing the bell of the redbrick building with the sign *St Michael's Shelter and Kitchen*. Had the station man really meant go dawn? Stay till dawn. *Yes! Go dawn.*

A curly-haired, rail-thin young woman answered, earnest and warm. She wore a striped apron over her navy T-shirt and jeans, a roll of tinfoil in one hand. She ushered him into a small reception area with certificates and photographs on the walls, briefly addressing a heavily tattooed, pink-haired lady at the front desk, who was slotting sheets of paper onto a clipboard. The desk was filled with leaflets; an open jar of peanuts sat at the edge. On one wall, a full notice-board contained a staff family tree. Beneath that stood a grey radiator making a *Suump!* sucking sound as though a magnet kept trying to land inside it. *You find Mae?* Daishuku asked, addressing the thin woman. *Mae come here?* He searched the woman's features. She tucked the tinfoil beneath her arm, a furrow appearing on her brow. *I'm afraid we haven't had a Mae here this evening. You're welcome to stay the night, though.* Gently, she drew him into the large hall. It smelt of soups, bread, warm spices, like somebody's kitchen, a hearth burning slowly in the guts of a red home for vagrants. There were bodies everywhere; a musty scent lingered in the air. At one end, lines of people queuing for food, slack badminton nets piled behind a row of volunteers serving from pots and pans. At the other end lay bodies in sleeping bags, blankets over them, breathing to mechanise the hearth. After eating a bowl of mildly flavoured chicken soup, Daishuku scanned his surroundings, watching for Mae to appear in the gaps between figures, at the end of the clinking of cutlery. He saw her face unfolding from the roll of tinfoil, crinkled, Mae as a tiny tattoo running up the receptionist's arm, in the jar of peanuts trying to break through holding a soiled blueprint, inside the radiator attempting to embrace an elusive magnet. He tried to hold all these sightings of his Mae but couldn't. It was red mist slipping through his fingers, faint trails that amounted to nothing, limping around the hearth. He fell asleep, between memories in the wrong order, a blanket over him, barely reaching his feet.

Later, the pain in his chest woke him up. And somebody had stolen his shoes, inheriting the wind in his soles, a shrill whistling at the opposite end reclaiming it as an ancestor. The pain he felt rocketing through his body was unbearable, searing. His nerves hummed as though a thousand knives were pinned against them. The ache in his head threatened to split it, like an unsweetened coconut. He convulsed, curled into a ball amid other sleeping bodies. His skin tightened. The age spots vanished. The wrinkles smoothed. His muscles became more defined, his hair thicker, the grey disappeared. Daishuku was getting younger.

When the morning staff took over, they found his clothes sagged, the area bereft of a body, his blanket crumpled over the fleeting sights of Mae, a large, bright, blinding cavity in the floor, which felt a little like looking at the sun.

Backwards into the chasm. Here. Daishuku was twenty-five, walking through acres of cornfield. The tips of tall stalks bent in the breeze, the thin sticks planted beside them on either side a guard to stop the winds wreaking havoc. The corn when it grew as expected was sweet, ripened from the dew and rain and good intentions, from Daishuku tending his father's land in the heat, under downpours, when the cold made his hands gnarled. At the edge of the land stood a bamboo house, a bamboo house with insect legs planted in the ground in a precarious union, where the outcome was a possible uprooting into the skyline or collapsing from baskets of corn piled on the small porch, the empty chair where his mother used to sow becoming a pit stop for the grey cat leisurely trailing invisible small territories. Daishuku tugged the hoe over his shoulders, his footsteps quickening, his left arm pushing the weight of stalks away, like malleable green curtains the land coughed up. His fingers knew the softness of the soil, its dusky hue, the measure of water on the stalks, the shafts of light falling through, the sharp, occasional thin cuts, the tiny bulbs of blood like stagnant ladybirds waiting for permission to move. The bamboo house trembled. He paused, listening, heard the crinkle of a straw mat, a cream puddle in one path. He listened for Mae the bruised Murasaki Shikibu to press her petals against the blade of his hoe.

He heard the swoosh of stalks pushed back, a wrinkling amid a sea of green, the air cool on his neck as his body went into alert mode just in case. He stepped to the side, obscured by some stalks, his grip tightening on the hoe. The small scar from an incision on the inside of his left wrist itched. He resisted the urge to scratch it, taking deep breaths instead. In the distance, the door of the bamboo house flung open, shuddering as the costumes of previous occupants crinkled in the doorway. The gentle patter of footsteps approached, then a whistling sound, their signal. He smiled, relieved. A rush of warmth heated his skin, stirring him inside. He dropped the hoe, stepped back into the line of vision. Mae appeared, a sheepish expression on her face, Her slender frame belied a toughness that slowly revealed itself. Her dented, stubborn chin, high forehead, slash of curved mouth spoke of an unconventional beauty. Her dark, silky knot of hair was tucked underneath a wide straw hat. Dressed like a man in her slightly baggy, black Haori suit, she carried a rolled-up mat tucked beneath one arm, a small bag of sliced oranges in the other, the juice like a burst artery of sweet nectar. She spread the mat on the floor, took off her hat. *If only our warring fathers could see the resolution to a small war can come through the children.*

Daishuku laughed. Mae was prone to random philosophical musings he found oddly endearing. He was less naïve.

Their fathers hated each other too and the men who came before them, he said.

They lay down, the sway and bending of stalks a lullaby. She fed him two slices of orange; he licked her fingers, making a popping sound, which amused her. Her shirt flapped against her stomach, a pouch hidden by baggy clothing. He pressed his hand there for kicks that were yet to come. Looking beyond them, he imagined Mae's stomach rising through the green, expanding, anchored by his hand. The tips of stalks snapped around them. He listened for the sound of a grain of corn in a growing tiny fist. Mae kissed his wrist, promised to insert the orange pips in his incision so she could watch them bloom into fruit that would distort in quiet spaces.

The cat on the bamboo porch separated into parts. The costumes worshipped a stalk growing from a crack in the door-way, christened with a thick line of orange dew.

The war between the two families began generations back over land when their great-grandfathers had been best friends. The land that bordered Niigata was at least four hundred acres, had an apple orchard, a run of chicken houses, a well, a saw mill. An emperor's son had gifted it to Daishuku's great-grandfather, Hiroku, for intercepting and saving his life one night on a dangerous road when two bandits ambushed him. Hiroku had in turn told Akira, Mae's great-grandfather, about his new small fortune. A promise was made, a handshake exchanged, a plan to toil on that land together, to yield its fruit to build an inheritance for their families. But Hiroku was a gambler, a drunkard.

He could often be spotted stumbling from the gambling houses, clothes dishevelled, reeking of sake, mumbling about his ancestors, his wife's continuous lack of interest in him, the unpredictable behaviour of his children, a streak of recklessness he wrestled with, particularly appearing in the men of his lineage. It skipped the odd one here and there but nevertheless reared its head eventually. It was rumoured Hiroku owed several debts. They mounted, one on top of the other. Great stone burdens that dented his shoulders, changed his once-proud walk.

One night, high on sake and false confidence, he gambled the emperor's gift away.

He cried all the way home, drunkenly waving his arms like a windmill's interpretation of a panicked man. At home, he broke the news to his wife Azumi who, glowering in anger, threatened to cut his body into little pieces, then dump them in the well they'd never drink from. His children grew to resent him for the loss of their inheritance. When the news travelled, a furious Akira vowed never to speak to his old friend again. And so a rift occurred between the clans; a rip that expanded, gathering blood clouds in its wake. Hiroku continued to drink. Azumi became a stranger in his bed. The children grew. The years passed. His friend Akira never reneged on his promise. In their seventies, their hair whitened, bodies stooped over canes, words slow from their tongues, one cold night Akira saw a heart bleeding on his bed mat. Thinking his old eyes were playing tricks, he poked it with his cane. The heart dodged the poking, rolling away into the night.

The next week, Hiroku died of a heart attack, pieces of his heart scattering in the rift.

On the evening of his twentieth birthday, Daishuku headed to his family's outhouse clutching a lantern, a task he'd become accustomed to since the incidence of bandit raids increased over the month. They thrived on the highways of Honshku, catching wealthy travellers passing through off guard. They weren't killers but nevertheless used coercion, the threat of violence to terrify their victims. The notorious Paniko gang even struck homes on the outskirts. Families were on alert. The squeaking of the lantern slowly swaying in his hand merged with the soft whispers of the cornstalks. In the preceding two weeks, Daishuku had noticed items missing from the outhouse: a beautiful golden fan, a wooden tobacco case bearing a dragon's motif, an ancient Sho. A creaking sound in the outhouse pricked his ears. He heard rummaging, then stillness, as if the intruder had anticipated his approach. After the awkwardness of adolescence, he'd blossomed. He was above average height, with elegantly handsome features, which belied what most would consider a lower social status as a farmer's son. Thick, expressive brows often gave the impression that he was scowling when deep in thought. His long hair was piled into a loose topknot. He set the lantern down carefully, waiting calmly, aware of the pocket knife strapped to his ankle should he need it. He kicked the door open. The thwack jolted the assailant who spun round.

You must be a weaker strain of the Paniko, sent to rob chicken houses and the vulnerable, Daishuku said, by way of greeting.

Dressed in black, topped off with a Sugegasa hat, the assailant flew at him. He was slighter than Daishuku expected, though fast and agile. They wrestled on the ground. Amid the flailing of arms and blocking of punches, Daishuku stopped. He was certain his chest had brushed against breasts.

Be still! he instructed, pinning the intruder down by the shoulders. He removed their hat. Midnight hair cascaded down. A choppy fringe, restless brown eyes were revealed. There were dirt marks on her face, plus an expression of deep annoyance, mouth curved into a sneer. He stood up, stepped back, his body humming as recognition hit him. *You are Kitamo's daughter.*

She scrambled to her feet, brushing the dust off her clothes. *Yes. Congratulations. The dunce gene skipped you. And you are Makoto's son. Stay back, peasant! Before I gut you like a meal from the Tenryu river*, she warned, rolling her sleeves up, hand clenched into fists.

What exactly is the Paniko's ideology? What is in the manifesto, if you have one? Or is it just a front for directionless opportunists? Daishuku mused, walking back towards the doorway, blocking her exit.

Halfwit, the Paniko run these regions! Soon, we'll have government officials right where we want them, she spat, walking towards him, fishing out a folded sheaf of weathered brown paper from her chest, bearing scribbling on the back: a map, which had England circled in red. She held it up to him as though it was a challenge.

He snatched it from her. *Ah, you plan to extend your thieving beyond these territories*, he said, bemused. Her nostrils flared.

She pointed at the map's red circle, the creases formed, gathered like the lines of a sleeping storm. *One day, I will travel there. I will build things you can't imagine while you are here drinking sake with goats! Becoming the worst version of your ancestor.*

He grabbed her arm, steering her outside. *Come again*, he added, holding her gaze, daring her to. Then Mae the bandit woman was running through the cornfield, light from the lantern a waning orb. Her hair trailing behind was a raven's abandoned wing; her lips pursed over his pocket knife like a bit between her teeth.

Backwards into the lacuna. Here he was ten, accompanying his father, Makoto, to make his round of deliveries in the town centre. He sat on the stoop of a shop, which sold carved wooden shoes that looked like small ships, an old Shakuhachi instrument, a green glass bowl twinkling at the rim, large maps of places he'd never heard his father mention. He pointed to one hanging map. He saw the figure of a small girl crossing the miniature-shaped countries. She held a dagger, waving it from side to side at a crinkled sun, which loomed at the edge. The sun shrank. The girl's hands faded. The dagger spun, the countries rearranged themselves. The girl disappeared. He waved the store owner over, his finger jabbing at the map, which felt smooth beneath his touch. The old man, who wore an eye glass, slapped Daishuku's fingers away, peered at the map, saw nothing. He didn't know it then but Daishuku had witnessed the strands of time colliding. The store owner gave him a sweet to stop his hands wandering. He ran back outside, searching for his father in the stream of people milling about, wondering who the girl from the map was, sucking the soft-centred black sweet, unaware of the bright liquid seeping into the roof of his mouth. The street swirled. The sound of a car engine revving caught his attention. He ran towards it, a brown beetle that reminded him of a giant locust. The man at the wheel lit a stick of tobacco, rolled the window down. On the dashboard were two dice pieces, a wilted purple furan, a box of matches. The scrawny man drummed his fingers against the wheel as he smoked, waiting. Daishuku slowed down passing the car, guided by an instinct that made his stomach tumble. His skin tingled. A lump in his throat formed. He passed the women dyeing cloths in buckets before wringing them, determinedly twisting the material as if they'd crawl away from their clutches, like dyed, hand-spun cobras. He wandered through the smoke, the sizzle of street food cooking in large woks, the men and women stirring, wiping their brows, negotiating with hagglers. The scent of spicy Sukiyaki lingered in the air. He spotted his father in a damp alleyway behind the rubber factory, arguing with a man in a silken, cream suit. The man held a bowl of Miyabi soup in his right hand. The scene seemed unsteady somehow, as if a ripple in the ground would cave their footing. His father's expression was drawn, his shoulders slumped. Steam blew from the factory pipes, like a smokescreen. The man waved his fist in his father's face. His father shrank back. Then the man's face paled. The bowl fell from his hand. The soup spilled. The chopsticks clattered to the ground. His father ran, almost knocking into him at the entrance. Daishuku gasped from the impact. His father picked him up, instructing him to be quiet as he ran. This was the closest he could remember them being, his father holding him in flight.

The man stumbled out of the alleyway to the waiting beetle, clambered in. The engine revved once more. Daishuku looked beyond his father's shoulders at people swarming, separating into clusters, like a symphony the engine had accidentally set off. The sound began to thin as though marooned on a distant shore. Soon enough, his weight became too much for his father's arms. Their hearts beating almost simultaneously, he watched for the alleyway's steam to deliver dice and a dead furan into their route of escape.

Daishuku watched the policemen approaching their home from a distance, on the bend, like uniformed ants, getting closer and closer, their proudly pressed uniforms lightly covered with dust, the gold buttons like shrunken badges catching the shattered ends of a fallow summer. The stiffened uniforms were stretched tautly over their bodies, as if they'd abandon the figures, leave them naked, the uniforms walking through whispering corn in a separate ambush. For days, the stalks had shivered in warning, their tips grazing each other in collusion, rust crawling up the tassels. And a withered reflection sucking from the rust till blind, till mired in the soil, the dirt, in the minuscule grains trying to morph into a valve; a release.

Daishuku ran to get Makoto, who'd lost his appetite for days, whose reflections wandered through their home trying to eat slivers of light on his behalf. Standing by the window with his father, Daishuku pointed at the soldiers. His mother, Reiko, emerged from the mat in their bedroom screaming, asking Makoto what shame he'd brought on the family. Her face whitened. Crestfallen, she splintered. Hundreds of her heads were shrieking in the stalks. Her kimono gown multiplied, burrowing in the soil in search of roots to mimic. Daishuku covered his ears; his heart was beating so fast he thought his chest would crack open. He looked to his parents for reassurance but each was unravelling. He knew that moment would change everything. He just couldn't understand how. Almost in a stupor, his father, Makoto, walked slowly to the front doorway. The policemen came. They dragged Makoto to the ground, on his knees; Reiko cried, circling uncontrollably. Powerless, Daishuku ran to Makoto, a bruised boy desperately trying to grab his father's hand one last time.

He stood at the edge of the bamboo house. A broken siren became a fold of sleep.

Makoto had poisoned a man to whom he owed a great debt.

The bamboo house collapsed.

Backwards into the current. Here. Daishuku was a tiny sperm curling, darting, shooting. Flanked by a flood of scenes that were small membranes finding their elasticity. The scenes attempted to keep up but they were loaded with concoctions of pain and joy and longing, the results of which were little erosions, a caving here or there, a withering at the tip, holes off centre a finger could slip through, a dribble of ink, the lines of a small country. The membranes beat in the current, limped along obediently, bound by barely visible threads glimmering occasionally. Speeding, the sperm was ahead, sharply turning, twisting, gathering momentum, a white tadpole drunk on its own movement. Unaware that, one day, it would be a man who'd fall in love with a woman called Mae, who'd carry a stalk in her mouth to England, who'd give him a son there. And that the son would follow the root of the stalk back to Japan, only to go missing clutching his father's dagger, like a last lifeline. Mae, the mother, would die of a broken heart, the father would never recover from her loss.

Upstream, the sperm encountered memories it would claim in the future, memories that waited patiently to deceive it, to present themselves as voids, rearrange components on cold city streets, underpasses, in borrowed clothing that collapsed into puddles of colour, into folded points between dimensions and as reflections mirrored in oil spills. Shooting forward, the sperm continued on its destined trail.

It was a piece of glass in the vein, a spot of blood travelling through a season of snow, a musical chord colliding with an infant's silhouette.

Daishuku was beginning again: a slither rumbling the boughs, rupturing a haze of memories and membranes. Heading for the cold womb precariously balanced on a curb, flooded with water, light, and the angles of several resurrections.

(DYING OF) THIRST

Gemma Weekes

1.

the gospel must begin   in the middle and ugly   just like this
with my feeling that life had its back to me
standing in the chill   in the trashbagged alley by the back
entrance of the Wendigo Club   where I screamed at my
manager Portia   to drown out the trouble   I felt coming
like   dogs feel a storm

'Where the *fuck*,' pronounced so hard the words bounced off
the sidewalk and rolled into the gutter, 'is my rider?'

'You got everything you wanted…!'

'No, I did *not*! Where's the pineapple juice?'

because I'd worked so damned hard to matter   and it was
time everyone knew I *mattered*   and Ms Portia Devlin didn't
get it   had never suffered like I had   to be a real *someone*   a
real person with insides   who drank real goddamned juice

'They had three cartons of it…'

'*Fresh squeezed* is what I asked for!'

she was about to find out what suffering *was*   if she kept
fucking me over

my stomach was all acid   I should have been relaxing
before my performance and instead I was out in the piss-
smelling alley   having to do everybody's job   and it was all
one long drawn-out indignity

'Mardou…'

'I need it for my *vocal* cords!'

'I'm on it! It'll be there by the time you get back to the

dressing room. Rob just went out to buy it…'

'It's disrespectful. I put it on the fucking rider!'   I had to
yell to get the words past the tension in my throat   the world
behind Portia shook   and contracted

'If it was Kerouac's white *ass* doing a performance here, would
they have "just made a *mistake*"?'

If I were a better mother to myself, I'd have remembered:
Be suspicious of what you want

and if I'd known how dangerous it was to get what I wanted
I'd have taken off right then   running toward the sea
over cracked and bleeding sidewalks   giving flowers to derelicts
humming Miles' *Kind of Blue* under a sky reddened by city lights
until concrete gave way to the beach   belonging to myself
the way the sea belongs to itself at night   polluted but alive
I wouldn't have been afraid of the Kid or so contemptuous of
what I already had

'Are you really still pissed about the Kid…? He's hot shit right
now, Mardou. We can't afford to –'

'If that's what I *meant* then that's what I would have *said*!'

'But it's clear you're still –'

'I don't need you to repeat yourself!'

the wind muscled in on our conversation   slicing through
my dress   carrying with it   the rotten memory of struggle

'Look, Mardou.' Portia sucked on her cigarette in that anxious
way she did when nervous or mad   her pale mouth puckered
like an asshole   'Do you understand how *huge* this is?'

          tossing her dishwater hair   blowing clouds of toxins
'You're a prizewinning, bestselling author and performance artist. You've landed The Wendigo Club! Could you even get *in* here
three months ago?'

'So I should just be grateful like a good little nigger?'

'The juice is probably already in the dressing room. I'll have a
word and make sure this doesn't happen again…'

her eyes hard and unflinching   the way a manager's eyes
should be

windows into   an emptiness so vast   it could only fill itself
with money

those eyes were why I hired her
I wanted all the   coin   I could stuff into every gaping schism
every fracture   every laceration   of my life so far
I wanted to sweat quarters   and fart dollar bills   I
wanted to be so armoured with money
that if a motherfucker scratched me   I bled green
and I was so damned close
less than an hour before   I'd been a goddess   sliding up to
the kerb in a limo like Venus surfing her clam shell   stepping out
of the scent of leather into clouds of praise
MARDOU!   The who's who of NYC   pressed cheeks and
palms with me   slipping me business cards and compliments
touched my hands   arms   waist   hair
YOU MUST MEET SO-AND-SO   SUCH A FAN
bouncers who'd once blocked my passage   now bowed and
scraped
ushered me   with muscled nods   into a red room fat with
couches   slick with mirrors   artwork yawning open from
every wall   each a window into   someone's skull

and then I saw HIM   ZEUS
he had come!
god of the underworld glittering   at the bar like a shard of
glass
club owner and suspected pimp   philosopher   aficionado
of illegal substances   cinephile   art appreciator and patron
skin white as a fresh-bleached skeleton   and cheekbones
to match
rarely seen even here   at his own establishment   in a suit
that cost the GDP of a small country   youngest heir of the Wards
a line of vampires that could be traced   all the way back to
medieval Europe
all my hard work   had been for this
but before   I could reach his side   Zeus shifted to reveal a
young man standing next to him
I recognised him right away by how he stood which   was
like his mother

soft-bent neck of his mother   in his long black coat   soft
black skin   his skyward column of hair
      it was The Kid
      fuck fuck fuck
      they spoke intently   the Kid laughed as if he were shy
his mother's quiet accusing laugh   soft and suspicious of
      everybody   because soft
      I had seen him   from around corners   from safe distances
      I'd seen him   nodding out   on park benches in the Bowery
peddling his ass to lonely old men
      fuck fuck fuck   I hung back
      what was the Kid doing there?
      just the shape of him made me feel poor and   crazy like his
mother
      who   rumour had it   was in the hospital with a broken soul
      I pulled Portia close: 'Do you know that kid?'   pointed him
out   told her I didn't want him at my party
      'He's too hot to throw out.'
      and maybe I knew it and didn't want to know it   had
heard and unheard his name in elevated circles   had seen
and unseen his   poems   scrawled all over downtown   like
an advertising campaign   for giving up
      'Trust me on this,' Portia said now in the alley   lighting up
a new cigarette with a flame   that reminded us   with sudden
heat   how dark it was   darker than it should ever be right in the
thick of downtown   'You are The Voice of The Black Experience The Conscience of The White World!   By the time
I'm done, if you say 'jump', a thousand idiots are gonna crack their
heads on the ceiling. Even Zeus.'
      I wanted that   I wanted it so bad it made me dizzy
      'Spare me the fucking sales pitch.'
      but the Kid's face had ruined everything   infecting the
present with the past   uncertainty rose in my gut   like a meal
that didn't agree
      it said   *this is going to hurt*

2.
if I'd known what was waiting for me   in the gutter of my
success
 I would have allowed my suffering to make me generous
 I'd have not been so afraid of the sheer drop   in Abla's eyes
and of the way she needed me
 12 years before she came to Paradise Alley   after two unsuc-
cessful phone calls in the pink flush before evening   when all
the ghosts of the day hung in the air
 shouted me from the street   MARDOU
 standing there   dark black and soft   The Kid silent clinging
to her hand   my godson   still bandaged from the accident
 he had been hit by a car just weeks before   seemed always
trying to die   even then
 'Please,' she said   in shapeless trousers and shirt unlaced
shoes and all her heart in her face   my friend since we were little
girls in Harlem   through a million triumphs and horrors
 'We need to stay with you for a while. You were right, Mardou!
In the beginning you said... you always said...'
 'Right about what?'
 'Kent wants to steal my son. I've lost him once already...
please...'
 my heart beat hard in my throat   my lover said he might stop
by and I was ashamed   I imagined his words   *I'm surprised you
know such a woman*
 ashamed   and   *ashamed* to be ashamed
 I despised her in that moment   the unpretty face greasy with
tears and sweat   her bowed posture
 all I wanted was to be left alone   with my lovely soft depression
 and the promise of getting drunk   and fucked
 'I can't.'
 Martin Luther King was freshly dead   and would not save us
 'I thought you hated it here, anyway!' I said spitefully
she always said so   the strange junkie whiteboys and pretenders
and what she called my worship of them   but who was she
 to judge   who slaved every hour to make   her husband

the Haitian son of a lowly farmer   feel like an aristocrat and
an American?

Was I any more of an invention than she was?

'Please,' she said   shuffling forward   with no pride or malice
'I *can't*.'

how she clung to her kid in the street disgusted me   I clung to
no-one that way

and certainly not anyone who loved me back

not even my blonde-curled daughter   gone years before
disappeared without a trace   into her father's whiteness

that she could not bestow upon me   that she could not protect
me with

and instead   lead strangers   to mistake me for the nanny
or a kidnapper

it was on a similar autumn day that my daughter's father

made a gift of our child   to his wife   who had all the
money   but no good eggs

'I was there for you, wasn't I?'   Abla said   as if life works
that way   'When you needed somewhere, I helped you.'

'I helped you too,'   I said   we'd held each other together one
long winter after her first son had died   my daughter taken   and
summer gone completely as if never to return

she had convinced her husband to let me stay rent free in the
basement   so he could outsource the chore   of grieving with
his wife   hardened and shuttered as he was

we snuck marijuana and danced   painted and wept

until she fell pregnant again

and now her tired shoulders   the top of the boy's afroed head
the scent of the caramel tree   the sky sinking into nightfall   all
of it spoke with one voice   and called me COWARD

but I was not safely suburbed in Brooklyn

had no big house on Pacific Avenue like they did   no front
parlour   spare room or walk-in pantry

could not look after her as she had once   looked after me

I didn't owe anyone anything   I belonged only to myself and
that was all I wanted   and all I had

I didn't   invite them to my front door   but met them in the
central courtyard of my building   with its heavy washing
lines   and playmates for The Kid
    we sat on a bench   untouching   as if her misery and bad
luck were contagious
    I told her again that I could not keep them
    'Go home and talk to your husband,' slid easy out of my mouth
'I'm sure this is just a misunderstanding,'   said despite my belief
that   her husband was   a thin-souled prick   a social climber
authoritarian   and potential psychopath   so stingy in every
way he probably   saved his piss in bottles
    but that day I wanted her to leave   more than I wanted her to
be happy
    or even survive
    'You know I'm not one to beg, but I'm begging you, Mardou.'
Abla tried to appeal to me a last time   though it was clear she
didn't really think it would work
    The Kid staring from a corner of the shadowed courtyard
with those big deep eyes   and their horrid undertow of hope
    if I'd known what would be waiting for me   I would not have
been
    afraid to let those eyes   change me
    we would have   eaten pizza by the slice and   slept all together
warm in my small bed and laughed   and been safe
    my whiteboy lover didn't show up   anyway and
    I had no money for wine
    I had nothing   at all   that night

3.
inside the Wendigo club   I walked underwater toward the bar
    the party flowing over my head aglitter with gyrating bodies
    moving too frenetic or languid   for comfort
    screaming earnestly at each other   about things they would
instantly   forget
    sickness rose in my throat   I could see neither   Zeus nor the
Kid

wildly   I searched for them   went even to the men's bathroom and to the fire escape   and to the melee   of the dancefloor
where a gorgeous blonde girl danced   as if possessed   hair in
her face   her body   all angles
    the DJ demanded   TOTAL OBEDIENCE   if we were gonna
have a GOOD TIME
    said THROW YOUR HANDS IN THE AIR   GO CRAZY
GET UP   GET DOWN   and
    staring at each other's teeth   was how these fuckers knew
they were having a GOOD TIME
    dance was ruined for me years before   as soon as I knew it
was expected of me   that I shuffle   hustle and jive on cue
making it a performance
    for other people   I was doing for free and
    oh to be free of the rage that stiffened my body at parties   and
drove me to monetize myself
    to be like the blonde girl   miming electrocution   under the
disco lights
    to once again enjoy my   self
    the way I once did   long ago summers in the basement of
Abla's house
    when Portia appeared I snatched her posh liquor   downed
it   asked for another   'Didn't you say you don't like
drinking before performances?' she said
    terror throbbed in my molars   tickled the ear canal   both
sides of my head   radiated freezing   from the glass of
bourbon   ached in the palm of my hand
    travelled up my arm   threw my heartbeat off-signature
itched through my sharp shoes into the balls of my feet
    stiffening my knee joints   so I stood frozen   amidst the
fashionistas and artpushers   and literati
    in the dreadful certainty that my dream would be stolen
    The Kid   was surely saying things about me   nasty things
to sour me in Zeus' eyes   he would say   I was a pretender
that my activism was an act   my courage restricted to the kind
that put me in front of an audience

a saviour   without the heart to save   even my friend who
loved me
    that I was a fraud   who had stolen his mother's story
his mother's voice
    I dug my fingernails into my arm to prove   by the pain I felt
that I *was* real   and if I was ever not real   then tonight would
make me real
    my name emblazoned on the front of a prizewinning book
champagne flutes rioting with bubbles   these classy Deleuze
heels   this white Guattari dress
    white because white dresses are only for brides   and for
those who have more than one dress   and now I could
afford several
    the club was filling   I was crowded from every direction by
names
    and the bodies they were attached to   John Blame my
publisher   Sienna Gerber from Channel 22   Colin Provokian
who owned the art gallery on 43rd street   Andy the high class drug
dealer
    'Mardou!'   Portia's hand landing on my shoulder with shock-
ing muscularity   like a bird of prey   its claws around a mouse
'Don't be nervous, darling!'   the fact that her   random
collection of features had a *name*   suddenly   gave me vertigo
    'You're going to be fabulous!   You're always fabulous!'
    and they had all come to see *me*   MARDOU LEE   I had made
it   a *somebody* after a lifetime of languishing in the existential
equivalent of a sofa crease   the closest I'd gotten to VIP.   being
Very Invisible Person
    'I fucking *know* I'm fabulous!'   I yelled so loud   I felt the
tendons stand out in my neck   'I'm a Black woman living in
America. I can't afford nerves.'
    and Portia laughed with all her teeth as if I were her own Black
baby
    'John will be introducing you soon. Do you want to go and get
ready?'
    I slipped   one unsteady foot in front of the other   into the

relatively quiet back room reeking of mould   smoke and sex
where I could drink my fresh-squeezed pineapple juice in peace
     The Kid would sabotage me   I was sure
     my reflection   stared back at me from the wall   impris-
oned in glass   and was not on my side
     lightbrown skin   darker than usual in that light a leaden grey
     eyes careworn and puffy   mouth tense   cheekbones
protruding like
     some kind of   wrong-minded love letter   to a history I
did not know
     and where had my softness gone? where was the little woman
the ingenue?   I hated this person
     my reflection and I   stared at each other   sunk to-
gether into our chairs   Abla's words repeating   on me
     I was there for you, wasn't I?
     'Shut the fuck up!' I said aloud
     'I don't owe any of you anything! No-one!'
     a knock came at the door and I   jumped   as if Alba herself
might crash through   the mirror
     I didn't breathe 'til it was just Portia saying
     'Ready?'

4.
I suffered
                    that was the performance
     I wailed   screamed   yelled   pleaded   cursed   jiggling my
Black ass out from the back room of the Wendigo   naked and
greased like a cut of meat   ready for the pan
     wearing only gold chains walking a cold filthy floor under
hot lights   to ascend the stage before a sea of gleaming teeth in
rapt faces
     how delicious the fizz of guilt   as a reminder of their power
     I was   power   inverted   delectable
     everywhere my eye landed was a mirror

hunger staring   back a million times from every surface and
my face itself a surface
    a story is a surface   I said   a person is a surface   I said
a culture is a surface
    where was ZEUS?   I felt for him   with my blood   with
the black in my eyes   the brown in my skin   with the coil
of my hair
    do we not   in the end   all want to be food?
    I drew him to me   he came for only the fiercest and blackest
of Black pain   the kind that reached from a central void to
match   in its depth   the emptiness of the vampire
    this pain was delicious to him and all those of his line   he
watched   his eyelids weighted with pleasure
    he would elevate me   fatten me on money and attention   that
I might show others how to hurt so beautifully   how to bleed
their longing into the air   populating it so densely with wounds
that all Zeus need do was poke his tongue from between his teeth
to taste the misery
    I knew he would come   and he did   how could he resist?
    we were one
    I shook and kneeled   that was the performance   I pissed
myself   so urine ran down my leg and pooled around my feet
    that was the performance
    and I shook and wailed
    and it felt good   like peeling a scab
    and weaponized myself   against myself
    this is how I would become real   and solid upon the earth
detonating myself along the fault line between surface and the
depths   by being the ultimate n i g g e r
    the first   to level the insult   at myself
    I would be the elevated one   ZEUS would sink his fangs into
me
    drain me of all melanin   that I may be ultimately nothing
but myself
    free to be nothing and everything   free to walk the Earth
unharassed

the   n i g g e r   self   left shrieking on stage
and Mardou   no longer Mardou   gone home to a house
bigger than the street she was born on
WOW!   LADIES & GENTLEMEN!
performance done   there was thunderous silence   followed
by explosive applause
AUTHOR OF *BLACK PUSSY/WHITE ART*
WINNER OF THE DUTCH WEST INDIA PRIZE 1981
MARDOU LEE!
I saw then   out of my nakedness The Kid was watching too
      tears bleeding down his face

5.
and had he not been like my own?   slept in the crook of my
arm
      giggled and danced for me   in innocence
      had I not filled my palms with his skyward hair   w h e n
it was soft and fine as candyfloss   squeezed his ripe cheeks
      had I not cleaned him of shit and snot   tucked him into his
bed
      diverted from him   the harshness of his father's words
with jokes
      sung him ella fitzgerald   and the beatles
      had I not fed him animal crackers and warm milk   named
for him   the colours of flowers and cars and crayons
            had he not been like my own when my daughter was gone?
            we are all   the children we once were

6.
something hard exploded against my cheek   hard and then wet
      my fingers came away slimy
      another missile launched   smacking against my abdomen
      a   golden-headed woman   pushed   through the crowd
      screaming in her outside voice   NIGGABITCH   to an
accompaniment of dead   gasping silence
      it was the beauty   who had been dancing

she threw another egg   and no-one moved to defend my
body
   'What are you doing?' I moaned
   the audience relaxed into delight   at their own cleverness
at getting the joke   and began to applaud
        AH THE SHOW IS NOT OVER!
   when the blonde woman ran out of eggs
   she threw each of her   blue shoes
   right   then left   tearing my skin
   why was she doing this   who'd danced so carefree?
   I struggled to escape   but was blocked in every direction
by applauding people
   I searched   for The Kid but he had gone   who
   could have saved me
   ZEUS stood   at the back of the crowd   all   colour concentrated in his smile
   I yelled for the girl   to stop
        and the crowd took   my protest as an invitation to
join in   throwing shoes   handbags   loose coins   a wig
a pack of rubbers   a newspaper   a tampon
        this was genius
   'She's not real! She's made up!'
        first tentative   but soon
   soon more unleashing
   loving screams WHORE   NIGGERWHORE
   words running together   indistinguishable or incoherent
with joyful rage
   released suddenly   and with a great force of momentum
        BLACK CUNT   BLACK CUNT BITCH
   'This is genius! GENIUS!' Portia screamed   as blood oozed
from my painted lips   my invented eyebrows   my tight
shoulders
   everyone who was not participating   was laughing and
clapping
   Did Zeus not know   he would need me alive   to feed on?
   'Please!'   I yelled   but had already been yelling

cried out   but had already been crying   'This is not the
show!'

'Oh my God!   Isn't the name of the show   'This Is Not The
Show?'   Fucking Genius!'

no no no   Zeus did not need to feed on me   there were
more lining up to take my place   there was no shortage
it was a vampire's market

the blonde leapt on stage   wiry strong   with heavy palms
and sharp nails reaching her fingers   round my neck   breathing
into my face and

it was my own face looking back at me   only pale
edged blonde   eyes rimmed black

and   so skinny her collarbone was   a brutal hollow at
the base of her throat

it was HER   who I had given away
the blond curls   hanging in my face
my baby I had called Persephone after my favourite story
she had come with The Kid

I fell under her blows   too powerful for her size   as if
she were legion   as if she were   the size and weight
of a Mack truck

I gasped   her violence was a kind of love   the most
honest applause
I had ever gotten
the truth
of all the rage I didn't
know   how to spend
she smashed her   fist against me
until I dissolved

INCANDESCENCE

Nii Ayikwei Parkes

Things had been going badly at Abu Salim. The inmates glowed with cheer, their sallow cheeks elastic and animated over their bones. The guards had questioned over one thousand men – *why, why?* – using every trick they had learned in their long careers as jailers and torturers, and every single prisoner – even if they were in separate wings and had not seen each other for over a decade – gave the same response.

The answer had the guards doubting their years of training and torture: *Prisoner 13874*, said every man. *Ziad*. When told that Ziad was in solitary confinement, that he had been for five years, the inmates laughed. Laughed. Laughter under torture; who ever heard of such a thing?

And yet when they went down narrow steps to check, there Ziad was, as he always was, staring at the single bulb in the cell, left illuminated to ensure Prisoner 13874's sleep was never complete.

It was small and terrible acts such as perpetual lighting that had given the guards at the old fort their reputation. Like other such prisons around the world, they were known for hooding, rectal rehydration, pop torture using the worst Seventies songs, waterboarding and cramped confinement – but it was their attention to the smallest deprivations that made them unique.

So Ziad was not given the water a good Muslim needs for his ablutions, but fragments of newspaper. He wiped gingerly, conscious of the ink and the transient news that might be absorbed by his backside. The discarded clumps of paper piled in a corner of his solitary cell, clustered like the first incomplete structures of a new city.

Unsurprisingly, the lights kept dying out. Ziad would watch the wide-bottomed bells of the bulbs turn darker over time, a gradual shift from the pale yellow stain of a new smoker's fingers to a light charcoal. The transition was barely perceptible to an ordinary user, a bulb only noticed when it failed to do its duty. After flicking the switch a couple of times to be sure of what was already clear, a hand would reach for the spent bulb and twist it out of its usual orbit. Ziad watched the guards fetching a high ladder to reach the light fixture dangling from the eighteen-foot ceiling; once the bulb was out, darkened fingers would shake it, setting off the distant, unmistakeable death rattle of a broken tungsten filament. For Ziad, each bulb was a fallen sun, a broken regime, each change tossing him into a new universe. Although it hurt his eyes to stare, the slow undoing of the bulbs was his way of marking time. From the first yellowing, he counted down its eventual demise. If they'd used good quality supplies at the old fort, each regime of light would have lasted as much as three months, but the average time was no more than two.

He knew he'd outlast many more bulbs. He wouldn't break.

Ziad was meant to burn out in the inert vacuum of solitary confinement, but he had made his peace with his position. There was no anger to burn, just resignation. He would not apologise for something that was true just to see the sun again.

If the guards valued literature, they would have realised that what they provided him with to clean his buttocks was entertainment. It also told Ziad what the guards confiscated; he got their leftovers – what they didn't read or study or couldn't imagine. For instance, there was a paper that appeared every month with jokes and crossword puzzles in French, which was clearly meant for one of his fellow inmates. The language reminded Ziad of Rousseau, reminded him of what it was like to speak to a room full of philosophy students. From these fragments of newsprint he read about a massacre in Dunblane, Scotland; a major oil spill on the east coast of the United States of America; plane accidents far and near: in Peru, Nigeria, the USA, Congo, India and the Dominican Republic. He read squatting over the metal bowl provided for him, his thighs solidifying as he learned about strongmen like Mugabe and Museveni winning elections in their petrified countries.

It wasn't common for him to touch the paper after he had used it to clean, but on this day the photograph on the balled-up news-print was so unusual that Ziad wrinkled his nose and reached for the crushed sheet with his left hand. Using a foot to trap the corner of the paper, he stretched it out, his shit streaks making unintended art on one side.

Luckily, the image was unobstructed because it was on the reverse. As he'd thought, it was a picture of a bulb, but it didn't look like any he'd seen before. It whispered from the middle of an advert by a company called Shanghai Xiangshan Limited, looking for a local distributor for a new kind of light bulb that used a fraction of the usual energy.   It was a spiral; like a fluorescent tube, thin as meshabek, wound into the form of a bulb – a shapeshifting light. Ziad stared at the picture for a long, long time, then crumpled the paper again, kicking it onto the week's mounting excretory heap.

At first, Ziad tried to forget what he had read, to block out the outline of the bulb, bury its skull shape under the skin of time. He managed three days before he started tossing and turning in the bright-yellow night, thinking of the possibilities of a bulb that could last two whole years! Even better, it used less power, which meant it was unlikely to leak as much heat into his cell as the bulbs they were currently screwing above his head every two months.

One day, without thinking, he asked one of the guards if he had any knowledge of the new kind of bulb replacing the tungsten filament ones around the world.

'No,' was the leather-skinned officer's gruff reply. 'What do you need to know about bulbs anyway, 13874?'

Ziad let it go immediately. Leather Skin's tone made him consider how profoundly this calibre of man resisted change. They loved stillness in all its forms. If Ziad's prisoner number changed, they would lose their minds. They wouldn't call him by his name because it might remind them of someone they knew and cared for and separating a name from emotion can be as difficult as separating food from its flavour.

He returned to his usual routine: rising daily to the distant muezzin's call that somehow breached the walls. As he was not provided with the means to wash properly, Ziad took great pains to clear his mind and open his heart before kneeling for his Fajr – one of only two prayers he managed to adequately prepare for, in a day. After that he sat in meditation until he heard the hatch of his cell door being opened. Twice a week, a gloved hand reached in to remove the used metal bowl that carried his excretions, topped by its mountain of crumpled newsprint. It was Ziad's task to remember which days this collection was made, or he risked being beaten with a knotted rope. For this reason, he had, over time, developed a memory system: he had marked seven grooves in the concrete floor with the sides of the metal bowls that came in and out of his cell, and he moved a tiny ball of compressed paper along the grooves each time the muezzin's morning call came. He knew that every third day the bowl was collected.

What he could count on daily was a bowl of tasteless gruel, slid in through the door hatch with a stack of torn-out newspaper sheets and a metal cup filled with water – Ziad saved a small amount to clean himself for Asr. The rest of his time he spent in his mind: replaying entire conversations with his wife, his late father, his mother and his sister. In between, he stretched and hummed songs his grandmother used to hum – and often lay on his back, looking directly at the light bulb, as if in defiance of all the adults who had ever told him not to do so as a kid. He watched the lights blaze, fade and die.

Ziad lived in this cycle of light, sometimes unable to separate himself from the constant glow, feeling disconnected when a bulb died.

He felt like his limbs were floating when two guards came to change the latest bulb. One bore a tall ladder, which he held steady as his spindly-armed colleague unscrewed it. The room seemed to spin counter-clockwise with the dead bulb. Ziad heard his own voice asking whether they had considered using one of the new bulbs he had read about.

A quick slap reset his head. Both guards glared at him, then the Spindle spoke. 'You seem to be enjoying confinement too much 13874 – you need to do some work.'

That evening, Ziad was crammed into a group cell with seven other men. After prayers, when the lights were off and they lay sweating in the sweltering space, Ziad said, 'There are bulbs that don't produce as much heat as these ones.'

In the morning, doing laundry under a scorching sun, Ziad thought about Shanghai Xiangshan bulbs and how they worked. His hands quickly grew sore, fingers catching on the buttons of the guards' uniforms he washed. How did a thing use less energy, yet have the same presence, the same effect? How was something fully present when three-quarters of its life force was absent?

He remembered the afternoon of his arrest. Could it even be called an arrest? It was a kidnapping. His wife Safiyya didn't know until three weeks later, what had happened to him, where he was. He was simply walking towards the main gate of the university when two students fell in step alongside him, greeting him. Before he could finish a response, they manoeuvred him into the backseat of a Peugeot that appeared from nowhere. As they covered his head, it occurred to him that one of the men looked familiar. It wasn't until he had already been in jail for four months that Ziad remembered the face. He had seen him in his lectures. The man wasn't one of his students, but he had blended in so effortlessly – a near invisible presence.

As present and absent as a new Shanghai Xiangshan bulb.

Ziad carried the wet uniforms to the Drying Room, which was

just a cloth-covered wood frame that let in the heat of the sun, but not the dust of the barren landscape. As he hung up the thick jackets and trousers, he tried to guess which ones belonged to which of the guards he had encountered in his two-year stay at Abu Salim. Which of these hanging suits was cut to fit Spindle or Leather Skin? How much of themselves did they pour into the starched hold of their uniforms?

His mind returned to Safiyya. He was not allowed visitors, so he had not seen her since the morning of his kidnapping, when he kissed her growing belly and promised that he would be back home early. After his arrest was on the news, three weeks after he had been locked up, he was instructed to write her a letter with his confession, explaining why the revolution was right to imprison him. He wrote: *I was radicalising students as aggressively as I kissed you on our first date*. Of course, they hadn't kissed on their first date, but if the revolution insisted on falsehoods, then he would communicate the truth through falsehoods. Safiyya would, at least, know what to tell their child when they asked where their father was, but Ziad's heart ached for her. They were supposed to experience having a child together, but instead she had been all alone in labour and now she was probably soothing a crying toddler, with no one to yell *Take your child* at. He wished himself next to her, his fists clenched with the pain of his own powerlessness.

Later that afternoon, after a lunch of spiced lentils and bread, Ziad watched as four sets of prisoners from his wing played football, like boys unburdened of the responsibility of going home for dinner. Clusters of guards watched them – both for entertainment and signs of mischief. Ziad sat with rows of other prisoners, their legs in front of them, their buttocks on the sand beyond the markings for the two football pitches.

There was a collective gasp as the head of the prison arrived to take up a seat four metres from Ziad. The guards all seemed to stand straighter. The prisoners had seen him on TV before. He was one of the young stars of the revolution – competent, confident, clinical – and now a captain. He clapped as one of the footballers, a former professional who had tried to defect during an international tournament, dribbled three opponents and lobbed over two defenders and the goalkeeper to score. The entire passage of play was reflected in the unblemished, magnetic sheen of the captain's revolutionary sunglasses.

Ziad couldn't help himself. He rose, dusted sand off his buttocks, walked towards the young revolutionary, and bowed his greetings.

'Captain, have you heard of the new kind of bulb from the Shanghai Xiangshan Company?'

Two burly guards put their hands on their holstered pistols and ran towards Ziad, but a slight shift of the head by the captain told them to stand down.

The young captain was known for not travelling with a body-guard even when in the grimy tangle of the city. He was confident in his ability to look after himself. In his black sunglasses, Ziad saw his own face for what it had become: a thing of sunken sides filled in with rough beard growth, keen, curious eyes glowing from the depths of its decline, and a mouth – he watched his chapped lips explaining that if the prison switched to the new bulbs it would save money and the guards wouldn't need to disturb the prisoners so often to change bulbs.

Ziad watched as the captain's frown deepened, then relaxed, then returned – and he noticed the man's left-hand signal to the guards that the prisoner in front of him was crazy. Still, Ziad was not ready for the fall. The captain was so swift, his left leg shooting out like a switchblade and breaking the direct contact between Ziad's legs and the ground. He stood over the prisoner as one who didn't know that his youngest aunt had sat in the same primary school class as the man at his feet.

'Are you telling me how to run my prison?' he spat.

In the time it took for the captain to sit back down, Ziad was bundled back to his former solitary cell, confirmed as an unhinged radical, back to his incandescent bulb.

Prisoner 13874 returned to his routine: rising daily to the distant muezzin's call that somehow breached all the walls, clearing his mind and opening his heart to kneel for Fajr and sitting in meditation until he heard the hatch of the door to his cell being opened. It was a routine largely unbroken until almost two years later when Spindle and his companion came for their two-monthly visit and replaced Ziad's burnt out incandescent bulb with a Shanghai Xiangshan bulb.

Ziad had been waiting for the day because he already knew that the revolutionary government had started replacing incandescent bulbs in their offices, barracks, bases and prisons the year before. The young captain had suggested them as a trial when he moved from Abu Salim to a larger prison in the north of the country. The prison saved so much money in six months that the captain was first put in charge of procurement for the entire armed forces, then promoted to Major, then made Minister for Trade. One newspaper fragment suggested that the company importing the Shanghai Xiangshan bulbs belonged to the family of the young Major, but who can know the truth in a revolution? It was like the story of the new guard who had been sacked from Abu Salim five months before the Shanghai Xiangshan bulbs arrived. When Ziad was found lying shirtless on the ground in the Drying Room while the new guard was on duty, the poor officer was accused of moving Prisoner 13874 without clearance. No matter how much he denied it, none of his colleagues believed him.

'I never touched the door, I swear!'

'So why is the prisoner out here and not in there?'

'I don't know; ask him. I swear, it must have been someone else.'

Ziad tried to confirm the guard's story, but who listened to prisoners? He was silenced with a knotted rope and shoved unceremoniously back into his cell.

If Leather Skin had peeked in the cell when he pushed Prisoner 13874 in, he might have believed his unseasoned colleague. But, as it was, Ziad staggered in as the incandescent bulb cast his shadow in two directions.

The guards at Abu Salim were unsettled, not just because the inmates glowed with cheer. They were uneasy because, once again, Prisoner 13874 was causing people to tell strange stories.

How could a man who was kept alone in a cell that you could only reach by going past two guard stations and down a narrow flight of steps be going around the three wings of the prison to tell stories? Even worse, it was a man who had clearly been losing his mind since the head of the prison had kicked him to the ground and sent him back into confinement after just two days out. Every strategy to get information out of him had failed.

Of course, Ziad always had the lights on because, after close to seven years, he still refused to publicly confess to his crime of polluting students with counter-revolutionary ideas. They had blasted his cell with loud music from Lynyrd Skynyrd nonstop for three days only to find him sitting upright meditating beneath the light. They had beaten him with water-soaked ropes that made intricate patterns on his skin, but he didn't scream once. Electric shocks elicited small giggles from him and he treated waterboarding as if it were a day out at sea. Three officers had crowded into the cramped solitary cell to berate, cajole, threaten and insult him, but Prisoner 13874 countered with phrases and questions elicited from his childhood and his years of study of philosophy:

Where was the moon when Juha pulled it from the well?

Time and numbers are nothing but modes of thought – many philosophers said that and they still died, but it's true

How could Um Bsisi have avoided his trials?

If Aristotle believed that an eye is not an eye if it cannot see, what human function, if lost, will make us no longer human?

The guards were beginning to suffer a fracturing of their faith in their own skill as officers of the Revolutionary Prison Service.

'Maybe it's because he is a philosopher,' Leather Skin suggested when a handful of senior officers gathered for lunch.

'It could be,' another guard agreed. 'Every prisoner has a weakness. Normally the ones who can take physical pain are not as strong when we work on their minds, but this one...'

Leather Skin cut in. 'I'm telling you, it's the philosophy!'

There were nods all round and then a period of silence as they tore into their lunch.

'Have you noticed how he's started gaining weight?'

A chorus of nods.

'Maybe an emotional wound,' said the most senior officer in the room. 'Didn't he once write a letter to a wife?'

'Yes,' Leather Skin confirmed.

'Good. Let's find her!'

And, like wolves, they tore into their food.

The news they got back was better than they could have hoped for. Not only did Prisoner 13874 have a wife, but she had two children and at least one of them could not belong to the man, because the child was two years old and he had been in prison when the child was conceived. The guards whispered amongst themselves with glee. What man would not be broken by such betrayal?

Again, three officers crowded into Prisoner 13874's cell. This time, the mission was clearer: they taunted him to the limits of their imaginations. They questioned his virility and his sexuality; they stripped him to 'check' if he had male genitals; they braided his hair, put flowers in it and asked him to serve them. All through it, Ziad was unmoved.

'What do you have to say, 13874?' Leather Skin asked.

'What you have done here just tells me how you treat your wives,' Ziad responded, his face impassive, mildly aglow.

Leather Skin slapped his bright cheek, his breathing suddenly ragged, but he held the other guards off from attacking the prisoner.

Ziad settled into a kneeling position with the ease of a clothed man.

'Aren't you going to ask us if we are lying about your wife?' one of the guards asked.

'Why would you lie? I trust she and the children are well.'

The guard caught the eyes of Leather Skin and his other

compatriot. They shook their heads as one. It was perhaps in that moment that they decided to do what had not been done at Abu Salim in over fifteen years. They would arrange for a prisoner to be visited by family. A man may be able to ignore a reality that is spoken, but how could he refuse the evidence of his own eyes?

A light-bulb moment is understood as an instant of deep illumination, a flash of the most profound insights after a long period of contemplating a problem or studying a phenomenon. The less explored possibility is the sheer blinding impact of a light bulb filling a space with its incandescence.

To heighten Prisoner 13874's humiliation, the prison officers set up his visit with his family in the large central compound, where prisoners of all the wings of Abu Salim were taken to exercise or play sports – or to be inspected by visiting revolutionaries of the ruling council. It was the site of Ziad's last official public outing, when his legs had been swept from under him by the young revolutionary who was responsible for the proliferation of Shanghai Xiangshan bulbs across the country. Even if Prisoner 13874 wanted to forget what he saw, he would have hundreds of witnesses to remind him. All the prisoners were brought out, a handful squinting in unfamiliar daylight after years in confinement.

Ziad was ushered to the centre of the field in clean brown overalls, towards a table set up for the visit. The table had four chairs around it: three on one side for the visitors and one on the other for the prisoner. Prisoner 13874 was halfway to the table when the gates to the compound opened to let his family in. There was an ephemeral scatter of dust riding the wind, catching rays of sunlight and dancing in the incidence and refraction of it all.

In the years to follow, the prisoners would debate which reality elicited the longest lasting confusion on the faces of the guards. First, a girl who was supposed to have never seen her father tore away from her mother and the guard to run directly into his arms. Her joyful yelps were those of a child who knows her father well. The prisoner lifted her up and held her like a sack he had carried many times. Before the surprise of that moment had passed, the wife and the second child – a boy – came close enough for all to see. The boy's keen eyes were nobody's but Prisoner 13874's; the boy had his whole face. All their working lives, the guards had thrived on having more information than the prisoners: in their training, they were taught to slip in and out of spaces, to wheedle their way into people's heads, vanish in market places, appear beside suspects, upset logic.

Now they knew what it felt like; they were on the other side, illuminated in their bewilderment.

Ziad's bright eyes moved over the forest of his wife like a pair of fireflies celebrating the brilliance of flight. He fell to his knees. He held her hands as luminous dust danced around them and placed his lips on her belly – full and round as a bulb.

WRITERS' AND EDITORS' BIOGRAPHIES

Patience Agbabi FRSL is a Fellow in Creative Writing at Oxford Brookes University and an Associate Member of the Faculty of English at Oxford University. Her latest poetry collection is *Telling Tales*, a multicultural retelling of *The Canterbury Tales*. Her debut middle-grade novel, *The Infinite*, was shortlisted for The Arthur C. Clarke Award for Science Fiction Book of the Year 2021. It won the Wales Book of the Year: Children and Young People Award 2021.

Muli Amaye is from Manchester, UK. She is the coordinator of the MFA Creative Writing at The University of The West Indies in Trinidad. Her first novel, *A House With No Angels* was published by Crocus in 2019. She writes short stories, novels and poetry.

Alinah Azadeh is a British-Iranian writer, visual artist, performer and cultural activist. She has had short stories, poetry and articles published and broadcast. She is the inaugural writer-in-residence at Seven Sisters Country Park and Sussex Heritage Coast, UK, for South Downs National Park, leading *We See You Now*, a decolonial literature and landscape project supported by Arts Council England, which includes the podcast, *The Colour of Chalk*.

Judith Bryan's 1998 Saga Prize winning novel, *Bernard and the Cloth Monkey,* was republished in 2021 for Penguin's *Black Britain: Writing Back* series, curated and with a new introduction by Booker-prize winner, Bernardine Evaristo. Judith's fiction and nonfiction are published by Penguin, Bloomsbury and Peepal Tree among others. Her first play, *A Cold Snap*, was shortlisted for the Alfred Fagon award. She is a Hawthornden Fellow and Senior Fellow of the Higher Education Academy with over twenty years experience teaching creative writing. She has two historical novels in progress and is working towards a first collection of short stories.

Patricia Cumper was born in Jamaica and moved to the UK some twenty five years ago. She writes for the stage and radio. She was Artistic Director of Talawa Theatre Company and won an Outstanding Contribution award at the 9th BBC Audio Drama Awards 2020 for Outstanding Contribution. She is currently producing The Amplify Project, a series of podcasts in conversation with Black British Writers. She is a trustee of Utopia Theatre Company and a council member of the Arts and Humanities Research Council: at heart she is first and foremost a storyteller.

Joshua Idehen is a poet, teacher and musician. A British born Nigerian, his poetry has been published alongside Linton Kwesi Johnson and Anthony Joseph. He recently collaborated with The Comet Is Coming and Sons of Kemet on their Mercury nominated albums, *Channel The Spirits* and *Your Queen Is A Reptile*.

Melissa Jackson-Wagner is a Guyanese-British retired academic who holds a PhD in Caribbean Literature. She has always worked to centre nuanced histories of Caribbean diasporas within academia and beyond. More recently, she has also worked as a consultant on issues surrounding multiracial identities. Her poetry has been published in *Wasafiri* and her artwork has been exhibited both in the UK and Guyana. She is currently working on her first speculative fiction novel.
Instagram: @dr.melissa.j.wagner

Peter Kalu's novel, *One Drop*, was published by Andersen Press in August 2022. He writes speculative and historical fiction. His short stories can be found in anthologies by Peepal Tree Press, Comma Press and Bluemoose.

Katy Massey's memoir, *Are We Home Yet?* was shortlisted for The Jhalak Prize 2021. She writes novels and scripts, as well as nonfiction, and produces literature projects which focus on life experiences which would otherwise go unrecorded. Katy was a freelance journalist before completing her PhD at Newcastle University. She lives in East Sussex.

Ronnie McGrath (aka 'ronsurreal') is a socially conscious Black visual artist, neo-surrealist poet, and novelist. As well as teaching creative writing at various sites throughout the country, he facilitates creative writing classes as a therapeutic tool for mental well-being and to assist the rehabilitation of people who suffer from alcohol and substance abuse. He continues the search for an 'authentic Black' form of writing that is unashamedly bawdy, experimental, edutaining and downright rebellious.

Claudia Monteith is a writer, artist and group facilitator, leading creative writing courses in Bristol. At present, she is writing a mother/daughter memoir, entitled *The Retelling,* and a blog on her website that explores the highs and lows of what it means to be kind and creative in a crazy world.

Chantal Oakes uses a collaborative arts practice to produce research and creative text for publication and moving image. Recent work includes articles in *Archives: Lancashire History Magazine, Asylum Magazine*, an essay for University of Massachusetts Press, *Black History Connections* (online), and a short story for *Closure*, Peepal Tree Press. Recent commissions include art pieces for Preston Live Arts Festival, Living City (online), Harris Art Gallery, Fish Factory, Penryn, and xviix (online).

Irenosen Okojie's experimental works play with form and language. Her debut novel *Butterfly Fish* and short story collections *Speak Gigantular* and *Nudibranch* have won and been shortlisted for multiple awards. A Fellow and Vice Chair of the Royal Society of Literature, Irenosen is the winner of the 2020 AKO Caine Prize for her story, 'Grace Jones'. She was awarded an MBE For Services to Literature in 2021.

Koye Oyedeji is a writer who splits his time between London and Washington D.C. He has contributed to a number of anthologies and literary journals. He is currently at work on a full-length project.

Nii Ayikwei Parkes is a Ghanaian writer and editor who has won acclaim for his work as a children's writer, poet, broadcaster and novelist. He has also published a leading crop of UK poets, including Nick Makoha, Malika Booker, Niall O'Sullivan and Warsan Shire, as founder of flipped eye publishing.

Jeda Pearl is a Scottish Jamaican writer and poet and Co-Director of Scottish BPOC Writers Network. She has performed at StAnza, Push the Boat Out, Hidden Door and Edinburgh International Book Festival. She was longlisted for the Women Poets' Prize 2022 and was awarded Cove Park's 2019 Emerging Writer Residency (fiction). She has works published/commissioned by Black Lives Matter Mural Trail, Not Going Back to Normal – Disabled Artists Manifesto, Shoreline of Infinity, Scottish Storytelling Centre and galleries, Rhubaba and Collective. Instagram: @JedaPearl; website: jedapearl.com

Aisha Phoenix is an African Caribbean British speculative fiction writer. Her short story collection was shortlisted for the 2020 SI Leeds Literary Prize. Her work has appeared in publications including Peepal Tree's *Filigree* and Inkandescent's ~~MAIN~~-*STREAM*. She has also been published in Spread the Word, National Flash Fiction Day, Leicester Writes, Brick Lane Bookshop and Bath Flash Fiction anthologies. She has an MA in Creative Writing (Birkbeck) and a PhD in Sociology (Goldsmiths).

Akila Richards is a poet, writer and spoken word artist, performing and collaborating in the UK and abroad. She has completed work to commission across artistic genres: in theatre, for audio, in moving images and for culturally creative events. Her recent poems and short stories featured at Dulwich Gallery, Brighton Festival, and in anthologies published by Peepal Tree Press, Waterloo Press and Penguin, as well as on digital platforms. Akila is editing her poetry pamphlet and novel for publication.

Ioney Smallhorne is a writer and spoken-word artist. She was shortlisted for the Sky Arts/Royal Society of Literature fiction award, 2021, longlisted for the Jerwood Fellowship in 2017 and shortlisted by Caribbean Small-Axe prize in 2016. Ioney's essay, 'Using Poetry to Push Back Oppression', was published in Leeds Beckett's academic journal, *Storymakers* in 2019; her poems have been anthologised by Peepal Tree Press and Nottingham Black Archive. She has an MA in Creative Writing & Education (Goldsmiths, University of London), is a part-time English teacher and facilitates performance poetry workshops.

Gemma Weekes is the critically-acclaimed author of the novel *Love Me* (Chatto & Windus), as well as proud mama, poet, playwright, multidisciplinary performer and screenwriter. She's written for BBC show *JoJo & Gran Gran* and with the Line Animation for clients including Riot Games, Acura, Chobani and Netflix. She is working on her second book, an experimental verse novel entitled *GRI-GRI*. She is represented by Rukhsana Yasmin at the Good Literary Agency.

Dr Reynaldo Anderson is an Associate Professor at Temple University in the Department of Africology and African American Studies. He is currently the executive director and cofounder of the Black Speculative Arts Movement (BSAM) and the co-editor of the following anthologies and journals: *Afrofuturism 2.0: The Rise of Astro-Blackness* and *The Black Speculative Arts Movement: Black Futurity, Art+Design* (both Lexington Books, 2015, 2019), *Cosmic Underground: A Grimoire of Black Speculative Discontent* (Cedar Grove Publishing, 2018), 'Black Lives, Black Politics, Black Futures', a special issue of *TOPIA: Canadian Journal of Cultural Studies* (2018), and *When is Wakanda: Afrofuturism and Dark Speculative Futurity* (The Journal of Futures Studies, 2019). He is also the author of numerous articles on Africana Studies and Communication studies and helped conceive the joint BSAM and NY LIVE Arts *Curating the End of the World* online exhibitions on the Google Arts platform (2020-2022). Dr Anderson is a member of the curatorial council for the Carnegie Hall Afrofuturism festival in New York City in February and March 2022. He has presented papers in areas of communications, Africana studies, Afrofuturism, and critical theory in the US and abroad.

Leone Ross is a novelist, short story writer and editor. Her fiction has been nominated for the Women's Prize, the Goldsmiths award, the RSL Ondaatje award, and the Edge Hill Prize, among others. In 2022, she won the Manchester Prize for Fiction for a single short story, 'When We Went Gallivanting'. The *Guardian* has praised her 'searing empathy' and the *Times Literary Supplement* called her 'a pointilliste, a master of detail…' Ross has taught creative writing for 20 years, up to PhD level, and worked as a journalist throughout the 90s. Her third novel, *This One Sky Day* aka *Popisho*, came out in paperback with Faber & Faber and Picador, USA. Ross lives in London, but intends to retire near water.

Dr Kadija George Sesay, FRSA, is a literary activist and independent researcher of Sierra Leonean descent. She is the Publications Manager for Inscribe/Peepal Tree Press supporting the writing of Black British writers, which includes the series editor for ground-breaking poetry and fiction anthologies, *Red*, *Closure* and *Filigree*. From 2001-2015 she published *SABLE LitMag*. She has edited anthologies of work by writers of African descent in all genres and published and broadcast her own creative work including *Irki*, published by Peepal Tree (2013). She received a grant from Arts Council England and a Society of Authors Award to research her second poetry collection, *The Modern Pan-Africanist's Journey*. She co-founded the Mboka Festival of Arts, Culture and Sport in The Gambia and founded AfriPoeTree a Selective Interactive Video of Poetry and Pan-Africanism. She has received an Honorary Fellowship from Goldsmiths, University of London and a Fellowship from the Royal Society of Literature.

Red: Contemporary Black British Poetry
Edited by Kwame Dawes
ISBN: 9781845231293; pp. 252; pub. 2010; price: £ 9.99

"Perhaps the most significant thing to be said about *Red* is that the poets in this volume burst through any constraining label with writing that throbs and pulses and seeps and flows."
— Margaret Busby

Featuring: Jackie Kay, Patience Agbabi, Nii Ayikwei Parkes, Raman Mundair, Maya Chowdhry, Dorothea Smartt, Fred D'Aguiar, Joshua Idehen, Linton Kwesi Johnson, Bernardine Evaristo, Roi Kwabena, John Lyons, Lemn Sissay, Grace Nichols, Jack Mapanje, Daljit Nagra, John Agard, Gemma Weekes, Wangui Wa Goro and many more...

Red collects poems that engage 'red', poems by Black British poets writing with the word "red" in mind – as a kind of leap-off point, a context, a germ – the way something small, minor, or grand might spur a poem. It offers the reader the freedom to come to whatever conclusions they want to about what writing as a poet who is also Black and British might mean.

The result is a book of poets ranging from well established and published writers to first time poets. Red does find its usual associations with blood, violence, passion, and anger. Sometimes it is linked with sensuality and sexuality. But there are surprises, when red defines a memory or mood, the quality of light in a sky, the colour of skin, the sound of a song, and much, much more. The anthology, therefore, succeeds in producing poems that seem to be first about image, and only then about whatever else fascinates the poet.

In this sense, *Red* is a different kind of anthology of Black British writing, and the richness of the entries, the moods, the humour, the passion, the reflection, the confessional all confirm that Black British poetry is a lively and defining force in Britain today.

Closure
Edited by Jacob Ross
ISBN: 9781845232887; pp. 240; pub. 2015; price £9.99

"Stunning new writing" – Maggie Gee, *The Guardian*
Listed in BuzzFeed's "22 Brilliant New Books You Should Read"

As the narrative mode across cultures and time, the short story form wings from oral "folktales" to myths of origin, from parables of caution to contemporary narratives of disclosure, disquiet and discovery. Humans have always valued the short story as a way to make sense of the world, and their place in it. *Closure* is essentially about human striving.

"Opening a short story anthology, there is often something to delight, something to surprise. There is also often something clever, self-indulgent, that speaks of a writer's skill but limited experience of life. Jacob Ross's careful selection of stories from black British writers restores a sense of connection with the detail of human fragility in our fragmented contemporary culture; with narrative, with the spirit. With the subtle, sometimes unconscious, responses of these writers to what Britishness means. This book is both an important contribution to the future development of the form and a celebration of some of our finest writing. Surprising, delightful and full of life." Cathy Galvin

Featuring short stories by: Monica Ali, Dinesh Angelo Allirajah, Muli Amaye, Lynne E. Blackwood, Judith Bryan, Nana-Essi Casely-Hayford, Jacqueline Clarke, Jacqueline Crooks, Fred D'Aguiar, Sylvia Dickinson, Bernardine Evaristo, Gaylene Gould, Michelle Inniss, Valda Jackson, Pete Kalu, Patrice Lawrence, Jennifer Nansubuga Makumbi, Tariq Mehmood, Raman Mundair, Sai Murray, Chantal Oakes, Karen Onojaife, Koye Oyedeji, Louisa Adjoa Parker, Desiree Reynolds, Hana Riaz, Akila Richards, Leone Ross, Seni Seneviratne, Ayesha Siddiqi, Mahsuda Snaith.

Filigree: Contemporary Black British Poetry
Edited by Nii Ayikwei Parkes
ISBN: 9781845234263; pp. 128; pub. 2018; price £8.99

Filigree typically refers to the finer elements of craftwork, the parts that are subtle; our *Filigree* anthology contains work that plays with the possibilities that the word suggests, work that is delicate, that responds to the idea of edging, to a comment on the marginalisation of the darker voice. Filigree includes work from established Black British poets residing inside and outside the UK; new and younger emerging voices of Black Britain and Black poets who have made it their home as well as a selection of poets the Inscribe project has nurtured and continue to support.

"I finished this new anthology of black poets in Britain with 'ghee on my lips' as Roger Robinson writes in 'Repast', with a sated appetite, but wanting more – more of the lives that came spinning from its pages. There are testimonies and remembrances here, poems of resistance and bombast, and hymns of love of all kinds. But what struck me most is the varied and accomplished craft of these writers – the link with poetics and traditions past, but always with an eye to renewal and invention." Hannah Lowe

Featuring: Tolu Agbelusi, Sui Anukka, Raymond Antrobus, Lynne E Blackwood, Sid Siddhartha Bose, Victoria Bulley, Michael Campbell, Nana-Essi Casely-Hayford, Maya Chowdhry, Rishi Dastidar, Tishani Doshi, Zena Edwards, Samatar Elmi, Christina Fonthes, Patricia Foster, Kat François, Nandita Ghose, Nikheel Gorolay, Keith Jarrett, Maggie Harris, Joshua Idehen, Sumia Jamaa, Pete Kalu, Fawzia Kane, Rachel Long, Adam Lowe, Nick Makoha, Roy Mcfarlane, Ronnie McGrath, Momtaza Mehri, Sai Murray, Selina Nwulu, Louisa Adjoa Parker, Aisha Phoenix, Barsa Ray, Akila Richards, Maureen Roberts, Roger Robinson, Selina Rodrigues, Seni Seneviratne, Ioney Smallhorne, Degna Stone, Hugh Stultz, Ruth Sutoyé, Keisha Thompson, Gemma Weekes.

ALSO FROM PEEPAL TREE/ PEEKASH PRESS

New Worlds, Old Ways: Speculative Tales from the Caribbean
Edited by Karen Lord
ISBN: 9781845233365; pp. 145; pub. 2016; price £8.99

'Do not be misled by the "speculative" in the title. Although there may be robots and fantastical creatures, these common symbols are tools to frame the familiar from fresh perspectives. Here you will find the recent past and ongoing present of government and society with curfews, crime and corruption; the universal themes of family with parents and children, growth and death, love and hate; the struggle to thrive when power is capricious and revenge too bittersweet. Here too is the passage of everything – old ways, places, peoples, and ourselves – leaving nothing behind but memories, histories, stories.

This anthology speaks to the fragility of our Caribbean home, but reminds the reader that although home may be vulnerable, it is also beautifully resilient. The voice of our literature declares that in spite of disasters, this people and this place shall not be wholly destroyed.

Read for delight, then read for depth, and you will not be disappointed.'

Starred review in *Publisher's Weekly.*

Edited by Karen Lord, with stories by Tammi-Browne Bannister, Summer Edward, Portia Subran, Brandon O'Brien, Kevin Jared Hosein, Richard B. Lynch, Elizabeth J. Jones, Damion Wilson, Brian Franklin, Ararimeh Aiyejina and H.K. Williams.